Praise for k a t e   c h r i s t e n s e n 's

i n   t h e   d r i n k

"Like Bridget [Jones], Christensen's Claudia Steiner is a mess . . . but Claudia is endearing because she remains appreciative of her own grittiness." —*Time*

"Like its protagonist, Christensen's book is funny and intelligent, filled with dead-on New York character types and locales." —*The Baltimore Sun*

"At a time when authors are penning bestselling memoirs about their alcoholic torment, and 12-step programs are as popular as SUVs, Christensen's take is refreshing."
—*New York Post*

"Hilarious, decadent, painfully honest, and sparkling with wit and originality, *In the Drink* is the perfect '90s love story, a tale for anyone who's ever had a few too many shots of bad whiskey, bad jobs, mornings after, and pinings for that person they can't stop thinking about. With this exuberant first novel, Kate Christensen bursts onto the literary scene."
—Cathi Hanauer, author of My *Sister's Bones*

"If *In the Drink* were a beverage, it would be spilling over with character development." —*The Weekly Alibi* (Albuquerque)

"Kate Christensen's language bristles with poetry; her wit crackles with insight. This rite of passage to the literary and sexual landscape of New York in the 1990s is easily one of the best first novels I've ever read."
—Arthur Neresian, author of *Manhattan Lover Boy*
and *Dog Run*

"Read *In the Drink* because it's about a girl who knows exactly how it feels to be us. For a change." —*Bust*

kate christensen

in the drink

Kate Christensen is a graduate of Reed College and the Iowa Writers' Workshop. She lives with her husband in Brooklyn, New York, where she is writing another novel. *In the Drink* is her first book.

Anchor Books

A Division of Random House, Inc.

New York

in the drink

kate christensen

FIRST ANCHOR BOOKS EDITION, AUGUST 2000

From "The Waste Land" by T. S. Eliot. From *Collected Poems 1909–1962* by T. S. Eliot, copyright © 1963, 1964 by T. S. Eliot.

Short excerpts from "The Suicide," "Recuerdo," and "God's World" by Edna St. Vincent Millay.

The Library of Congress has cataloged the Doubleday edition as follows:
Christensen, Kate, 1962–
In the drink / Kate Christensen. — 1st ed.
p.   cm.
ISBN 0-385-49450-5
I. Title.
PS3553.H71615   1999
813'.54—dc21   99-18876
CIP

Anchor ISBN: 978-0-385-72021-2

Author photograph © Matthias Geiger
Book design by Dana Leigh Treglia

www.anchorbooks.com

146086900

Anyone who has never floundered or failed
can be expected to have little patience
for those who do.

chapter one

"Dear Mrs. Skye," I found myself writing one afternoon, "Thank you so much for your fascinating letter. Of course I'm thrilled that you liked my new book as much as the first one, and I'm delighted to hear that you share my aims concerning the establishment of a strict death penalty in every state."

I stopped writing and yawned, then leaned back in my chair and stared up at the ceiling as if casting my eyes heavenward, praying for rain or succor. I noticed small heaps of dead moths piled up inside the chandelier's glass tulips, each as small and dry as a flaked-off chip of gray paint. I looked up through the glass at them for a while, wondering idly why, over all the thousands of years since the discovery of fire, moths as a species hadn't stopped getting sucked into lamps and fireplaces and candle flames and lanterns and streetlights—wasn't that exactly the sort of thing evolution was designed to correct? They deserved to sizzle to death on lightbulbs if they were too stupid to figure it out. It served them right.

I yawned again, flicked my eyes over the paragraph I'd just written and found absolutely nothing there worth reading. It was one-thirty. I got off work at five. Images from last night arose and faded: the International Bar, dark wainscoting beneath mottled-eggshell walls strung with Christmas-tree lights, my friend Frieda's face across the table, alight with laughter. "You're *kidding*, Claudia, you're making that *up*." Often after I'd got four or five drinks down my gullet, I would find myself telling stories about Jackie. My audience's laughter always made me feel much better about my job. Afterwards I rolled merrily home, fell into a deep sleep and awoke feeling like a brand-new daisy in a sunlit meadow, filled with fresh hope that maybe today was the day my real life would start.

That it wasn't, and wouldn't be any time soon, generally hit me every afternoon around this time. It was just hitting me now.

"Certainly," I wrote on, "taxpayers' money is wasted on keeping murderers alive, and would be put to better use deporting illegal aliens and making the streets safe for law-abiding citizens such as you and I. It is for intelligent, thoughtful readers like you that I write my books. I thank you again for your kind letter. Warmest best wishes, Genevieve del Castellano."

I printed out the letter and added it to the stack of claptrap awaiting Jackie's signature. When I rapped on her closed bathroom door, she called impatiently, "Well, come in, Claudia." I entered to find her sitting naked on the toilet. She held her hairpiece in both hands and clenched the phone between her shoulder and ear, talking through a mouthful of bobby pins. Her skin drooped in tissue-fine wrinkles from her bones. Her real hair was pinned into a topknot, giving her the look of a plucked exotic bird. Anyone else in this position might have been at a disadvantage.

"Hold on, Jimmy," she said. She put the phone on the edge of the tub, flushed the toilet and put on a dressing gown, in the interests of warmth, I was sure, rather than any modesty on my behalf. She took her sweet time pinning on her hair, chatting to Mr. Blevins, while I thought about the list of things I had to do today. "Just a moment, Jimmy darling," she said finally, and set the phone on top of the laundry hamper. I handed her a pair of reading glasses. She placed them on the tip of her nose, took the letters from me and scanned them. The hairpiece clung to her head like some small scared animal.

"I've told you a thousand times," she said to me, "you've got to give these people their full titles. *Ambassador* Bob Stevens." A fleck of spittle landed on my nose from the hiss of "Ambassador."

I had chosen not to address this particular ambassador as such because he was one of Jackie's oldest friends and I'd thought it would be an unnecessary formality, something I'd known her to deplore on other occasions, in a different mood. I couldn't explain this to her; she didn't have the patience for examples of her own inconsistencies, and in any case I should have anticipated today's standards. "Sorry," I said, gritting my teeth. "I'll change it."

"You American girls are so ignorant! What would he think of me? It's not your fault, but you just don't have the sophistication European girls have! Give me that." She snatched my pen and rooted through the stack, scrawling wildly. I watched her in silence. Finally she thrust it all back at me.

"Your hairpiece is askew, Jackie," I said sweetly.

"My what?"

"Your hair. It's on crooked."

3

She flicked the merest pointed glance at my own hair and said, "What are you waiting for? You have a great many things to do," and plucked up the receiver. "Jimmy dear, I have to go. I have this girl here and she needs me to show her—oh, never mind, I'll see you tonight."

Poor Jimmy Blevins had heard our whole exchange and must have known that I needed her like a machete in the head, but there was no possibility that he wouldn't choose to believe her. He was a plain little gray man in a suit, but according to Jackie he was the best dancer in New York, with a tendency, she had once confessed to me, to get erections when he held her closely. Her power to inspire them plainly titillated her. She complained about him: "They never give that Mr. Blevins fresh flowers, the ones he brought yesterday are already shedding all over the rug" (the fact that he owned a funeral home never seemed to occur to her as an explanation for this), and, "I can't bring Jimmy to that dinner, he's not good-looking enough, what will people think?" but whenever he didn't call for a few days Jackie would fall prey to one of her mysterious fugue states; she would ask me to leave a message with his secretary that she was "back in town."

I went back to my dining room office and slumped over the computer. Why couldn't she just sign the damn letters? I thought about what to drink when I got home. I had a bottle of vodka in the cupboard, and a few days ago I'd stashed half a bottle of gin somewhere safe—my underwear drawer? under the sink? Anyway, wherever I'd put it, it was still there. I rolled the decision on my tongue: vodka was clear and clean and lucidly numbing, but gin had that oily juniper-berry underbelly, a hallucinatory edge that sometimes took me out of myself. But gin was tricky, it could backfire if you weren't careful, and who wanted to be careful?

4

The phone rang. "Genevieve del Castellano's office," I said in my throatiest voice.

"I can't concentrate," said William. "It's getting worse."

A double helix of joy and despair twisted through me.

"I know what you mean," I said, laughing. "I have the same problem."

"No, you don't," he shot back.

"Yes I do."

"No," he said. "You don't work with Devorah." He almost groaned the name.

"Devorah," I said.

He took this as a sign of interest and elaborated: Devorah was a paperback bodice-ripper heroine brought to life, given a paralegal degree and recently hired by his firm. For the first time since I'd known him, I heard William say the words "olive-skinned" and "bewitching."

"Bewitching," I repeated hopelessly.

She was also twenty-two. I had lately begun to notice the new crop of young girls on the sidewalks and in the bars, making me feel supplanted and strange. Biology was cruel; I knew that as well as anyone, and I didn't need any reminders, especially not from him.

"What do you think," he said with a short chuckle, clearly under the illusion that I was his pal, his confidant, his sidekick in matters amatory, "should I call her into my office and bend her over a filing cabinet?"

"No," I said.

He laughed. For years we'd always discussed, frankly and in exhaustive detail, the people we were attracted to or sleeping with or trying to extricate from our lives; for several months last spring I'd been involved with William's old friend John Threadgill, and William spared me no detail of his unresolved

5

feelings for Margot Spencer, and the string of young, impeccably groomed, unforgivably humorless women he dated, obsessed over and eventually dumped.

It pained me to hear about all this, because I'd been in love with William myself for the past year or so. Of course I hadn't told him; I didn't want to ruin our friendship or chase him away. Anyway, I hadn't chosen to feel this way, it had been visited on me like a fever, and as with a fever, I would ride it out. All I could do in the meantime was send peacekeeping troops from reason to hormones and wait for deliverance.

"You want to meet at George's tonight?" he said. "Gus wants to join us. I just talked to him a couple of minutes ago."

"Gus?" I said, but I knew better than to complain. For reasons I couldn't begin to guess at, William loved Gus, and William was almost pathologically loyal to anyone he loved. I would have bet that Gus bit his tongue about me for the same reason. "All right, see you at George's," I said equably.

"Gotta go, I have someone on hold. Around nine or so?"

"Keep your mitts off the jailbait," I said, but he was already gone.

I opened the casement window as far as it would go and leaned out over the courtyard. The air smelled of dry leaves, an underlying tang of diesel exhaust. The wind rushed upward with a light chuckling, ivy leaves turning on their stems. The sky was darkening already. The bleakness of the waning afternoon held the promise of some alluring after-dark adventure, if I could just hold on until then.

Then Jackie's squawk issued from her bedroom, talking to her secretary, and that secretary was me. I reeled myself back in and followed the sound of her voice to see what she wanted now. What bound me to her, to coming here every day and going home to my little room every night, to the nocturnal escapes I devised for myself, was a centrifugal force so established that all my bodily systems had adjusted themselves to it. If it were removed suddenly, I imagined that I would stagger and collapse.

Nine years ago I had come to New York, fresh out of college, buoyed along by the idea that I wanted to be a journalist. But after a brief stint in the dun-carpeted offices of a midtown gazette, typing things for burned-out maniacs who stood over me frothing at the mouth, my starry-eyed notion of Claudia Steiner, Reporter on the Beat, had vanished into the ozone. I couldn't muster the requisite hard-bitten, white-hot urgency, the chain-smoking and yelling and cutthroat story-mongering.

After I quit, I carried around a hole in my chest where a driving ambition should have been. As if sensing this vacuity, the professional world presented a smooth cheek, offering no purchase as I slid from job to job—receptionist, dog walker, phone-sex scriptwriter, temporary secretary, waitress, house-cleaner, temp again. Each time I left a job I looked dazedly around, gulping in mouthfuls of fresh air before plunging bleakly on to the next one. What sustained me through each dull, grinding interlude was my knowledge of the ephemeral ease with which I would vanish from their consciousnesses and they from mine six months later when I moved on again.

I had never intended to make such a mess of things. It had happened incrementally and gradually; every day, I'd felt the gap widen between me and that parallel universe that contained the life I'd meant to create for myself, that exciting, interesting whirl of travel and fabulous dinner parties and satisfying work. Over the years, I'd begun to take a perverse pleasure in seeing just how bad my life could get before the whole thing blew and, as an interesting corollary, just how severely I could punish myself for having been so arrogant as to think that my untapped potential and vague desire to succeed were of interest to anyone but me. Since I had run out of other options, this experiment served as a sort of substitute for ambition.

Three years ago, I'd come to work for Genevieve del Castellano, socialite and best-selling author. I was still there. I had my reasons, but they were all I had.

I found Jackie trying on a black cocktail dress in front of her wall of mirrors. She presented her back to me. The zipper stuck halfway up, and her flesh lapped over the material. "It'll go on," she said calmly, folding the wings of her shoulder blades together. The zipper cut into my fingers and wouldn't budge. She scooped her breasts higher in the bodice, repositioned her shoulders, and said, "Now try it." It slid up easily. She did a tripping little waltz, humming, swishing the full skirt; she was as small and fine-boned as a girl, and her husky tone-deaf voice was so guileless I had to laugh. She always looked a little taken aback when I laughed at her, but flattered, as if people rarely found her funny. She laughed along with me although she didn't seem to know why. "Does it make me look fat?"

"Not at all," I said sincerely.

"It's ancient," she said, pleased. We smiled at each other. "I had it made in Paris twenty years ago. Those new designer dresses disintegrate if you wear them twice."

The second dress went on easily, a sequined number she'd just had made by one of her designer friends. It had a stiff, crenellated skirt and a complicated bodice that stood away from her chest like a shell. She took one look at her reflection and said, "It's absolutely hideous."

I said with emphatic earnestness, "No, it's beautiful," but I knew what was coming.

"Don't patronize me, Claudia; a *child* could see how impossible this dress is. I'd like to send it back right this minute."

"Should I call them?" A slow hot bubble welled in my head and burst against the top of my skull.

But to my intense relief, she said, "Juanita might be able to cut off the sequins, or take it in, or . . . we'll see." As I helped her out of it, she added, "By the way, that new waiter we hired for my dinner last night turned out to be a *black*! In he walked, black as you ever saw! Well! My *jaw* dropped. He sounded fine over the phone, didn't he? Probably because he's a homosexual and they all sound alike. I couldn't very well tell him to leave, I had guests arriving. I had to spend the whole evening in the pantry. I wasn't going to leave him alone with the silver. And I had to serve most of the courses myself; I didn't want him to touch anything with those hands, no telling *where* they'd been, and they've all got that AIDS now. Can you *imagine?*"

And the thing was, here in the buffered, hermetic vault of her apartment, I *could* imagine. "How awful," I heard myself saying soothingly.

She bustled back into the bathroom, unaware that our little colloquy had sent a jolt of self-loathing through my gutless viscera. I had sympathized with her. I had bolstered her view of the world and herself. Technically this complicity didn't hurt anyone, but its macrocosmic and historical implications were not lost on me. I should have told her how insanely self-centered she was. I should have defended the poor waiter.

I trudged back to my desk. Several minutes later I heard her slippers flopping along the foyer. I rattled the computer keys busily, although one second before I'd been picking my split ends and darkly considering my own spinelessness.

"I have a project for us," she announced.

For the rest of the afternoon, we worked on compiling the photographic section for *Detective in Décolletage*. The idea was that these photographs would bolster the veracity of the story, but Jackie allowed into her books only those pictures in which she looked her absolute best, no matter how everyone else looked or whether or not it had anything to do with the plot and characters at hand. As a result, the photographic sections of her books were an oddly assorted mishmash of unrelated characters, unintelligible scenes, blurred faces identifiable only with the aid of the caption below. Their collective authority served to reassure the reader that the author was the same woman as the narrator of the story. She reigned over the squinting, the decapitated, the compromised, the out-of-focus, her features crisp and radiant, her hair perfect.

With my help (which consisted mainly of saying either "Beautiful" or "Not your best"), she chose for her latest book a stack of snapshots and newspaper photos of herself standing alongside several of the book's more famous characters. The people in the photographs were engaged in activities which jibed well enough with those of the characters in the book: lunching, golfing, hunting, yachting, and smiling in self-satisfied little groups at charity balls and parties. She extracted from its gilt frame on the guest bedroom table the crown jewel in this particular collection: a photograph of Jackie and Giancarlo del Castellano with their close friends Ferdinand and Imelda Marcos, taken in 1977 in Manila.

"The trip to the Philippines comes in Chapter Seven," Jackie informed me, as if I hadn't put it there. "Giancarlo and President Marcos got on splendidly together. Ferdinand wasn't nearly as bad as the liberal press made him out to be. And I don't believe for a minute that Imelda had any idea what he was up to. Wives of our generation never paid attention to those things, that's what no one seems to understand."

The foursome stood with the sun full in their faces. I suspected that Jackie had masterminded the photograph by commanding the photographer to shoot before anyone else was ready: the President and First Lady had clearly been caught off-guard, but Signor del Castellano, whatever else he may have been, was the sort of man his wife could trust always to meet with perfect equanimity any shutter that went off in his direction. The Marcoses looked squat and unprepossessing next to their glamorous guests. The del Castellanos had both had the foresight to wear sunglasses and stylish white hats, so their shaded faces looked attractively smooth, while their hosts were caught squinting, baring their teeth in almost canine aggression. Standing on a slight rise, Jackie looked triumphant in a white flared-leg pantsuit. Although I knew that the two women were about the same height, she looked nearly a head taller and far slimmer than Mrs. Marcos, who appeared to have been edged into an adjacent flower bed.

"Take especially good care of this one," said Jackie, putting the Marcos photo into a large brown envelope, separate from the others. "I have no negative and this is my only print."

"I'll guard it with my life," I promised impatiently. What did she take me for?

"Well, I certainly hope you won't have to do that," she said.

I checked my watch: it was time to start packing up for the day, but there was still her incoming mail to open and sort. This consisted today of several invitations, a fan letter, something from the IRS, a bank statement, a bill or two, the latest bulletin from Media Watchdog and the usual assortment of junk mail. I always separated junk mail into its own pile. I had once, early on, mistakenly thrown out a notice for a sale at one of her neighborhood stores, and the next day she'd gone out and bought a new answering machine somewhere else for eight dollars more than the sale price; in the elevator, her next-door neighbor had seen her opening the package it came in and had asked her whether she had gone to the store in question, they were having such a marvelous sale. Jackie had said no, were they really? and then the whole thing came out, and I caught hell, and as a result she now insisted on seeing everything.

I left the mail on the kitchen table in two piles, one junk, one everything else, then put away the folding table and computer trolley in the pantry. I stored the two envelopes containing her precious photographs on the shelf where I always kept my current work. And then I was free to leave for the day. As I crossed Central Park, I hummed to myself, the same breathy, tuneless notes Jackie had waltzed to. The darkening early spring dusk smelled fresh and empty; headlights came on one by one until the traffic was a blur of streaming light. Lit interiors stacked high above the edges of the park glowed through the bare treetops. I came out of the park onto Central Park West and headed up and over to my building.

I lived on the fourth floor of a former residential hotel that had been constructed cheaply and hastily after one war or another to house a sudden influx of immigrants willing to live anywhere. The stairwell was a trembling shell of flaking plaster, a fragile husk my mounting or descending tread always threatened to implode and send sliding into a pile of rubble in the basement. The stairs sagged in the middle, eroded like bars of soap. The plaster curlicues in the upper corners of each landing had been reduced by attrition to sad grayish ridges, more fungal growths than embellishments. There was an elevator, but it was a scary, creaky old box, splitting at the seams and frayed at the cables, whose upward speed was slower than climbing on foot.

When I opened my door and turned on the overhead light I got a brief impression of vanishing movement, the usual squadron of cockroaches sliding into hairline cracks in the kitchen wall. Seven years in this tiny room with these creatures had dulled my squeamish loathing of them. I still set out Combat disks every few months, but this was more out of habit than any expectation that they'd die out. We'd struck a kind of deal: they roamed at will through my apartment all day, but skedaddled the instant I came home. Like the Israelites in the wilderness, they depended on manna from the sky and the whims of an incomprehensibly larger being who could squash them underfoot if they got out of line. A cross-section cutaway of my wall would have revealed a seething, lustrous blanket of generations upon generations living out their lives in this wall without any awareness that beyond it lay streets, sky, light, trees, countless other walls and worlds like theirs.

My kitchen was wedged into the entryway next to the coat closet. It consisted of a waist-high refrigerator with a tiny stainless-steel sink and two burner coils built into its top. Affixed to the wall above this contraption was an old metal cabinet that held plates, bowls, cups, a can of coffee, a three-year-old box of cornflakes, nearly half a bottle of vodka and a box of sugar. I filled the kettle and turned a burner to High. As the coil heated, a stray roach, senile or stupid, came twitching its antennae slowly along the wall. I considered its shiny, flat, greasy shell, the obscene way its feet adhered effortlessly to the vertical surface. It wasn't strictly an insect the way ants or bees were insects: it had no charm, no organization, no industry, no purpose whatsoever except to repulse everyone who saw it. Even a mosquito was preferable to this vile machine; even a fly. No worthwhile species cannibalized its dead, ate its own excrement, exuded oily fluid so it could slither through a crack as narrow as paper. Their lives were myopic, disorderly, without the least affiliation to the natural world or progress or any aspiration at all beyond fulfilling their appetites. I reached down and removed a shoe and took aim. It slammed against the wall and the roach fell dead behind the refrigerator. This brought scant satisfaction, since its corpse would only provide food for the others and enable them to hatch plenty more just like it. I put my shoe back on, washed my hands, then measured several scoops of coffee into the aluminum pot. I took the milk carton out of the refrigerator and sniffed it; the milk was still good, even though the expiration date was yesterday. This gave me a greater pleasure than killing the roach had, but it was of the same low-life caliber.

"Delilah," I called. I had a cat, ostensibly. I'd got her two years ago as a kitten, a cute little tabby I'd hoped would throb with affectionate purrs on the pillow by my head at night. But she immediately fled under the bed when I brought her home, and stayed there. I knew she was still alive because her cat box always had one neat, litter-coated turd in it when I got home, and her food and water disappeared at a rate I couldn't attribute to the cockroaches; also, once in a great while, when I'd been sitting very still for a long time, one gray paw protruded warily from under the bed, testing the air currents; as soon as I exhaled or moved even slightly, the paw was retracted. I longed to have her curl in my lap and bat playfully at my book like other people's cats, but it did seem fitting, in a grim, black-humor sort of way, that my cat avoided me even though I was the only game in town.

While the kettle began to shudder like a stationary revved-up engine, I paced around. My room was ten by fourteen, total square footage one hundred and forty. I had become as inured to the limits of my principality as I was to its vermin population; its crowded desolation was a comfortably accurate reflection of my internal state. Any opulence or decorative strategy would have required a concomitant upgrading of my inner landscape, and this wasn't something I felt I could do right now. Next to the bed were a table and chair, a dusty armchair squatting under a standing lamp, and a bookshelf containing a thesaurus whose cover had fallen off, the paperback poetry anthologies left over from college English classes and one hardcover book consisting of my prose and Jackie's name and photo. My tiny closet was a black hole into which clothes were sucked and never seen clean or whole again.

I snapped on the radio. I had set it the day before on a salsa station; music came ratcheting out at me, furious and festive. I turned up the volume and sashayed, one hand on my stomach, the other in midair, three mincing little steps east, three west, five over to the stove, where steam was coursing from the kettle's spout and quite possibly making it whistle, although I couldn't hear it over the music. I poured the water into the top compartment of the coffeepot, then turned the radio down so I could hear it dripping through. The sound reminded me of the trickle of a stream, rain on leaves.

I topped off my coffee with a dollop of vodka and brought it over to my desk. I downed half of this weird but bracing mixture before I went through my mail, which had been accumulating, ignored, on my table for the last week or two. Month or two, really. My own mail was easier to sort than Jackie's, consisting as it did entirely of computer-generated warnings from Visa, another Visa, Sallie Mae, a third Visa, NYNEX, Con Edison, and so on. I couldn't pay them. And I owed the IRS countless thousands of dollars more, since Jackie didn't withhold anything from my paychecks. I'd had no contact with them since I'd started working for her. By informing them of the amount I owed, I'd only cause them to expend a lot of trouble and postage to no avail. I didn't have any money to give them. Even my bank overdraft was tapped out.

These things were clear enough; what confounded me was why. Where did my money go? It seemed to have a leaching-away quality that other people's money didn't have. When I deposited my weekly paycheck in the bank it dribbled out like water from a leaking barrel. No, this wasn't strictly true; I myself withdrew it in forty- and sixty-dollar increments, and spent it on rounds of drinks, takeout dinners, taxis home from the East Village. When I'd started working for Jackie, my debts immediately spiraled out of control, and I made no effort to rein myself in: my spending habits, which had been profligate before, became suicidally self-destructive. I took taxis to work if I overslept; if I didn't get around to dropping off my laundry at the corner Chinese place (another new luxury I allowed myself), I would charge clothes on my own Bloomie's card when I ran errands for Jackie. When Jackie gave me two weeks off in July, I treated my friend Frieda to a vacation in Mexico, including airfare. I was acting according to an intuitive conviction that better, richer days were just around the corner. I had got a taste of the high life, I spent every weekday in direct contact with it; some of it would eventually rub off on me, it had to.

Down in the street I heard the fierce energy of children's shrieks; I felt old and weary. Then I reminded myself, as I tended to do in such moments, that I was a best-selling author, even though almost no one knew it. My second book was almost finished, and then I would write my third. Everything would be all right as long as I kept going in this direction, as long as I had a paycheck. My debts, Jackie, the question mark constantly hovering above my head, all were insignificant little pebbles in my way, easily kicked aside when the time came. I would come out from under Jackie's wing the same way Margot had. Very soon, I would start thinking about what I would write if I could write anything I wanted, and then I would write it, and then—

I roused myself with the sudden decision to take a bath, my usual remedy after wallowing for any length of time in my deep financial shit.

To my stupefaction, in the bathroom mirror was a fresh-faced blonde. This reflection had nothing to do with the way I imagined I looked—bleary, bloodshot, prematurely aged. Gusts of despair, gallons of alcohol, had washed through me without leaving any horrific mark that I could see. Recognizing this, I was seized with a sudden hope that my life might not be doomed after all. These moments visited me every so often from out of nowhere, brief bubbles that immediately burst and vanished.

I climbed into the steaming tub with the shiny, aromatic *Cosmopolitan* I'd bought at a newsstand on the way home, unfolded my limbs, rested the heavy magazine on my bent knees, leaned my head against the rim. Steam beaded on the glossy paper; my muscles relaxed so much it didn't seem possible that they had ever been so tense. I breathed in and out slowly, read an informative story about nail wraps and facial peels, about which I knew nothing but was willing to learn; I liked the author's big-sisterly, confiding tone. I felt pleasantly drunk. Then the phone rang.

Evidently, as far as Jackie was concerned, I dissolved into the cosmic tide every evening when I left her house and hung in limbo by the umbilical cord of my telephone until I was reincarnated in her doorway the following morning. Her voice on my answering machine filled the four walls and found the scruff of my neck. "Claudia, it's Jackie. I urgently need to know where on earth you put those copies of my book that came today. I've turned the place upside down!"

I jumped out of the tub and stared at the machine. It did no good to screen these calls. If I didn't pick up, I'd worry all evening that she thought I'd lost her books and then tomorrow I'd have to hear about how she'd been awake all night stewing. I finally picked up the receiver and said as if I'd just come in, "Oh, hello, Jackie."

"Yes. Claudia dear. Now, I've looked everywhere, but everywhere, and I simply can't find them. I have to send one to that man who sent that adorable letter, that wonderful man in Paris, what was his name—"

"Henri Severin," I said. "I already sent it. They're on the floor of the pantry where you told me to put them." Water ran down the insides of my legs and pooled at my feet.

"Oh, Claudia, I've told you twenty times, you must unpack them when they arrive! I can't have all those boxes around, it's so low-class."

I mumbled something, doodling with a wet finger in the dust on the answering machine.

"Now, another thing, I was awake in the middle of the night last night thinking of five things I asked you to do that I never heard a word about and I couldn't remember what they were! You *must* attend better to everything I tell you. Oh—" Her voice aimed itself at something beyond the receiver. "Jimmy, don't mess those papers, I've got them in a special order. All right," she said, to me again, and hung up in mid-sentence.

By now my bathwater had stagnated and I was too antsy to get back in anyway. I got dressed and went out and bought a Styrofoam container of red beans and yellow rice from the Cuban-Chinese place around the corner, then stopped in at a bodega for a quart of Triple-X lager. Over dinner, I leafed through some of my old college poetry books. I wanted to watch TV, but my morale wouldn't allow it. Instead, I stumbled on Wordsworth's "The Prelude" and submitted myself to a soothing and purgatorial dose of blank verse:

> O, blank confusion! true epitome
> Of what the mighty City is herself
> To thousands upon thousands of her sons
> Living amid the same perpetual whirl
> Of trivial objects, melted and reduced

To one identity, by differences
That have no law, no meaning, and no end—
Oppression under which even highest minds
Must labour, whence the strongest are not free.

Poetry had for years served as my own private equivalent of davening under the gimlet eye of that scurrilous, moody Jehovah with his monobrow and fistful of lightning. It was like tapping into some eternal spring of guidance and companionship: an hour or so of poetry made me feel that I'd atoned for whatever wrongs I'd most recently inflicted on the natural order. Meanwhile, the red beans were piquant, mealy, savory, the rice rich and salty, and the lager ice-cold, perfect with the food. Jackie would have had no inkling of how good this meal was. She would have turned up her nose at it; too Hispanic, too earthy and low-class. She could only enjoy food if it was out of season, had a French name and was prepared by a man in a toque. I sat at my little table, wriggling my feet comfortably in their warm socks, sprinkling more hot sauce every now and then, feeling the happy skittering of my pulse that meant I was going to see William tonight. I would rather see William than anyone else in the world. I wished I didn't feel that way, but there it was.

chapter two

Jackie and I had been thrust together three years before by our mutual need for each other: she was desperate, and I was available.

Shortly after Jackie's first book, *The Sophisticated Sleuth*, made it onto the best-seller list, Margot Spencer, her former secretary, had given notice, leaving Jackie in an absolute panic: her Rumpelstiltskin was about to vanish, abandoning her with a head full of straw. She had exhorted Margot to find her someone exactly like Margot, who, eager to discharge this final duty and get on with her life, had called me out of the blue to tell me that she knew of someone who needed a secretary and to ask if I needed a job. "I think you'd be an ideal replacement for me," she offered.

I doubted this very much. Margot was the kind of person I had always viewed with an uneasy admixture of intimidation, incomprehension and envy, one of the chosen few whose lives seemed to progress along a brightly lit superhighway without even the most fleeting inclination toward dark alleyways. Her chiseled face was designed aerodynamically, like the prow of a ship; the planes of her long limbs were angled like oars. During her tenure with Jackie, she had written articles and essays in her spare time, several of which her agent had sold to magazines. An autobiographical essay for *Vanity Fair* about her childhood in Greenwich, Connecticut, had won her a nice big contract with a reputable publisher to be expanded into a book-length memoir, *In the Land of Silk and Money*. This in turn had led to more and flashier magazine assignments and a contract for a second memoir, this one called *Innocence Abroad*, about her junior year of college, when she'd lived in Paris and studied at the Sorbonne and suffered from an eating disorder— it seemed like a terrible waste to me to be an anorexic in France, of all places, but she'd no doubt had her reasons, one of which may well have been that it would net her a hefty advance one day.

Margot and I were maniacally friendly to each other, as if an infusion of artificial warmth would overcome the natural hostility neither of us wanted to acknowledge, but which lay like a frigid spring under our every interaction. We had met through William, with whom she had had a year-long affair when she was a senior at Barnard and he was in his first year of Columbia Law School. She'd dumped him just before summer vacation; I privately suspected that their relationship had served as her experiment with the lower classes, but of course there was no way to verify this theory. Margot treated William with a detached friendliness, but he accorded her an almost reverential respect that made me want to shake him, hard, until his head cleared. Meanwhile, he worried about me and confided in me and listened to me, which was fair enough, except that it wasn't enough for me.

But if Margot thought I was capable of replacing her, I certainly wasn't going to argue, especially after she mentioned the pay (eighteen dollars an hour) and promised that although I was hired to be Jackie's personal secretary, my true purpose would be to fulfill her multi-book contract. "She's not very literary, to put it mildly," she said. "All I have to do is mention that you're a writer and she'll hire you over the phone. I'm telling you this for your own good: you'll write her books for her, but the fun of writing them is the only reward you'll get."

"I see," I said blithely; I had just been laid off from a particularly awful waitressing job.

"No you don't," she said. "I'm warning you, she's impossible. She'll drive you crazy."

I laughed. "How bad can she be?"

"How bad can she *be*," she repeated bemusedly, as if she didn't know quite where to begin, then launched into an account of humiliations I couldn't imagine someone like Margot having to undergo at the hands of one old lady on the Upper East Side. That old bat wouldn't dare tell me in front of three of her society-lady friends that I reeked of garlic; she would never make me take her niece's poodle's bloody stool sample in a taxi to the veterinarian, or kneel down to zip the fly of her jeans; if she did, I would just tell her to go to hell. Margot was obviously more sensitive, more serious than I was; I could put Jackie in her place. Anyway, eighteen dollars an hour—"Do you really think she'll hire me?"

Margot said sympathetically, "I'll call her right now."

Jackie called me ten minutes later. "I trust Margot completely," she said, "and I need someone right away, so I'm not even going to interview you or ask for any sort of résumé. Just come at nine on Monday morning, and we'll take it from there."

I showed up at her Park Avenue building wearing my only

suit, a matronly and unfashionable navy-blue affair I'd bought at a Salvation Army several years before to wear to an interview for a job I didn't get. The doorman, who'd been alerted that I was coming, said a cheery hello ("I'm Ralph," he said, "and you be careful up there!"); the elevator doors opened onto a small vestibule flanked by two doors marked 4A and 4B. On the wall between them hung a dark, authentic-looking oil. Antique urns filled with freshly cut lilies sat by both doors; I reached down and touched a cool, waxy funnel. The wallpaper was cream-colored, faintly flecked with maroon, the air scented with traces of a perfume I didn't recognize. A chill crept along my arms.

She opened the door and we looked each other over. Her face was impenetrable, her hair a bronze lacquered shell. She wore a tailored Chanel suit, the same navy blue as mine, but the resemblance ended there. The phrase "hired sight unseen" hovered unspoken in the air between us; I was suddenly aware that I hadn't combed my hair after my windy walk through Central Park. She sniffed deeply and lifted her nose a notch higher, apparently resolving to make the best of things. "Well, hello, Claudia, come in," she said in a hard, deep voice that didn't match the rest of her. I shook the hand she offered; it was cool and bony and smooth as a lizard. She ushered me into her foyer (gilt, mirrors, marble) and opened the door to the coat closet. As I hung my wool coat between two glistening furs, she said, "I'm so sorry, you'll think I'm very rude, but I'm absolutely crazy today, I have an interview in twenty minutes and a lunch meeting with the man who's translating my book into French. I've left a list of things for you to do, but I don't have time to go through it all. I'm sure you can figure it out. We'll have time to chat later. Margot spoke so highly of you. Right in there. I've got to run."

She disappeared down the hall. I examined my reflection in

the enormous mirror over the marble stand, finger-combed my hair and smoothed my blouse, then skulked through the arched doorway into the dining room. Dark green velvet curtains covered the window; daylight filtered in around the edges, giving the room an undersea murk. When I pressed the wall switch, the chandelier above the large oval table leapt into light, illuminating the place in which (although I couldn't know it yet) I would spend a good part of my waking hours for the next several years. The room was high-ceilinged, formerly elegant, now a little worn around the edges, as if its decline had been too gradual to be noticed by someone who saw it every day. The wallpaper, a repeating Mediterranean landscape of meandering river, olive and cypress groves, church spire in the hazy distance, was peeling behind the radiator and near the baseboard in one corner. The Persian rug was frayed and faded in several places. The table, covered by a dark green tasseled cloth, was spotted with fallen petals from a vase of browning yellow roses; ten or twelve straight-backed chairs with worn green cushions were lined up against the far wall, as if to make room for a junior-high dance.

By the window stood a folding table and plain wooden folding chair, and a small computer table on which were a laptop computer and miniature printer: my new office. I sat at the folding table and stared at Jackie's scrawled list for a while, then shuffled through the papers next to it, which I guessed were related in some way to what she wanted me to do, if I could only read her handwriting. I got up and opened the curtains and squinted at the list again. One of the items appeared to be, "Order three books from editor, Gid Row," and a phone number. I dialed it. "Hello," came a curt male voice after half a ring.

"This is Genevieve del Castellano's secretary," I said hesitantly. Her name was hard to say all at once; I had to take a break halfway through. "May I speak to Gid Row, please?"

He asked in astonishment, "Is this Margot?"

"No," I said, "my name is Claudia Steiner. Margot left. I'm new."

He chuckled; I pictured a fat clean pink man with a highly intelligent face. "With a name like that, you should be the castrating bitch on a soap opera, but you sound more like the ingenue. It's Gil Reeve, by the way, unless she's calling me names."

"Oh, I'm sorry," I said. I double-checked the instructions. "I think she wants me to order three copies of her book."

"Jackie will tell you to call me for every little thing, but you'll learn who does what before too long. I'll switch you over to Janine. Hold on."

Janine said without much enthusiasm that she'd send the books. This was the day's sole achievement. At five o'clock I found Jackie on the phone at her desk in the sitting room. I stood in the doorway until she hung up. When she asked what I'd accomplished that day I said apologetically, "Well, I tried to figure everything out. I looked through the hard drive on the computer and went through some file drawers."

"That's all you did, all day long?"

"And I ordered the books you wanted."

She gave me a look I would come to know very well, a wide-eyed vacuum of a stare that sucked me in and immobilized me. "You didn't do *anything*," she said finally.

What could I say? She had been expecting a real secretary, someone who would bustle in and take charge. I wasn't capable of taking care of myself, let alone someone else. I folded up my desk and wheeled my computer table into the pantry under her direction ("Make sure you put it away every night, Claudia,

25

I don't want visitors to see my dining room looking like a common workplace"). Then I put on my coat, said a meek good night and stomped home. I sat at my table and devoured the contents of a white carton, a glutinous mess of miniature corn ears and crunchy beige disks left over from the night before, not at all improved with age. After dinner, I looked through my closet and despaired at the lack of suitable outfits, Jackie's Chanel suit hanging miragelike before me. Finally I gave up and went to bed, where I lay awake, my thoughts revolving without going anywhere, for several hours.

I wanted to succeed at this job. I had spent my entire youth in a small town in the Arizona desert, then escaped to an even smaller liberal-arts college where everyone was similar in many ways to everyone else. Although I had lived in New York for six years when I met Jackie, I had managed to remain astonishingly unworldly; I'd confined myself mostly to East Village dive bars, midtown office buildings, and the shabbier areas of the Upper West Side. I had never left the States. I had never encountered anyone remotely like Jackie, except in books and movies. I knew, intuitively, that I needed to be slapped awake, and she had struck me right away as just the person who could do it. She was a die-hard Republican, a lapsed Catholic, a European aristocrat and an American celebrity. Her picture appeared in magazines and the society pages of newspapers; she was a guest on talk shows. Her tables and desktops were crowded with gold-framed pictures of herself with movie stars, bullfighters, jockeys, politicians, her handsome late ex-husband, her playboy sons.

I spent the first few weeks in a blur of confounded agony, teeth gritted, shoulders hunched as if I were bracing myself against a gale-force wind. Everything Margot had predicted came to pass. I was not in fact tougher than Margot, and Jackie was not in fact an old bat, she was a terrifying, glamorous semi-lunatic who had it in for me for reasons I couldn't fathom. Nor could I entirely grasp the reason for my presence in her apartment. The logic behind her requests was as inscrutable and unfamiliar as her handwriting. Who was the Countess Robles and why was I calling to tell her that "the dress wasn't long enough"? What exactly did I mean when I called the travel agent to ask about the Florida tickets and make sure they were "the right flight"? I tried to improvise around the bits of information Jackie gave me; I felt too cowardly to risk asking for explanations and being pinned to the wall by her exasperated stare.

In most of my other jobs, I had been just another bored nobody playing computer games and sending faxes, leaving at five without a backward glance, the time colorlessly subtracted from my life like money from the bank. Being alone with Jackie all day in those airless, cloistered rooms transformed me in my own imagination into the heroine of various archetypal dramas, all sharing the common thread of subjugation and silent forbearance. I was bound to rocks, banished to the underworld, imprisoned in towers, mistaken for a frog, sent on impossible quests. Our days together took on a tunnel-visioned, hothouse compression I had heretofore associated with hostages and their captors; I typed and filed, scurried and fetched, bathed in a light that shone only in my own head.

Later that evening when I walked into George's, the place was empty except for the three lonely-guy regulars who'd grown their tailbones down into their bar stools and the weeknight bartender, a formidable giantess named Wanda. She didn't talk much and rarely smiled, but she knew how to toss Macallan over ice cubes until it was silky and cool but minimally diluted, then slide it at just the right instant into a tumbler. This was important because, as part of his fledgling power-elite persona, William was cultivating a taste for perfected single-malt Scotch.

He came in right after me, looking harried and rumpled and carrying his briefcase, straight from work, still in his suit and tie. The sight of him momentarily daunted me. He looked like such a grownup. How had maladjusted little Billy Snow turned into this handsome lawyer, and what, exactly, was I to make of my own situation in light of his success? We were two seeds planted in the same soil, but he was useful and edible, and I was a weed.

"The usual?" he asked, taking out his wallet, a streamlined calfskin affair stocked with platinum credit cards.

"Okay," I said, although I didn't much care for perfected whiskey; all that chilling without diluting did something to its chemical makeup that made it more potent and mood-altering than whiskey drunk either at room temperature or on the rocks. But no matter: I would have what William had, in hopes that his mood and mine would align themselves, two compass arrows drawn to the same magnetic pole.

We hunkered down at a little round wobbly table. As we got a few mouthfuls under our belts, he sighed and rubbed his head. "I brought so much paperwork I might as well have camped in my office," he said.

"You're going to work here?"

"No," he said. "I brought it to fool my conscience. As long as it's with me, I'm safe." He had a crease in each cheek, not exactly dimples, but hollows that deepened when he smiled. I felt light-headed, as if I'd inhaled a balloonful of helium. I exhaled but it didn't go away. "Those old-boy fucks," he was saying now; I'd been watching his mouth with involuntary hunger instead of listening to what he was saying, and so had missed the topic change, but I suspected that he was referring to the senior partners at his firm. "They cornholed each other at Choate, married each other's sisters, they probably borrow each other's clothes. Every day I have to go to the men's room and look in the mirror and say to myself, I'm as good as anyone from a Connecticut charm school. But even though I look and talk and dress just like them, and now I even take a leak just like them, they know I'm an outsider, they can smell it in my DNA."

"How do they take a leak?"

"Like soldiers. Shoulders squared, weapon in hand, ready, aim, fire. I used to just slouch and dribble at the urinal like a wild animal until I noticed someone looking at me funny. Regulation pissing! Can you believe it?" He shook his head, half angry, half proud of himself.

"I have to watch Jackie on the john, too. What's up with that?"

"Speaking of Jackie, I ran into Margot the other day."

I smiled uneasily. "Really? How was she?"

"She was unfriendly. Well, not unfriendly exactly. Sort of polite and distracted. After about two minutes she said, 'Well, nice seeing you again.' Nice seeing you again. Like I was some asshole who had tried to pick her up at a party." He studied his hands, which were cupping his glass and rolling it back and forth against the table. "Next time you talk to her, maybe you could ask her what I've done to offend her."

"William, we aren't friends. If it weren't for Jackie, we would have nothing to talk about. Anyway, speaking of Jackie, she gave me another lecture today about American girls. So what if I didn't grow up knowing a bunch of dukes and earls and viscounts? In what way are viscounts useful?"

"They're like peacocks. They can't sing, and you can't eat them, but they look great in the yard." He took a mouthful of whiskey and held it on his tongue with a sensual grimace that should have made me tell him to cut out the yuppie affectation but instead ignited the little pilot light in my loins. "Ian Macklowe's secretary just quit, in case you're interested."

"Ian Macklowe," I said. A wave of depression crested and broke over my head. "That senior partner who gets three-hundred-dollar haircuts? Who buys his girlfriend hundred-dollar pairs of white cotton underwear? I can't work for that scumbag. My God!"

"You'd make fifty grand a year," said William. "I'd recommend you even though you keep telling me what a shitty secretary you are. You can type, can't you?"

"I'd be totally miserable."

"You're miserable now."

"What do you mean? I'm writing a book. I can't just leave."

He looked at his glass, which was almost empty, and then at mine. "Well, there's always the next round. You in?"

"Why not."

We smiled at each other. To keep myself from leaping at him and devouring him alive, I looked over at Wanda, who was upending a case of Rolling Rock into a bin of ice. Her features were crumpled with the effort into a dented button at the center of the vast white pillow formed by her brow, cheeks and chin. If I had expected the sight of her to steady me, I was disappointed; I floated on a heady, expanding current that almost lifted me from my chair.

"Well hello, you two," said a voice above us, a sharp clear needle piercing the roar. Gus Fleury. His hair was slicked artfully back from his brow in one cohesive wave. A veneer of sweat gleamed on his sharp face. His hair gleamed; his sharkskin jacket gleamed. He was drinking a thick concoction in a tall glass, a swirl of chalky pastel-colored liquids.

"What's in that drink?" I asked. "It looks like barium."

"Crème de this, crème de that," he said, seating himself at

our table. He had emerald-green, almond-shaped eyes, which he widened or narrowed as necessary for maximum theatrical effect. "Don't tell me you've never heard of a Vanderbilt, Claudia."

The moment, or whatever it had been just now with William, had evaporated. "I bet you haven't," said William. "How's it going, Augustine?"

"If you call me that again, I swear I'll put a contract out on you, and I have connections, as you'll hear. I'm in a complete panic, thank you. I'm trolling desperately for a new site for my play. It was supposed to go up next week."

In the mid-eighties, during his final semester at NYU film school, Gus had shot a low-budget movie about East Village drag queens, *Apocalipstick*, which became an art-house hit, won a prize at Sundance and was snapped up by a major distributor; he'd made an additional small fortune from foreign, video and cable TV rights. Because he had invested all this money wisely, he now had the luxury of producing one "original" play after another without having to worry about overhead or profit or the opinions of downtown-weekly theater critics, one of whom had described his work as "precious, icky tripe" and another of whom had written, "The show began with a snot-nosed, self-important whimper, and I have no idea how it ended, because I ran away."

"We had a factory building in Dumbo," he was saying, "but last week the owners, two Jersey wiseguys who wouldn't know artistic integrity if it kneecapped them, heard there was nudity involved. They told me, and I quote, 'No naked fags or no deal.' I told them she's not technically a man any more, but that cut no ice with Dom and Vinnie, and I frankly didn't want to end up feetfirst in a bucket of concrete at the bottom of the East River. So we're homeless now."

"A lot of plays have naked men in them all of a sudden," I

said to no one in particular. "I don't get it. Women can be nude and in total command of the situation, but men without their clothes on look like wet cats. I think Eve ate the apple to give Adam a little dignity."

"*The Waste Land: A Musical Tragedy,*" said Gus to William. "I wrote the music, for synthesizer and drum machine, very seventies, a sort of disco extravaganza. The text speaks so clearly to that whole era, you know what I mean?"

"No," said William, "I don't have a clue. All I read is law crap. Come on, Gus, give us a few bars."

"Let's see." Gus made a show of resting his pointer finger against his cheek and rolling his eyes ceilingward while he mentally scanned the score. Then he took a deep breath and whined in a breathy Bee-Gees falsetto, wagging his head to indicate the drum-machine beat, " 'Here is no water but only rock, rock and no water and the sandy road. Here is no water but oh-honely rock, rock and no water and the sa-handy road.' "

I laughed. William didn't.

"Eliot's text is *chillingly* apropos," said Gus piously. " 'I had not thought death had undone so many,' for example, and the drowned sailor, the sterility, the aura of decay. 'Consider Phlebas, who was once handsome and tall as you.' "

"Apropos of what?" I asked. "Disco? I don't get it."

Gus turned to me as if he'd forgotten I was there, which he probably had. "Of course, Claudia," he said, "you *have* heard of metaphor."

Now William laughed. I looked away as if I'd just seen something mildly interesting at the bar, even though there was a hockey game on TV and Wanda was sitting on a stool in the back, smoking a cigarillo and reading the *Post*. Gus talked on and on, but I wasn't listening; I wasn't even pretending to.

"Blah blah blah, me me me," he said after a while, as if to

sum up the essence of his personality in six words for anyone who hadn't caught on yet, then rested his chin on his hand and gazed at William through intensely green, deeply interested eyes. "So what have you been up to, career boy?"

"Not much," said William. "Churning out the bullshit, billing the hours."

"Stalking the paralegals," I blurted; I was in the grip of a merry recklessness and something else, a hard emptiness underneath the whiskey glow that made me finish what was left of my drink in one gulp and smile edgily at no one.

"Watch out," said William, nudging Gus, "she's on the warpath tonight."

"I'm not that bad," I said defensively. Then I saw by the startled look that flickered across his face that he'd only been teasing me back. "Oh," I said with a brittle laugh. I closed my eyes for a second and felt the room begin a slow reel, then opened them again and squinted at Gus, who gave a wide-eyed start, as if he'd just remembered something of enormous interest and couldn't wait to share it.

"Have you heard the good news about Margot?"

"What good news?" asked William.

"Her memoir just won the Clark Foundation Award," said Gus. "It was totally unexpected. A bolt from the blue. It couldn't have happened to a better person."

Steep black cliffs closed in on me from the corners of the room. "That's a lot of money, isn't it?" I asked. My voice sounded hollow.

"Not to mention the prestige," said Gus. "She can pretty much write her own ticket from here on in."

"Can she," I said. I felt him monitoring me for my reaction, and did my best to look unperturbedly back at him. There was a smudge of mascara on his lower left eyelid, but I didn't tell him.

"That's amazing!" said William. "Good for her. She deserves it." I heard in his voice equal parts respect, wistfulness and affection.

I burst out in a harsh voice, "She probably knows someone on the committee."

They looked at me.

"That's how it works. Of course she's a good writer, but it's amazing the way she seems to have connections to everyone who can help her. She schmoozes like the rest of us breathe. She's known all the right people since she was born." With an enormous effort, I made myself shut up.

"Is that so," said Gus. He studied me for a moment with a canny appraisal that made me cast about for a way to modify what I had said. I didn't look at William; I hadn't been able to look at him since he'd laughed at me.

"She's lucky," is what I came up with. "We need all the help we can get."

Gus raised his eyebrows at me over the top of his glass. "We certainly do," he said. He drained the last drops of his drink; the ice cubes rattled against his teeth. A peculiar look crossed his face then, a flicker of queasy self-doubt. "Excuse me just a moment," he said. He set his glass, empty now except for a sticky adherence, on the table, and stood up. The bar had become very crowded in the last few minutes. He leaned into the press of bodies behind him until they parted enough for him to insert himself and disappear among them.

"FYI, Claudia," said William, "there's no such drink as a Vanderbilt. He loves to make people feel like barn animals for not having heard of something he's just invented."

"How hilarious that must be for him," I said. FYI? Did he think he was writing me a memo? "Why are you friends with him?"

"Why is anyone friends with anyone?" he said mildly, and went off to buy another round. Behind the bar, a string of flashing colored lights pulsed like tiny hearts right where real hearts would have been if the bottles of alcohol had been human figures. High overhead, propellers mixed air with smoke and sent it downward; faces bloomed in the dim light, talking and sending smoke ceilingward. A country song ambled out of the jukebox. The metallic plaint of the slide guitar stirred up a squall in my chest; the whiskey spread a thick, fuck-it-all paralysis through me that made me go limp in my chair. I was so envious of Margot my arms ached, but it was the pure, hopeless envy of a paraplegic watching an Olympic runner win another gold.

Oh, buck the hell up, I told myself. What would it matter in a hundred years? It would all be over by then; maybe no one would even be around to know or care. We were all just shoring fragments against our ruins.

The jukebox went silent. Where was William? God, I loved him. The same hopeless paraplegic feeling doused me again. The process by which men and women fell in love and coupled off had always been about as clear to me as quadratic equations or Masonic rites. I'd grown up without being exposed to many actual men besides teachers, who didn't really count. I had cobbled together a composite picture for myself out of the limited source material at hand. My mother had naturally weighed in heavily with the opinion that the male sex was a lower order without common sense or the capacity to behave responsibly, but Gothic novels and fairy tales had inculcated in me the equally strong but contrary expectation that either a prince of some kind would carry me off to his castle or Mr. Rochester would eventually marry me if I waited for him to go blind. By the time I was eight years old, I'd absorbed the idea that courtship and marriage happened when the perfect man came along and chose you from the lineup. All you could do, as the girl, was stand there and wait.

After living for so many years with such precise and deeply ingrained expectations, being confronted with an actual flesh-and-blood man was like trying to understand a spoken foreign language whose dictionary I had read. Every now and then I caught a glimpse of a familiar word, but these brief flashes of comprehension never evolved into an ongoing conversation. Getting drunk and having sex with strangers seemed to open lines of communication in a physical, temporary sense, but I never remembered afterwards whatever it was I'd learned. William and I were friends, but there seemed to be no bridge between friendship and romance.

The jukebox exploded; the crowd yelled at each other, blowing smoke. I looked around in a panic, feeling as if my eight-year-old self had been whizzed through the intervening years and set down here at George's, alone and drunk.

William returned then from the other direction. I took the fresh glass of cold whiskey he offered me and took a sip; it tasted like cold sweat. "Thanks," I said. "This is the last thing I need, but thanks."

"Where's Gus?" he said. He looked around, puzzled, as if the presence of Gus weren't an odious burden to be avoided at all costs. The whiskey rose in my gorge, now tasting like bile.

"The Waste Land: A Musical Tragedy," I said passionately. "How pretentious can you get? He's so fucking full of himself."

"I'm back," came a voice from just above our heads. Then Gus seated himself primly, sipping from a brand-new Vanderbilt.

"There you are," said William.

"This play is just not going to happen," said Gus. He

looked frustrated. "No one can give me any leads. There is no available space in all of New York City."

"You can use my apartment, if it comes to that," said William.

Gus put his arm around William's neck and kissed his cheek. "Is he the most beautiful thing you ever saw?" he asked me.

I nodded mutely, aware of the electric proximity, under the table, of William's leg to mine; I pulled my knee away from his just before it made contact. When we'd finished our new drinks, William said, stretching and yawning, "Well, kids, time to go and do my homework."

"Pity you can't stay," said Gus. "I think I'll drift over to the bar and chat up that blond boy who's been giving me the eye."

"Are you going toward the subway?" I asked William.

"Sure," he said. "I'll meet you outside; I've got to go to the john."

"By the way, Claudia," Gus said as I was putting on my coat, "maybe you should come and see *The Waste Land* before you decide it's pretentious. You just might be surprised." His pointy dog teeth stabbed his lower lip. We exchanged a frank look; I recognized in his expression the fact that he didn't like or respect me very much, either.

For some reason, now that the animosity between us was out in the open, I was filled with a sudden strange goodwill toward him. "Fair enough," I said. "And good luck with the blond."

"Some people don't need luck," he said, batting his eyes.

"We all do, remember?" I said, and made my way out of the bar to the sidewalk, where I took deep breaths to clear my lungs. Rain dropped out of a white sky and ran through the gutters. I hadn't brought an umbrella; icy raindrops struck my forehead and trickled into my eyes and went down the back of my coat collar.

As I turned to the plate-glass window that fronted the bar, I thought I saw blue light sliding along the top of an oily pompadour right next to William's face. William's eyes were closed, and he was smiling. It looked as if Gus had his face buried in William's shoulder, but the air was smoky, and the crowd was thick. I shook my head to clear it, then looked into the bar again just as William emerged through the door a moment later. "Sorry," he said, "there was a line."

I felt even drunker out here in the cold, wet, windy street, like a marionette lurching loose-jointedly along. We were walking along St. Marks Place, past basement boutiques, fluorescent-lit fast-food joints, a fleabag hotel. We dodged a clump of drifting Trustafarians, their pimply teenaged suburban skin pierced, tattooed, track-marked, dirt-encrusted. "Hey," I blurted with soggy belligerence to one tall, emaciated lad who stepped into my path, or maybe I stepped into his. "Go home to your mother."

"Steady there." William steered me away with his hand on my elbow.

I leaned against him. "What was Gus doing to your neck?"

"When?"

"Like a vampire, right before you came out of the bar."

"Gus is a vampire."

"Well, it was disgusting," I said, but without much heat; I didn't care what we said as long as I was leaning against him. I slid my arm around his waist and he rested his arm across my shoulders; through the layers of his clothes and coat his body felt sturdy but malleable, as if it could hold its own against mine but would accommodate anything I cared to do to him. One of his shirt buttons bumped against my tooth. I closed my eyes dreamily, gave myself over to a haze of happiness, and let him lead me. He didn't seem to mind.

When he brought us to a stop I opened my eyes. We were, I saw, on the island at Cooper Square, standing at the curb, waiting for the light to cross Lafayette.

"Do you want me to get you a cab?" he said.

"Let me just stand here for a minute."

"Okay, but don't fall asleep, because I don't think I can carry you home."

"I would never ask you to," I murmured contentedly.

The light changed and people flowed by us, but we made no move to cross. We were swaying a little, holding each other upright. I put my face on his neck, right where Gus's face had been. I nuzzled my nose against him and closed my eyes. His pulse beat under my mouth, intimate and strange. It felt wonderful; my breathing slowed. I drank in the smell of his skin, raised my hand to the back of his neck and crushed the bristly hairs at the nape. I felt his head move against mine, heard the crackle of hair in my ears, the crunch of his coat. When I looked up at him, his face was a blur, his eyes one long eye. When I moved my mouth closer to his, a warm, living, pliant creature surrendered itself to my lips fleetingly and was gone. It happened so fast I wasn't sure I hadn't imagined it. Then we were standing a few feet apart, looking at each other. "Whoa," he said, laughing. "What was that?"

My face was burning; the cold rain felt good on it. The memory of his mouth recoiling from mine replayed itself viscerally. My mind felt as if a dark curtain had gone down in it. "I'm sorry, I just couldn't help it," I said, or meant to say; my words were probably indistinct, because my mouth wasn't working right. "I can't believe we've known each other for—why haven't we ever slept together?"

"Claudia," he said with a gleam in his eye, a rakish deflecting flash of—not amusement, surely, I must have been imagining it, "you are smashed."

"Could you hail me a cab?"

He raised his arm at the oncoming traffic and a taxi shot to the curb. He handed me into it, gave the driver a bill and told him my address. "Keep a good tip, and give her the change," he told the driver. When the man began to protest, William said, "Hey. You have change. It's a rainy night. Take care, Claudia, I'll call you tomorrow." He shut the car door and went off into the night, heading down the middle of Lafayette with his coattails billowing behind him, his briefcase bumping against his leg. Where was he going? He lived way up on York in the East Nineties.

Colored lights blurred together in one long streak all the way uptown. The driver stopped in front of my building, hit the meter, and turned on the overhead light. I waited passively, relaxed in the warmth of the cab, for what I didn't know. He handed me some money and I waved it away. My head lolled against the high back of the seat. "That's all right," I said, as if I were the Queen of Sheba, which was how I needed to feel.

"But he gave me a hundred bucks." He pushed the wad of bills at me.

Oh, William. He couldn't afford that. His mortgage and law-school loan payments made my own debts look like a joke. Did he think I was some kind of charity case? Damn him. Fuck him, in fact.

"Keep it," I said regally, as if it were too much of a nuisance to have to cope with change so late at night. The moment I got out of the cab, it tore off down the street and slid, fast, around the corner. I lurched to the front door of my building and fumbled with my keys. I took the stairs slowly, pausing on my way up to lean my head against the wall. At the top of the second flight I sat down on the landing and leaned against the wall and stared at the earwax-yellow paint of the stairwell. I couldn't face my apartment. All those unopened envelopes were still on the table where I'd left them. The cockroaches. The unmade bed.

Oh, shit, I thought, remembering. I stood up and climbed the stairs rapidly, dreading everything.

chapter three

I came in: no roaches in sight, and no Delilah, but I knew they were all around somewhere. I stood in the middle of my room, feeling unspeakably lonesome. I don't know exactly how long I stood there, but at some point, the phone rang. I went over to the telephone and picked up the receiver with a pang of joy. He was calling to apologize for laughing at me, for sending me home. To tell me he loved me.

"Claudia."

"Ma?"

"Am I calling too late?" She always stayed up until the "wee-wee hours," as she persisted in calling them, grading papers or reading the latest anti-Freudian propaganda and gritting her teeth.

"No," I said. Oh, well. "How are you, Ma?"

"Oh, I'm all right," she said, then added something in German, which I pretended not to understand. "Everything all right with you?"

To my enormous shame, I heard myself asking her for a loan. "It's just that my rent is overdue," I said. "And I'm afraid he might actually evict me this time."

She sighed. "Ja, liebchen, I can't lend you any more money. It's not that I can't afford it; I don't think it's goot for you to owe me so much."

She was absolutely right, as always, but I had never quite allowed it to register in my mind that she expected me to pay her back the same way Visa or my bank did. I'd always managed to lull myself into a false sense of immunity, assuming that simply because she was my mother, she might call it a loan but would staunchly wave me away if I ever actually tried to pay her back. Her expenses were nil, and her salary as a tenured psychology professor at a state university got bigger all the time. How expensive could acrylic sweaters be? How else was she going to spend her savings, if not on occasionally bailing out her ne'er-do-well daughter? I liked thinking of myself as her ne'er-do-well daughter; unfortunately, she didn't.

"Maybe it might be time to find a better situation." She was talking through a mouthful of something that sounded like oatmeal but was probably instant chocolate pudding. "Maybe it's time to decide what you really want to do."

Now we were at the heart of things. It had taken under a minute to get there. "I have a good job," I said obdurately. "I'm writing a book."

"I know how hard it is to establish a career as a young person," she said as if writing a book were roughly on the same level as washing dishes in a diner. She had endless theories about youth and its attendant delusions and weaknesses; what would she tell herself about me in a couple of years when I could no longer be considered a "young person" by any stretch of interpretation? What theory would she trot out then? "I did it myself, five years in that city, without anyone to help me, only hard work. I know exactly what it's like."

This was true; my mother had lived all through graduate school on powdered milk, and had lived in a room the size of an elevator, but this was meaningless to me right now. Her poverty was over, and mine was upon me. I listened mutely as her sergeant of a jaw put the spoon through its paces. She was wearing, I was sure, the usual green khaki flood pants and neon-bright acrylic sweater pulled straight down as far as it would stretch over her square mannish hips, not to hide them, but because she thought that was the way to wear a sweater.

"You know," she went on, and I braced myself, because I knew many things, none of which I wanted to hear from her, "maybe it's time to consider going to graduate school."

"I don't want to go to graduate school," I said. I scratched my head to dissipate some of the pent-up static electricity in there; I knew all my lines for this conversation, even stone-drunk. "And I don't think graduate school wants me. We have a mutual understanding."

She laughed with the gruff formality of someone not used to joking around. "Anyway, I'm coming down to New York soon, there's a conference. The first Saturday in April. Maybe you might have time for dinner with your old mother? Not too many dates with all the hendsome men?"

"Of course I have time," I said. "We can go to that Ukrainian place you like, remember?"

"Oh, they're all alike, all the cockroaches they got back there, no one washing hands. Better maybe we should stay in, better we cook for ourselves, you're probably too busy that night anyhow."

"If you want, we could eat at my place, but my kitchen isn't much, remember."

"I'm not sure whether we'll go late, in which case I don't want to keep you waiting, so we might as well wait until the next night if you can do it then. I wouldn't be able to concentrate, knowing you were standing out there, so hungry."

"I live here. I can distract myself. I like to watch people. I'll be okay."

And so it went, for five more minutes or so, until finally she agreed that if the conference went late she could assuage her conscience with the knowledge that I'd buy myself a hot dog. "On the steps, then," she said.

"Six o'clock."

"Or later."

"Or later, it doesn't matter how much," I said.

All of our conversations, even in better times, were patterned according to an identical blueprint. She pushed me to the brink of my patience but never quite over it, and I hid behind a shield of grim daughterly cheer that kept her at bay but never pushed her away entirely. With just the slightest increase of pressure from either side, the phone line would have sizzled and shrunk like a lit fuse toward both of us.

After I mouthed a farewell and we hung up, I noticed that the light on my answering machine was blinking. I pressed the play button with a lump high in my throat. Jackie's voice rasped out at me like the croak of some awful bird.

"Claudia," she said; I felt my ribs tighten around my lungs, "I just remembered something else I meant to ask you when I called earlier, but I can't think right now what it was. You must come straight in and see me first thing tomorrow. I know it's very important, something you'll have to do right away."

I hit the rewind button and fell onto my bed, where I stared up at the blank ceiling and waited for the room to stop spinning. Tears pooled coldly in my ears. In the street below, traffic roared through the rain, rattling the white plaster membrane of my little room. The air held me wetly in its mucilaginous grip; I felt as singular, thin-skinned and swollen with humors as a yolk. A long time later I wriggled out of my jeans and threw them on the floor, then turned out the light and lay in the darkness for a long time, not quite awake, but not sleeping, either.

Shortly after I'd left Evandale, Arizona, for Swarthmore, my mother called me at my dorm and announced that she would be moving East the following year. This gave me the impression that she was following me, so I urged her to stay where she was.

"I am so tired of this place," she said.

"Then why did you stay there all these years?"

"Because of you, liebchen."

"Me?"

"Because I wanted you to grow up in such a beautiful place, and not have to make new friends in your formative years."

I snorted. "Ma," I said, "I didn't have any friends in my formative years. I couldn't wait to leave."

She laughed. "You loved Arizona! You had the childhood I would have wanted, at least I could give you that."

I thought it prudent not to contradict her.

Although she had lived in upstate New York now for years, I still pictured my mother in Evandale in that spic-and-span cuckoo clock of a house on its miniature, crew-cut, unnaturally green lawn surrounded by a white fence, near the edge of town, on a wide, quiet street that ended where the foothills began their rise to the mountains that ringed the northeastern end of the valley. On the other side of our backyard fence spread a rubbled waste of fissured sand, lizards, barrel cacti as humped and bewhiskered as old men, saguaros raising hairy arms at each other.

That barren expanse was called the Ventana Valley. Several parched, dispirited little towns adhered to its surface; Candlewick, the largest of these, offered in the way of culture an A&W, a Kentucky Fried Chicken, Babbitt's Supermarket and the drive-in movie theater. Evandale lay a mile or so off the highway, an abject little backwater with a prisonlike elementary school, a couple of small mold-smelling markets, several churches, mostly Baptist, and a brown, listless park. The Ventana Valley was, for travelers passing through, a tedium of empty miles to be crossed. For those of us who were stuck there and wished we weren't, it was a far deeper tedium of time.

My mother had designed her house with a spatial economy having nothing to do with the desert it sat in and everything to do with the crammed-together medieval Black Forest village where she had been born and raised: it rose neatly, narrowly from the sprawling flats of ranch houses with carports, a slender structure of gingerbread eaves, bay window, dormers, a pitched roof. Every house in town had low plaster ceilings, linoleum and shag rugs, except for ours. Exposed dark beams vaulted our high living room ceiling; our wooden floors and counters were waxed and buffed to an old-world glow. Along two walls of my mother's study, dusted twice a month, were the complete works of Freud, nearly every existing book about him, the writings of Jung and Adler for purposes of (unfavorable) comparison, and various other reference materials. She kept all her "light" reading on her bedroom bookshelves upstairs—sixty or more dog-eared Agatha Christie paperbacks and a collection of hardbound nineteenth-century Russian novels as thick as loaves of bread. Most of our neighbors owned several Bibles, subscribed to the *Reader's Digest* and kept a few brand-new paperback best-sellers on their coffee tables, which they donated to the church bazaar when they were finished with them. In such a climate, the prevailing attitude toward my mother was a mixture of suspicion and admiration. She was an egghead and a brain in a place where gleaning actual knowledge from books was accorded an odd kind of half-wishful skepticism: no one understood it, they didn't quite believe it could really be done, and so they both respected and derided anyone who seemed to know how.

At the age of twenty-three, Gerda Steiner had left Freiburg to pursue a Ph.D. in psychology at Columbia, and had become an American citizen several years later. I could see her, dressed in one of those enormous, belted, pleated, shin-length fifties skirts, tapping ferociously at her typewriter until nearly dawn in her tiny rented room up near Harlem, having the time of her life. If Freudian theory was the flame of truth, then she was the glass lantern that housed it, shining over a sea of darkness and illuminating its depths with oral compulsions, dreams about wigs and cigars, Oedipal complexes, repressed urges and desires.

She had loved westerns as a child; she'd sat in German movie theaters, sometimes through three showings of the same movie, staring awestruck at tumbleweeds and sagebrush and sand. All she knew of the American Southwest was what she'd seen in black and white on the enormous screen, but it was enough to instill in her a longing so powerful that she left civilization behind for the wilds of Arizona as soon as she received her doctorate. She founded her mission in the wilderness, the Ventana Valley Psychoanalytic Institute, in a dusty Quonset hut on a scrubby patch of land just off the highway near Camp Ventana. Whether or not she was disappointed by the realities of Arizona after the cinematic dream of her childhood, she got right down to business. She recruited students by advertising, made something of a name for herself on the lecture circuit, and published articles, no doubt highly opinionated and provocative, in Freudian journals. Her mentor from Columbia and lifelong admirer, Dr. Grover Highland, recommended her program to everyone he could. No one had ever been to Arizona in those days; it sounded as exotic and remote as Persia to suburbanites and city dwellers.

So, against all odds, my mother had managed to inspire an increasing number of people to leave families and jobs for a stint in the middle of nowhere with her. After three years, she'd hired several more instructors and moved to the former site of the Yavapai Country Club in Candlewick, a sparkling, stucco oasis where sprinklers threw arcs of diamonds over the old golf course. Practicing and would-be psychoanalysts flocked from all over the country to be psychoanalyzed and lectured on such topics as "Development and Resolution of the Narcissistic Transference," and "Eros Against Thanatos: An Analysis of Psychoanalysis," and even "What Women Want." Remembering this, I had to laugh to myself. What Women Want! All she wanted were her worshipful students, her tidy little house and stout walking shoes and pork-butt sandwiches every day at noon on the dot! What other woman in the universe wanted those things? How could my mother presume to speak for womankind? But she did, and they all listened, took notes, quoted her later in their own papers.

By the time she was thirty-six, she was the owner of the only gingerbread house in Evandale, the guru of her own institute and the unwed mother of a baby girl she'd christened Claudia after some maiden aunt of hers she'd always admired. My birth was the one part of all this that may not have been on her original agenda, but she set about mothering with the same single-minded efficiency she brought to everything. She changed my diapers and administered bottles of formula (breast-feeding was all well and good for ordinary mothers, but she herself was far too busy) between sessions and classes; whenever she needed a baby-sitter, she cast a net into her well-stocked pool of serious bearded men or earnest bright-eyed women, one of whom obligingly dangled a rattle in my airspace all afternoon for minimal pay, or maybe no pay at all; the honor of being chosen was no doubt more than adequate recompense.

I had no father, no brothers or sisters. My male parent had been a visiting lecturer named Charles Kirby who got sucked into my mother's orbit for reasons I couldn't begin to fathom; during their encounter, he had managed to produce a spermatozoon intrepid enough to penetrate the tough hide of her ovum. When she was done with him, she spat him out and he crawled away to perish, or so I imagined my conception as having gone. All she would ever tell me about him was that he was British, male and dead; he'd been hit by a car crossing a busy London street before I was even born. One day I came across a blurred picture of him in a 1967 course catalogue, the year he'd lectured at the institute. I was mystified by his gleaming blond handsomeness: why had he felt the need to consort with the likes of my mother? Although pictures from that era showed a younger, slimmer, smiling version of her, I found it nearly impossible to imagine the two of them together. "He was no one so interesting," she had told me. "He was so typical! Really, he was after only one thing."

"What thing?" I asked immediately.

Like any devout Freudian, she believed that the subject of sex was repressed at one's own risk, so she answered me frankly, but with a detached briskness: she was above such animal urges except for the momentary behavioral aberration that had produced me. Her body was simply the necessary housing for her brain. I never saw her naked, and I doubted that she ever minutely inspected, as I so frequently did my own, her nude reflection in the full-length mirror on the back of the bathroom door. She spent her life sifting through the muck of other people's psyches while consigning her own to the realm of things best left alone; the one bodily pleasure she allowed herself was food, which she enjoyed with unapologetic gusto.

As I got older, I became increasingly aware of the vast, unbreachable distance between the mother I had and the mother I couldn't help wanting. I was never petted or cuddled, except by the occasional baby-sitter-disciple who'd left her own kids at home in L.A. or New Jersey while she pursued her career, and so found in me a temporary stopgap for her maternal longings. Although she must have been aware of various experiments in which lab mice unlicked by their mothers became weak and listless and finally died, my own mother's attentions toward me were primarily expressed in determining the true meaning of my behavior: Freud had had some fairly strong ideas about childhood, and I was expected to conform to all of them. I did my best to comply, outwardly at least, but it made me feel a little cheap and apprehensive, as if she'd see right through me and call my bluff. When I was seven or so, she caught me admiring one of my bodily creations in the toilet bowl instead of flushing it down right away the way she'd taught me, and she informed me that I was going through a late anal fixation. "Sorry," I said, looking regretfully at the bowl. "Should I take some medicine?"

She flushed the toilet with a steady hand. "You should not worry at all. You're perfectly normal in this. You might find that you do it again, and if you do I want you to tell me, all right?"

"All right," I said.

The next day I forced myself to do it again, although naturally I'd lost my original private interest in the enterprise. I went into her study and reported my behavior with a nervously insincere half-smile. She took me into the bathroom and inspected the scene, which was just as I'd left it. "Interesting," she said, well pleased. She flushed away the data without another word and returned to her work. I shrugged to myself and went up to my room, where I sat for a while, doing nothing, feeling vaguely ornery and low.

Equally perturbing to me, but in a more tangible way, was the shining, fussbudgety legion of porcelain figurines arranged on every surface, upstairs and down, according to some mysterious taxonomy handed down through the generations. They were not to be disturbed or touched. My mother dusted them herself. They had been her mother's, and before that her grandmother's. My mother was their present custodian, and I would be expected to take over when the time came, but they had no real owner, they were more like household gods; they possessed, in miniature and en masse, a strange kind of power, a morbid Teutonic righteousness: I hated the purse-lipped little shepherdess and her gamboling sheep, the battery of obscenely fat cherubs with legs like marbled hams, a farm's worth of creepy cows and goats with mournful human faces, several groomless brides, smugly replete with bridehood, an army of pastoral lads and lasses wielding either buckets, hoes and rakes or fifes, horns and drums, all of them stout and apple-cheeked, deranged with joyful acceptance of their lot. I had recurring, powerfully enjoyable fantasies about shoving them all into a cardboard box, taking them outside into the desert, digging a deep hole and burying them under a saguaro. But since my mother had made it very clear that touching or moving or accidentally knocking one over was punishable by death, I navigated the narrow hallways like a tightrope walker, and rarely ventured into the living room, where every rickety end table and whatnot was jammed with them.

I had a few friends, but our alliance was merely the expedient and self-protective banding-together of outsiders: Reuben Grady, who breathed through his mouth and smelled of pee; Linda Flavin, a Jehovah's Witness who wasn't allowed to make Halloween decorations or wear gym shorts; Jessica Marshall, fat and smart; Bobby Gordon, fat and goggle-eyed; Billy Snow, the scary little deviant; and me. It never occurred to any of us to hang out together after school. It was enough to have to be associated with each other all day.

The only one of my fellow outcasts for whom I felt any affinity was Billy. His father, Ed Snow, was head administrator of the institute; he and my mother weren't exactly friends, because my mother had no friends, but they liked each other well enough to sit at a poker table together once every month or two, so Billy and I shared the nebulous bond of kids whose parents are associated in some way: we didn't know whether or not we liked each other, but when we passed each other in the halls or on the playground, we exchanged an awkward smile, as if we shared a guilty secret.

Although Ed Snow had a master's degree in administration from the University of Texas and an office job working for a bunch of psychoanalysts, he looked and acted like a character from *Deliverance*. He was a swaybacked, chubby, potbellied man with a white-blond buzz cut, a wide, soft face with small blue eyes set crookedly on either side of a pug nose. When he played poker at our house, his eerie high-pitched cackle disturbed the air currents and made my skin crawl. His wife had died when Billy was three, but no doubt Billy looked like her; Ed Snow was a rodent of some kind, a large soft sewer rat, while Billy was a mongrel, feral but intelligent, fine-featured and lanky, with coarse black badly cut hair and thick glasses taped together in one corner.

I was afraid of Billy, but I also admired him. His resistance was as outward as mine was covert. He lived with his father in a dismal house with a boarded-up window that Billy himself had broken and no one had fixed. In the lower grades his infractions were minor: poking girls, throwing spitballs at the blackboard. As the years progressed, so did his crimes, from setting trash can fires and stealing lunch money to ripping a toilet out of a boys' room stall and, in eighth grade as a sort of pièce de résistance, hot-wiring a teacher's Mustang during school hours and taking it into the desert for a joyride. He was always being sent to the principal's office. The teachers suspended him, threatened to expel him permanently, swatted him, sent notes home to his father, but nothing they did affected him in any way that I could see. His father beat him, everyone knew about it; he'd show up limping one morning, and squirm around in his chair as if he couldn't get comfortable, but not even that could quell him. He destroyed anything that got in his way, and anyone who teased or provoked him was sorry: he leapt at them, arms windmilling, trying to tear their eyes out. Most people left him alone.

In the second-grade Christmas pageant, Billy was cast as Joseph and I played Mary. As we trudged side by side from stage right to stage left and back to stage right, getting turned away by various innkeepers in doorways, Billy, as directed by the teacher, supported me with one hand around my waist and the other under my elbow, guiding me as if I were an extremely pregnant woman instead of a seven-year-old girl. I had until that moment thought of him as someone whose attention it was unwise to attract, but now he enfolded me like a precious, fragile thing and gave me a look of such pure and spellbinding tenderness that I was shocked out of my concentration on my role; I looked gratefully back at him, oblivious of the audience and the pageant, of anything but this compassion that had been visited on me from out of nowhere. When the pageant was over, Billy turned back into the same unpredictable psychopath he'd always been, with no interest in me or anyone else, but I felt secretly allied with him, whether he knew it or not, from that moment on.

The other person I admired, but not so secretly, was Lauren McDevitt, who lived next door. On those wonderful days when she had nothing better to do than to play with me, I jumped up from my book when I heard the doorbell ring and ran downstairs as fast as I could without disturbing the figurines. When I opened the front door, she seized my arm and compelled me outside to serve as the supporting cast for the various games she devised—explorers, travelers, foreign spies—whose general plot and parameters she would establish, and whose literary details I would then attempt to supply. My tastes tended very much toward the romantic and improbable and hers not at all, so these make-believe sessions always involved a lot of running and shouting and very little internal drama.

Just beyond our backyards was a rusted-out old sedan, half-buried. We climbed through a hole in her fence to sit in it and drive to faraway destinations; Lauren allowed me to keep up a running narrative while she occupied herself with shifting gears and gunning the engine through the scenery I was feverishly, joyfully describing: a bridge arched over a deep river that led to the outskirts of a city, into whose heart we rocketed. On we went, past a jumble of theaters, skyscrapers, apartment buildings, department stores. Finally Lauren had to remind me, "I'm driving, Claudia."

"I know," I said.

"So quit telling where we're going."

"Okay," I said, overpowered suddenly with a rapt adoration. "You're so beautiful," I sighed. "You have princess hair."

"Get off me, you lezzie," she said gruffly, pushing my hand away, shoving my head.

Throughout these long afternoons outside with her, I was

55

always conscious of being a speck at the bottom of a vast, ragged bowl of rock under the empty sky, buried in the silence and heat, surrounded by blank sand. The foothills, with their gray-green mesquite fur, rolled away to faraway mountains that sat sharp-spined on the horizon, unconnected to the valley floor, as if they'd been set down ready-made. The buttes and mesas to the west glowed deep red; veins of magenta and green spidered along rock formations shaped like tablets or giant hands, stacked in layers of cinnabar, crimson, brick. Masses of clouds echoed the rock shapes in their charcoal or ocher strata, wind-shaped crags so dense they looked mineral. The air was thick with the breath of sage and hot dust. At sunset the air hung low, striated like a weird plowed field of pigmented earth, backlighting the mountains with shirred, neon clouds, leaching all the color from the rocks, abstracting the bushes to dark cutouts. The wind moved like a huge hand through the valley, filling me with a restless, empty impatience I later identified as loneliness.

There was a factory just outside Evandale; I could see it from our yard. During the day trucks drove to and from its gates in a blur of smoke and dust, but at night it became a scaffolding of glowing white tubes and gold lights. There was a moment during sundown every evening when the factory lights came on but the sky was still wild with clouds and color; the factory's sudden illumination had no more effect than a flashbulb going off in a bright room, but as the sky darkened, its lights intensified until it floated on the sand floor of the valley like the fantasy city I dreamed of. When the factory lights got so bright they made haloes on our eyelashes, my mother appeared in the back doorway, stocky and imperious, yodeling "Hoo-oo!" out into the darkness, a sound that made Lauren laugh and me cringe inwardly with embarrassed irritation at my odd, foreign-born, hopelessly uncool, self-righteously backward mother. It was time to go in for dinner.

Through the years, my mother hired a succession of women to cook and clean for us. I didn't know any of them well, since they came during the day while I was at school. By the time I came home they were gone, and our laundry was clean and folded, the breakfast dishes were washed, our beds were made, the floors were swept. They also left pots of stew or chili on the stove, pans of enchiladas in the oven. The food they made was oddly repellent to me; a stranger's hands had cubed the meat, chopped the onions, wrapped the tortillas. My mother loved this food and ate it with tremendous enjoyment. It annoyed her that I wouldn't eat it: "Stop being so picky-picky," she commanded. "If you don't eat it you'll have to starve, there isn't anything else."

I gagged it down in spiteful silence, not that she noticed: she was too involved in her rehashes of squabbles with a few of her more contentious colleagues, in this case Mark Wickers and Susan Fletcher: "They asked permission to teach together a verkshop on the techniques of Skinner. Too bad for them, because Fletcher is not coming beck next year and Vickers is dem lucky he got that contract. I cannot bear these idiot people! They drife me crazy with their stupid ideas!" She glared at me as if I might be in secret cahoots with them. I fled upstairs the moment I'd dried my hands on the dish towel.

At eight-thirty, I went down in my pajamas to poke my head into her study to say good night. In books, mothers kissed their children, told them stories, sang them lullabies. I stood in the doorway, shy with dread, filled with hopeless longing, picking at a sliver of wood in the door frame, gazing at my mother. At the slightest hint of encouragement from her, I would have flung myself into her arms, buried my face in her neck and held on to her so tightly she would have had to peel me off her, one limb at a time, to rid herself of me.

After a moment, she looked up from her book, placing a finger on the page to mark her place. "You brushed your teeth?"

"Yeah."

"Face clean? You finished your homework?"

"Just about," I lied.

"All right then, up with you. Sleep tight, liebchen."

I waited just a moment. No dice. "Good night, Ma," I said then, and went upstairs.

After breakfast, a hurried bowl of cold cereal I forced down my throat to keep my mother from getting out the rectal thermometer, I waited as usual in front of Lauren's house until she came out. We walked the eight or nine blocks to school together. She was nice enough to me until we set foot on the playground, but then a formidable junta of girls coalesced around her, popular girls, secretive and snide, and she forgot all about me, as well she should have, since my political value to her was nil. I wandered off to the shady breezeway, where I sat until the bell rang, leaning against the cool cinder-block wall with a book propped against my knees.

The Saturday morning after my fourteenth birthday, which is to say, when I had reached what my mother considered to be the age of "sexual maturity" (I'd had my period for over a year already but hadn't been able to bring myself to tell her), she marched upstairs and knocked on my bedroom door, then strode into my room brandishing a thick white orthopedic-looking garment she'd bought especially for me. It bore so little resemblance to the lacy pink castoffs Lauren had been handing down to me for two or three years that I might not have figured out what it was if my mother hadn't demonstrated its purpose for me. Her means of doing so was typically blunt: "Claudia," she said, holding the Ace-bandage-like contraption to her own chest, "this is a brassiere for you, and you wear it so you don't flop all over the place." She had also brought along a box of maxi pads. Lauren had taught me to use a tampon already, but I watched in horrified, spellbound fascination as my mother held the pad to her crotch with the blasé practicality of a stewardess demonstrating a seat-belt fastener.

At some point early in our freshman year of high school, Billy Snow must have woken up one day and realized that no one was going to help him escape, so he'd better do it himself. He skulked through the halls with his books tucked under one big hand, the other shoved deep in the pocket of his pants so it wouldn't punch anyone. He never had a girlfriend, never went to a dance; his clothes were wrinkled and not quite clean, as if he'd worn them to bed, and he smelled strongly of cigarette smoke and unwashed hair. But he made every honor roll, and was a National Merit Scholar. He got into the University of Arizona on full scholarship.

I got into Swarthmore with enough financial aid so my mother didn't have to empty her savings account to send me there. During my sophomore year, when my mother joined the faculty of the New York State University at Albany, she turned her institute over to several of her staff, among them the treacherous, Skinner-reading Mark Wickers, who had managed to wriggle back into her good graces. She bought herself a Victorian house on a treelined street near the campus and started a private practice in addition to her teaching load. She'd been there, on the whole happily, ever since.

Five years after I'd graduated from college and moved to New York, I was at the farmers' market in Union Square one Wednesday evening, and there, standing over a table of apple cider, was Billy Snow. My first reaction, almost before I'd even recognized him, was a pang of relief at the restoration of a loss I hadn't known I'd sustained. The slope of his brow, his expression, the way he stood looked as familiar and poignant as if our long separation had been that of estranged spouses. "Billy," I said abruptly. He turned and saw me, and for an instant looked blank. "Claudia Steiner," he said then in disbelief, and his face came to life, smiling, glad to see me. We stood talking until we agreed that we were thirsty, and went to the Old Town Bar for the first of countless drinking bouts together.

He had graduated the year before from Columbia Law School and had recently become a junior associate with a firm whose name was a string of *Mayflower*-sounding patronyms, which explained why he was wearing a suit, and why he occasionally and only half ironically used corporate jargon like "no-brainer" and "comfort zone." But he still had that same edginess, the old restless balking at having to do what anyone told him. He was still trying to tame himself so he could get what he wanted.

"I haven't been back to Arizona in years," I said over a pint of ale. "I hated it there, Billy. I didn't even know it was beautiful until I left."

"I know exactly what you mean," he said. "I'm William now, by the way."

I turned over in bed and listened to the traffic in the rain. A few cold, clear truths rose one by one through my consciousness like a flock of birds: I wasn't even remotely worthy of William and I wasn't ever going to have him; I'd asked my mother to lend me money and she'd said no; I'd given all the change to the cabdriver; no one was going to pay off my debts; no one would save me from myself. I fell asleep to the soft beating of wings in my head.

had parted ways last spring after just two months together, but not before we'd had enough ravenous encounters in the backseats of taxis and dive-bar bathrooms and the vestibules of tenement buildings to provide me with leaping-off points for fantasies whenever I needed them. I switched the water flow to the bathtub faucet, turned it on full blast, and positioned my crotch directly under the plunging jet of water. I imagined that John was having his jovially brutal way with me in a meat-district warehouse loading zone on a winter night. We had drunk enough red wine in the course of the long night to obliterate the frost-cold air and the hard metal edges we kept hitting various parts of ourselves against. We were fully clothed, with only the requisite parts exposed, and we went at each other violently, with gritted teeth, half laughing, our naked warm joined flesh the only thing we were aware of, everything else a febrile blur.

After this fantasy had run its course I had a brief moment of dislocation, trying to reconcile the water faucet with the large, vivid man I'd just allowed myself to be ravished by. I got out of the tub, toweled off, blew my hair dry, threw on a reasonably clean wool skirt and cardigan to hide the torn seam of my blouse, gulped a cup of coffee, and headed out into the day. The cold bright air tingled on my face; the whiskey seemed to have metabolized during the night into another kind of drug, some bracing combination of caffeine and champagne.

Then, out of nowhere, a mental time-release mechanism triggered the memory of everything that had happened last night. I stopped in front of an OTB and stared pop-eyed into the paper-strewn, sweaty interior. I met the eyes of a man who was looking out at me, but I was too stricken to know at first what I was seeing. Our gazes held a fraction of a second too long and then he lifted his eyebrows at me. I looked quickly away and staggered down Amsterdam, feeling as if I had irreparably ripped the fragile cloth my life was made of. I wanted to fall to the sidewalk and pound my skull to a pulp against the concrete.

Then I heard, as I occasionally did, the voice of Ruth Kos-wicki, my old therapist. "Oh, come now, Claudia," she said in my mind, "so what if the volcano erupted a little bit? Did you really think all that lava could just stay underground forever?" I could see her round, plain face, her dark eyes trained earnestly on me, hair falling from her bun around her face in gray and black strands, her rounded bosom heaving with the intensity of her empathetic response to me. She wore muumuus and sneakers and seemed to have a permanent cold; she poured cup after cup of chamomile tea from the teapot on the table next to her, sipping at it with rabbity little nipping motions. She had reassured me eight times over the phone when I'd called to set up my first appointment that she wasn't a Freudian; only then had I consented to see her, and only because I was desperately depressed and had no idea where else to turn. Her most fervent speeches made me itch to burst out laughing; her assurances and reassurances made me squirm with childish skepticism, but I kept going back week after week because somehow I knew that it did me good to chafe under the gooey warmth of her mothering. When I quit the receptionist job I'd had at the time, I lost my benefits, stopped going and hadn't seen her since, but she still managed to descend on me free of charge every so often. "Why do you think you don't deserve to have your feelings known?" she said. "So what if he knows how you really feel?"

"Shut up, Ruth," I muttered, but I felt obscurely better. I walked along West Eightieth Street, crossed Central Park West and set off across the park. Yesterday's promise of spring had been retracted overnight. Ice rimed each spear of long grass around the pond by the Delacorte Theatre. Although I was wrapped in a coat and scarf and had swaddled my head in a woolen cap, the icy wind penetrated the porous tissue of my bones and froze my legs to numb logs. The low rays of the morning sun knifed through the naked trees and blinded me. I bent squinting into the wind, hugging my coat around me, ears aching, eyes and nose streaming.

When I arrived at Jackie's, her maid was preparing the breakfast tray. Juanita, who'd come to the United States more than ten years ago, had not felt it worth her while to learn any English, which struck me as both xenophobic and admirable; Jackie communicated with her in sign language and a rudimentary Spanish invented from her knowledge of Italian and French. She paid Juanita less than half the going rate for maids, and was able to justify "supporting" one of "those illegals" by telling herself how much money she was saving; in the interests of further economy, she had Juanita come for the mornings only. How Juanita spent her afternoons or how she managed to support her children on the pittance Jackie doled out to her I had no idea, because Juanita and I were unable to share any but the most fundamental and nonverbal solidarity. No doubt Jackie preferred it that way.

"Good morning," I said, hanging my coat in the broom closet. My face burned and my nose ran, thawing in the warmth.

"Buenos días," Juanita said, knocking the top off a soft-boiled egg. "Cómo estás?"

"Okay," I said. I went to Jackie's room, knocked briefly on the door and went in. She was in her pink satin bed jacket, propped up against six or eight pillows, holding her reading glasses in one hand and a newspaper in the other.

"Good God!" she said when she saw me. She shielded herself with the newspaper as if to fend me off.

"What is it?"

"Oh, it's you, Claudia! Good heavens, you scared me! You look so fat with that hat on! Your face, I mean. I thought you were a stranger!"

"Sorry," I said, and removed the hat, which I'd forgotten I was wearing. I ran a hand over my hair to calm it down; it crackled and stood up against my palm.

She laughed breathlessly. "What a shock!" she said, fluttering a hand against her breastbone. "You looked like one of those women."

"I'm sorry," I said. What women?

Juanita came in with the tray, which held the soft-boiled egg in an egg cup, four crustless triangles of dry white toast, a pot of marmalade, a teapot, and an assortment of tea things and silverware. Juanita set the tray on the bed, and Jackie waved her away. When my eyes met Juanita's on her way out, we kept our expressions carefully impersonal.

Jackie shuffled everything around the tray until it was organized to her liking. "What are you standing there for?"

"You said you wanted to see me first thing when I got in."

She looked vague. "I suppose I wanted to tell you—never mind, I took care of it last night. Go on, you've got plenty to do."

I set up my table in the dining room, wheeled out the computer and printer, and looked through my work from yesterday. The photographs were right on top of the stack. I checked to make sure they were all there. They weren't. One envelope, the one with the picture of Imelda in the flower bed, was missing.

I didn't worry at first; it had to be somewhere. I went back out to the pantry and checked the shelf. It was empty. I looked through everything in the pantry twice, three times, a fourth. I searched the filing cabinets, the cupboards, all of the piles of papers on the counters. I checked my stack of work again. Then I stood by my table and stared at my computer screen.

I think I may have had a mild heart attack; my heart did something awful and pain shot up my left arm. My vision blurred. The subtle pressure I was under constantly in this apartment intensified all at once. The ordinary bad mood I'd been in until a few minutes ago now appeared to me the way the flu must seem to someone who's just been told she's terminally ill. Outside, people went about their untroubled business. In here, I breathed deeply and tried to think. It couldn't simply have disappeared. She must have taken it out for another look last night; she probably had it in her bedroom. Or she'd changed her mind about it and put it back in its frame.

I tiptoed down the hall to the guest room, swung the door open, and went in. The sight of the empty black cardboard in the gilt frame made me feel faint. I crept back along the hall and stood unseeing in the middle of the dining room. I couldn't search her bedroom until she went out to the hairdresser. I couldn't ask her where it was: she would be extremely upset and angry that I'd lost it, which wouldn't be at all helpful to me right now. As long as she didn't know, it was possible to maintain an outward appearance of calm.

I survived somehow until eleven by sitting in front of my computer in a trembling daze, typing nonsense and deleting it. When she finally left for the hairdresser I raced to her bedroom. I looked under her bed, between the books on her bookshelf, through her drawers, on the table by her toilet. I went to the utility room and showed Juanita the other envelope. "Un otra como ci?" I said desperately. "Have you seen another envelope like this one?"

She looked puzzled, released a stream of Spanish, smiled apologetically, and went back to her ironing.

I searched the kitchen, the living room, the guest room, the dining room, the pantry again, all the wastebaskets, and my pile of work for a fourth time. The messenger was coming at four o'clock to take the photographs to Gil Reeve. I had four and a half hours to find the envelope, and I had already looked everywhere. I wanted to bolt out of here and never come back.

I forced myself to sit down again at my table. The work she'd left for me to do sat before me, untouched. I had put the photographs on the shelf. Hadn't I? I was sure I had. But maybe I hadn't. I had been tired and in a hurry, and frazzled from doing battle with the publicity files. Jackie's favorite adjective for me was "careless"; her second favorite, "disorganized." I would hear them both, and quite possibly some others, very soon. I braced myself. The area behind my eyes ached.

Jackie's wrath swept through her like a sudden storm flattening anything in its path, which was all too often me. She'd screeched once that I was spending her money like a drunken bandit because I'd left the heater on full blast in the dining room when I went home one night instead of lowering it economically; she'd called me muddleheaded and crazy when I forgot to give her the message that Mr. Blevins wanted to bring over some flowers, so he just showed up that evening while she was entertaining another date. I was impractical, I was a dreamer, I was abysmally unorganized.

Even though I deserved them, these excoriations undid me. I sat at my desk afterwards, smarting as if I'd been brutally slapped, staring at the list in front of me through a screen of silent, impotent tears. It gave me no comfort that she reacted exactly the same way when the dry cleaner didn't have her gloves ready in time for the Pattersons' dinner party, or her neighborhood grocer ran out of her favorite flavor of frozen yogurt: forty-odd years of luxury had not obscured the fact that she'd been born in a row house. Nothing ever would. If she'd grown up as the daughter of a rich, aristocratic family, she might have learned graciousness and forbearance, but marrying into one had made her vulnerable and narrow.

I'd learned soon after I'd come to work for her that Jackie's origins were nearly as obscure as my own. She was born in Englewood, New Jersey, in 1925. Her given name, bestowed on her by a mother who was clearly burdened with a romantic nature, was Genevieve Ursula, but her nickname was courtesy of her father, Jack Timmins, who had obviously hoped for a son. As a girl, Jackie Timmins wore saddle shoes and lipstick and a parochial school uniform, read romance novels, drank sodas at the drugstore counter with her girlfriends, sang along with the Andrews Sisters and Lemmon Brothers on the radio and prayed for the brave boys overseas, none of whom was her boyfriend. She left high school the summer after her junior year to pursue a secretarial career in Manhattan, and in those years seemed to be headed for a marriage to a Wall Street trader or a doctor, which would have been a big step up from her Jersey row-house origins. But just after she turned twenty-one, Giancarlo del Castellano came riding up on a white horse and radically altered this destiny.

He was thirty-two, from an aristocratic Milanese family who owned vast pieces of Northern Italy. He had just been appointed to a diplomatic post in Paris and was looking for a wife, the one accoutrement he lacked for professional success. He met Jackie at a party in Manhattan given by the president of the company that had just hired her. She was Catholic, virginal, dewy-eyed, demure and, with the help of a low-cut dress and an upswept hairdo, a knockout. She was exactly what he needed. He danced with her all night, then married her three months later and carried her off to a life of almost absurd wealth and glamour.

Jackie reminisced to me about that life with a half-incredulous insistence: the flocks of uniformed servants, polished marble stairways, the fantastic, excessive dinner parties; the bullfights and horse races, where they sat in the best boxes. "Everywhere we went, they treated us like royalty," she told me. "And we were, Claudia. It's not like America over there; they're very class-conscious, very traditional, and they respect their upper classes, they don't try to pretend everyone's the same. You had to remember every minute that people were watching you. Even the servants; they saw everything and gossiped with each other. I was young and used to taking care of myself, I didn't want all those women fussing around all the time. It was hard for me at the beginning. Having everything done for you is not as easy as you might think."

I could see how it wouldn't be easy at all. It would have made me extremely nervous to have someone like me walk in off the street and take over the most intimate details of my life. I wouldn't have wanted a stranger in my house all day, watching everything I said and did. But the more I knew about her, the better I could do my job; she had to entrust me with complete access to her files, her bank accounts, her closets and medicine chest and telephone book. I had permission to forge her signature on her checks when I paid her bills. I wrote my own paychecks. She gave me a set of keys to her apartment so I could come and go as necessary when she was out of town. I had the run of the place.

Conversely, the less she knew about me, the better for both of us. I tried not to reveal anything about my life outside her apartment, to manifest only the qualities she needed to project onto me. To this end, I modeled myself after the personal secretaries I'd seen on *Masterpiece Theatre*, bespectacled girls who blended into the background until their mistresses needed them to take a letter or reserve them a berth on the Orient Express. Whenever she asked a direct question about my life— did I have a boyfriend, what did my mother and father do, where did I plan to go during my two weeks off—I smiled brightly and answered in a chatty, obfuscating stream of non-information, then turned the topic back to her. As a result, she knew only my phone number and where I'd gone to college, and she might have had some general idea of my age.

About two years before, once I'd begun writing what was certain to become a best-selling book, even a crappy one under someone else's name, I had begun to view my secretarial duties with increasing resentment, and I was neither professional nor dedicated enough to check the consequent downhill slide of Jackie's accounts, her filing, her correspondence. This was fine as long as I didn't screw up too badly, but losing the photograph was maybe the worst thing I'd ever done, and there was nothing I could do now but wait for her to find out.

She returned at noon on a gust of cheerful energy. "It's as cold as the North Pole out there!" she said, coming to stand in the doorway while she took off her coat. Her face was flushed, her eyes were bright, her hair was freshly poufed. "Did you call that man?"

"Which man?"

She looked sharply at me. "Right there on the list I left you. He's waiting for my answer. I told him I'd call first thing this morning. Call him immediately and tell him, just the way I wrote it."

A nanosecond later I heard her in the utility room, saying something in her pidgin Spanish to Juanita, who laughed. I felt intensely jealous of Juanita. I stood up and made my unsteady way out to the kitchen and drank a glass of water. My nervous system jangled and roared. Jackie appeared in the doorway. "What did he say?"

"Jackie," I said shakily, "I'm a little concerned about something. When I came in this morning, one of the envelopes for Gil Reeve was missing."

We stared at each other for a while.

"Which one?"

My face was numb. "The Marcos picture," I said clearly, so she wouldn't make me repeat it.

"What do you mean, it's missing?"

"When I left I put both envelopes on my shelf, and when I came in I found only one of them. I thought you might have taken the other one to show someone."

"Why would I do that? Of course I didn't touch it!"

There was a bad silence.

"Well, you'd better find it," she said. "I told you not to lose it. I have no negative and no other copy."

"I can't find it," I said, "and I've looked everywhere."

"What do you mean?"

"I've searched the whole apartment and it's not anywhere."

"What," she whispered. Here it came. "Claudia. That picture is irreplaceable. The book will be absolutely ruined without it."

"I know," I said.

She gave a cry of rage. The skin of her face had been stretched over her cheekbones to her ears and sewn into a tight, shiny mask, too firmly pinned in place to express any emotion stronger than mild curiosity. A thick coat of foundation and powder further restricted its mobility, so she had to clasp her hands to her temples and grimace openmouthed to convey her fury. Her neck tendons strained against their moorings. Her mouth strove to expel the words stuck like apple pips in her throat. "This is insupportable! This should not happen! Do you see how much trouble you cause me? I cannot have a secretary who is so careless and sloppy with my precious things!"

She did an abrupt about-face and tapped to the pantry on her ludicrously high, small pumps. She looked top-heavy from the rear, like a thistle or a tadpole, some primitive unfinished thing. Her big bronze mushroom of hair and the broad shoulders of her suit jacket dwindled to a hard tucked-under little nub of a butt and thin, slightly knock-kneed legs. I lumbered behind her and stood wretchedly by while she began rifling through the filing cabinets, opening drawers and pawing through them, in search of what I wasn't sure. "What's this!" she snapped, holding up a piece of paper. "I thought you sent this letter ages ago! What's it doing here!"

"Oh, there it is," I said. "I thought you sent it."

She handed it to me wordlessly. I clutched it in my damp grasp. This was not my fault, but the reason was too long and involved to even begin to explain. A little later she held up something else. "And this! What's this doing here! This was supposed to have been faxed to Gil last week. There's no date stamp on it."

"I've never seen that before," I said faintly.

"What do you mean you've never seen it? I gave it to you to fax last week and you told me you'd done it!"

"I must have thought you meant something else," I said. Again, this was not technically my fault, but at the moment, everything was. "I'm sorry," I said.

She looked at me shrewdly, penetrating my skull to the gray waste underneath, her eyes as intelligent and quick as a bird's in the shallow plastic shell of her face. "I don't know," she said, "how you function in the world. You're not normal. It is impossible for me to understand the way your mind works." I stood there, a mute lump of apology. "Go and fax it to him this minute. And call Imelda and ask if she'll send us the negative. Use the New York number, she's in town right now. Tell her it was 1977, the trip we took to visit them, she'll remember. And be polite, those Filipinos are very well-mannered."

We reconvened a bit later. She seemed calm, but I knew it was only an illusion. "What did Imelda say?"

"Her assistant is asking her about the negative. I'm waiting to hear back."

"You faxed that list to Gil?"

"Ten minutes ago, and I called to make sure he got it."

"Tell me exactly what you were doing, right before you left yesterday."

"I sorted through your mail and left it for you on the table, then I put my things away and went home."

A lightbulb went on above that sleuthing head of hers. "I threw out that whole stack of junk," she said. "I didn't have time to look through it. The envelope could very well have been in that pile. I'm sure that's exactly what happened. Honestly, Claudia, you're a nice girl, very pleasant, but you just don't *think*." Her voice trembled with patronizing pity. "It's terrible for me to have a secretary I can't count on. If you worked in the real world, in a real job, I wonder what would happen to you."

I lifted the receiver and called the doorman. Ralph said with a smile in his voice, "Garbage? Louie went around and got it this morning, I'm not sure what time, I think around nine o'clock, a little later. It should all still be down there in the basement." I thanked him and hung up. "When did Juanita empty the trash?" I asked Jackie.

She went and consulted with Juanita, and then came back, looking pleased with herself. "Eight this morning."

The garbage men usually came before that; it might still be down there. If not, I was going to have to go to the Fresh Kills landfill on Staten Island and paw through a city's worth of cat food tins and used maxi pads until I found it. Louie the handyman took me down in the freight elevator to the basement, where he showed me thirteen or fourteen big bags of garbage lined up against the far wall. "Good luck, miss," he said, and clanked off with his tool belt. I undid the twist-tie on the nearest bag, removed my sweater and rolled up the sleeves of my blouse, then plunged my hands in before I could think about what I was doing. The smell was not unbearable, since this was recent garbage. In fact, I came across a half-eaten ham or turkey on rye that looked pretty good. I hadn't eaten anything today, I realized, and almost laughed at myself, kneeling there sniffing hungrily.

I mucked through orange peels, chicken bones, wads of Kleenex, cereal boxes, slimy vegetable detritus and no manila envelope. I closed the first bag and looked at the rest of them before selecting another one and pulling off the twist-tie. Thinking I heard something rustling inside, I took it apart warily and then reassembled it as gingerly as if it contained a land mine, but I found nothing alive or explosive, and nothing I was looking for. Long ago, Juanita had escaped to wherever she went at one o'clock, leaving me alone with Jackie, who was cooling her heels overhead, awaiting my reemergence from the underworld with the photograph borne aloft like a celluloid Eurydice. She shouldn't have trusted someone like me with something so precious, but that was beside the point. I couldn't return empty-handed. If she said it was down in the trash, it had better be down in the trash: the anticipation of what she would say to me if I failed to locate it there almost capsized me in advance. I dug through the next several bags feeling the encroaching dementia caused by overloading the neurological channels that reconcile internal knowledge with external reality. What was I doing? For whom, and why? How much was I being paid to root through umpteen bags of garbage? What amount of money, if any, would be enough?

As I was closing the tenth or eleventh bag, I heard footsteps behind me. I looked up over my right shoulder and beheld the merry face of Ralph. "Ralph," I said, "look what it's come to."

"What did she lose now?" he asked, chuckling.

"Photograph," I grunted, dragging the next bag toward the light. "In a manila envelope. She didn't lose it, though. I did."

"You know what she did the other night? Came running downstairs all in a tizzy about some flowers we were supposed to have for her to take somewhere. She said you'd ordered them. 'My secretary was supposed to have arranged this,' she said."

"I thought the hostess called and said she didn't have to bring them after all," I said as a big rock fell into my stomach.

"Yeah, I know. That's what I'm telling you. She's right in the middle of yelling at me when she remembers something, probably what you just said, and just stands there with her mouth open. Then she sails right out the door like nothing ever happened. What a cuckoo."

I sat back on my haunches and wiped my hands on the clean concrete floor. They left dark wet smears.

"Anyway, I came down to tell you, there's a messenger waiting in the lobby. Should I send him up to her apartment?"

"No! No. Don't send him up. Tell him to come back at four o'clock, the time he was supposed to get here. The package isn't ready yet." I gave an unhinged laugh. "It's in here somewhere."

"I got you," he said sympathetically.

"Thank you," I said, and almost blew him a kiss before I remembered what was all over my hands.

75

I found the junk mail in the next-to-last bag. I looked through it rapaciously: magazine offer, two catalogues, book club offer, sweepstakes entry, Nature Conservancy donation request, notice of a new French restaurant opening nearby. I laid them out on the floor before me, Tarot-like. I read every word on all of them with incantatory supplication, but they refused to knit themselves together into a manila envelope. After a while I put them all back and closed the bag. Bleary-eyed, I confronted the last bulging glossy blackish-green membrane. I knew that the manila envelope was not in it, and I knew that Jackie would want me to look through it anyway. She would have stood over me insistently while I scrabbled through it for something we both knew couldn't possibly be there.

I looked at my open hands. I turned them over and examined the backs, and then looked again at the palms. They were rough and dry, hangnails chewed off during my frequent bouts of fear and panic. They were covered in goo. I filled my lungs slowly with air, and just as slowly emptied them. Something snapped in me then. I heard the twang in my head. There was no reason at all to look in the last bag. It was not essential, or possible, or even desirable.

I stood up and tried to pull myself back together. My back and arms ached. The rip in my blouse had widened so much that the sleeve was almost detached. My skirt had a big splotch of tomato juice all over the front that had spilled from an upended can, and my hair was coated with slime from continually having to push it out of my face. I put my sweater back on, then rang for Louie and rode up with him to the fourth floor.

I opened the side door to the apartment and stepped into the pantry. I could hear the clink of fork on plate in the kitchen. I hesitated. She hadn't heard me come in; I was tempted to gather up my things and run. She would never see me again. I'd screen all my calls for the rest of my life. But what, exactly, was I afraid of? "Jackie," I said, walking into the kitchen, "it wasn't there."

She sat alone at her kitchen table under a pool of light from the hooded lamp directly overhead, eating the lunch Juanita had left for her. She looked up and saw me, covered in garbage, with a reeking cloud of hair and a glint in my eye. "It wasn't there," she repeated in a cautious, pacifying voice. "Well, you certainly looked thoroughly. You were down there almost two hours."

"I found the stuff you threw out. The envelope wasn't with it."

The phone rang. I went to the pantry to answer it. "This is Mrs. Marcos," said a faint voice. "To whom am I speaking?"

"Claudia Steiner," I said. "You got my message?"

"I don't have any negatives from that visit," she said.

"I'll put her on."

I stood in the doorway while they reminisced about what a wonderful time they'd had a few months ago, going out dancing with Mr. Blevins and Mr. Metcalf. "It was such a treat when you got up and sang with the band," said Jackie. "You have such a voice, Imelda dear. I know I've told you this before, but you should really—yes, yes, I know, one is so terribly busy all the time, I know it myself, I hardly have time to write my books. Well, listen, my dear friend, I'm terribly sorry to bother you over such a little thing, but my secretary misplaced that lovely photograph of the four of us together outside the—yes, wasn't it, I was just telling my secretary, such a wonderful visit. Well, if you don't have it, I suppose I'll have to use another picture instead, but it's a shame. All right. Thank you, dear. We will, very soon. Love to Bongo."

Slouching in opposite doorways at either end of the pantry, we eyed each other with the wary uneasiness of combatants too tired to go on with the fight, but unable to surrender. "Well," she said finally, "this is really the last straw, Claudia. I'm so exhausted the rest of the day is just shot. I had wanted to get going on the new book, but I suppose it'll have to wait until tomorrow."

"I need to wash my hands," I said. I went to the bathroom just off the foyer and locked the door. I stuck my hands into a stream of warm water and lathered for several minutes with expensive camellia soap, dabbed at my skirt with a dampened embroidered hand towel and more camellia soap, then took another warm soapy little towel and plunged it around my armpits. I found a comb in my skirt pocket, wet it, and ran it through my hair. I washed my face thoroughly and dried it on yet another monogrammed scrap of terry cloth, then left all the towels in a sodden heap for Juanita to deal with: I didn't give a shit.

Jackie was pacing up and down the hall outside the bathroom when I emerged. She silently took me by the arm and marched me the few yards to the foyer, to the marble table by the front door where all her outgoing mail waited for me to take it down and mail it. "Look at that," she said with insistent eagerness.

"What is it?"

"I don't know, what is it?"

"It's addressed to Doris Loewenstein," I said. "In your handwriting."

"Look inside," she said.

I shrugged and opened the manila envelope. She hovered right at my elbow. Inside was a note Jackie had scrawled to her accountant, paper-clipped to a thick form the IRS had sent her. Under the form was an eight-by-ten black-and-white photograph of four people, two short and dumpy, two tall and elegant. "Here it is," I said expressionlessly. "I suppose you must have thought the envelope was empty."

"Oh, of all the silly—" She gave a brief conspiratorial giggle. "I wrote that note right before I went to bed. I was half-asleep. Well, there we go. The mystery is solved. It's very lucky we found it, Claudia; I was afraid that things would never have been the same between us if you'd lost this picture. We'll have to hurry now, that man is coming to get it."

It took everything I had not to slap her. I should have slapped her.

At four-thirty, the messenger arrived and bore away the accursed thing. At four thirty-five, Jackie took off her suit and stockings and underwear, and sank gratefully into a steaming tub to soak away the day's cares.

She was fanatical about her bath. Juanita was under strict instructions to clean it only with a chamois cloth and super-soft liquid soap imported from England. A sterilized water tank had been installed next to the tub; a man came twice a week to refill it with distilled water, pure molecules of hydrogen and oxygen free of all minerals, chemicals and biota. He also changed the filter which had been placed at Jackie's insistence over the mouth of the tap in case the water met any germs on its short journey through the foot or two of immaculate copper pipe that ran from the tank. The cost of all this was enormous, but it was worth any amount of money not to have to bathe in "that dreadful city water, just absolutely disgusting, and it's full of I don't know what diseases, it makes me sick just thinking about it!" She said this with evangelical intransigence, her delicately flared nostrils borne aloft above the cloacal stench of the municipal water mains. I sometimes wondered what she thought about, lying there; I pictured the surface of her mind, seething with all the sharp and irritating discrepancies between what she felt and what she wished she felt. How soothing it must have been for her to know that the water she lay in held nothing but what it seemed to hold.

Just before five o'clock, as I was wheeling my computer table into the pantry, Jackie summoned me tubside. She lay immolated in water clear as plastic wrap, encased like a sandwich. "My dear," she said, smiling beguilingly up at me as if that terrible episode had never happened, as if a whole new Claudia blew in on the winds of each mercurial change of mood like a series of memoryless Venuses, "would you mind getting my radio for me?"

I looked down at her through narrowed eyes. She wore a puffy clear plastic cap. Her body was long and pale as a shoal of sand, her pubic hair a bloom of seaweed. I was suffocated by this terrible intimacy. No one should have been so bound to another person. No one should have needed someone to do the things she asked of me.

I unearthed her radio and brought it into the bathroom, where I plugged it in and adjusted the dial to the AM station that featured her old and very dear friends Sammy, Perry, Frank, Dean and Bing. "Put it where I can adjust the volume," she said. "It has a way of creeping up. If it gets too loud it'll give me a headache."

I cast a flinty eye at the plastic shower shelf that hung from the nozzle overhead, a rickety contraption she was too cheap to replace. It had descending shelves for soap and shampoo bottles, and prongs at the bottom for washcloths and back brushes. Its hook, which was all that kept it suspended from the showerhead, had a crack in it, and was on the verge of breaking. With black-hearted insouciance, I hung the radio handle on one of the washcloth prongs, taking care to give the radio provisional purchase against the tiles so it would stay put until someone touched it, at which point the hook could very well snap off and the whole thing, including the radio, would quite possibly come tumbling down right into the water. The cord might be too short, and she might catch it in mid-air or fail to

80

apply enough force to break anything. I had no idea what would happen, and I didn't care.

I put on my coat and scarf, but I stuffed my woolen hat into my pocket: I would never wear it again. I didn't say good-bye. As I left I heard, echoing against the bathroom tiles, the mellow, perfectly phrased voice of Frank Sinatra: "Night and day, you are the one, only you, 'neath the moon or under the sun . . ."

I gave Ralph a radiant smile as I walked through the lobby.

"How'd it work out?" he asked.

"Fine," I said as I swept through the door he held open for me.

"So you didn't lose anything?" he called after me.

"No, I didn't," I called back over my shoulder, and set off for home.

chapter five

That night, as I was sitting in front of my black-and-white TV watching an incomprehensibly manic sitcom, and just as my stripped nerves were beginning to feel the effects of a big bolt or two of vodka, the phone rang. I looked at it for a moment, then turned down the TV volume and picked up after the third ring. If she asked where her Post-its were I would hang up on her. "Hello," I snarled.

"Claudia?"

"Oh, hi," I said. It was Frieda Mackintosh. I'd known her since we were freshmen in college. I had no idea any more how I actually felt about her, because college friends weren't like other friends, they were more like family: you didn't choose them, they happened to you, and they were yours forever. "How are you, Frieda?"

"A little depressed, actually."

"What's wrong?"

"Nothing new. You know. Do you want to go hear that band I was telling you about? The Flukes? They're playing to-night, the one with the oboe. They probably suck, but I'm so tired of the old guitar-bass-drums combo I could just die."

"Where and when?"

"Eleven at the Blue Bar."

"The *Blue* Bar," I said.

"I'll pay your cover, Claudia. We don't have to stay if they're awful."

"All right," I said. "I'll meet you there."

"Meet me *there*?"

She was silent, breathing pleadingly into the phone. I always gave in, but I made a point not to make it too easy for her. "Okay, I'll come and get you," I said finally. "But you have to be ready when I ring the buzzer, Frieda. I'm not coming up."

But when I rang her buzzer, she buzzed me in. I waited a few minutes, then rang again, and she buzzed me in again. I pushed the building door open and climbed up to her fifth-floor apartment, rapped on her door, then opened it. "I'm sorey," her voice said in its Canadian accent from somewhere just beyond the door. "Really, Claudia, it's just that I don't know what— everything makes me look so—" I went in. She stood in the glaring overhead light of her kitchen. Her short black hair stuck out at several angles as if it had been slept on. She had a streak of dark blue paint on the back of one hand and wore a baggy gray smock over a knee-length black skirt; even so, she was ravishing.

"You're trying out for Cinderella?" I said.

"Claudia," she said desperately, "I don't think I can go anywhere, actually. I'm feeling so self-conscious. I don't know what's wrong with me, I just can't take it any more."

Frieda was six feet tall and freakishly beautiful. She had an extravagant but simple face with perfect bones, a wide, full

83

mouth, black hair and dark blue eyes, skin that was at once luminous and creamy, an iconic orchestration of flesh and bone that seemed to belong not to her but to everyone who saw it. She rode along inside, cringing. She tried to camouflage herself in unbecoming clothes, but no matter what she did, everyone stared at her wherever she went as if she were a giraffe. Why she couldn't get over her self-consciousness and enjoy being gorgeous was beyond me, but I tried to understand for the sake of our friendship.

"Sit down a minute," I said sympathetically, and squeezed my way through the stacked boxes to the refrigerator. I managed to get the door open enough to see what was in there: a withered lemon, a jar of mustard, three rolls of film, and most of the six-pack of beer I'd brought last time I came over. I plucked two from the cardboard holder, found an opener in a drawer, and handed one bottle to Frieda. "Drink this," I said as if it were medicine, which it was.

She sat droopily down on a stack of boxes and took a sip. In the six years she'd lived in this apartment, she hadn't yet got around to unpacking her boxes. She was always just about to, and meanwhile she had accumulated stacks of newspapers and magazines, each containing an article or photo she was always just about to clip, and more boxes filled with castoff clothes and worn-out shoes she kept meaning to throw away; more distressingly, in recent months she'd started picking up trash off the street: spools of thread, colored Chinese circulars, interesting-looking bits of wood and glass and metal. She stored them in more boxes, stacked on top of the ones she'd moved in with. When I asked her what she was collecting them for, she told me that she planned to use them in her paintings. Her painting studio, a spare bedroom in another apartment around the corner, was clean and austere, bare except for a table filled with jars of brushes and tubes of paint, several canvases tacked to the wall, and finished paintings rolled or framed and stacked neatly in a corner. Her paintings themselves were meticulously organized variations on an overall theme of spare Manitoban quietude in brown and blue, without one extraneous brushstroke. I couldn't imagine where her trash collection would fit in, and it amazed me that someone so particular about her work space was able to function in this apartment.

"Frieda," I said, partially to distract her from her own misery, "last night I tried to make out with William and he sent me home in a cab."

"What did you do, exactly?"

I told her.

"Well," she said, thinking hard, "either one day he'll come to his senses and realize that you're the one for him, or he'll be flattered for a while, then forget all about it."

"That's not all," I said. "I asked my mother for money, and she said no."

Frieda gasped. I could always count on her to side with me against my mother. "How could she? She's your mother!"

"And today at work I really lost it; I think I might actually kill Jackie one of these days."

"She deserves it."

"No one deserves to be *killed*, Frieda. Sometimes it's all I can do to restrain myself. I think there's something really wrong with me."

"With *you*? What about me? It's all I can do to leave the house."

"Frieda," I said firmly, "it isn't just you who gets stared at all the time, it's everyone. We're like dogs sniffing each other's butts, but we do it with our eyes."

"That's so disgusting," she said, and took a big swallow of beer.

Our friendship was predicated on this ritual of mutual self-laceration and assuagement. I wondered what would happen if I said to Frieda, "Why are you such a damn weirdo?" and she said to me, "Why are you always *drunk?*" and I said back, "At least I can go out in public by myself like a normal adult!" and she said, "At least *I* can get through a day without making a complete ass of myself!" I had no idea what would happen if we said these things, and I wasn't sure I wanted to find out. I preferred to muster the energy it took to be reassuring and sympathetic. My sympathy was sincere, but afterwards I tended to feel as if I'd sold her a bill of goods. Maybe I had no credibility with myself, maybe that was the problem.

It was already eleven-thirty when we came out of Frieda's building onto Rivington Street. Everything started right on time at the Blue Bar, that was one of the things I hated about the place. By the time we got there, the band was onstage and, according to the guy who took Frieda's money and stamped our hands, well into their set. As we pushed our way forward, Frieda endured a thicket of stares, but, probably because I was prodding her in the ribs, she bravely bushwhacked a path to a little clearing not too far from the bar. Three guys in torn T-shirts and horn-rimmed glasses stood crowded together on the tiny stage, posturing and grimacing as if they were all playing air guitar in a suburban basement somewhere, but managing to generate a lot of noise with actual instruments. The singer, a big girl with a brassy voice, held her mike stand in both hands and made strange cross-eyed kissy-faces at the mike when she wasn't singing. Standing off to one side was the oboe player, a short bespectacled black guy in a suit who looked as if he'd been borrowed from the Philharmonic. The comical snort of the oboe was a nice touch, I thought, but Frieda turned to me, shaking her head. "What an incredibly ridiculous idea," she said. "I can't believe it. Rock oboe. Want to go?"

"We just got here," I said. "Let's have a drink."

"That's okay," she said. "I just had one."

"A beer isn't a drink." I insinuated myself through the crowd to the bar and bought two vodkas and gave the bartender a dollar tip, which left twenty-odd dollars in my pocket, and just under thirty in the bank.

"What's this?" said Frieda when I handed her the glass. "I thought I said—"

"To your health," I said, and tapped my glass against hers.

"Hey, there's John Threadgill," said Frieda. My mouth went dry. "And that guy, what's his name—"

"Gus Fleury," I said unhappily, trying to hide behind her, a bad idea.

John slid his hand up the back of my neck and kissed my cheek. "Well, Claudia," he said. "At last we meet again."

"Hello, John."

I hadn't seen him in months. He smelled like himself, and his cheek was stubbly; he stroked the nape of my neck in a firm-fingered, dexterous way reminiscent of things he had done to other parts of me. I tried not to think about the fantasy I'd had about him this morning, but I could feel my crotch getting warm, opening hungrily like a flytrap. I had never understood why this happened every time he got within ten feet of me. He was a large, ruddy, barrel-shaped poet whose head was crowned with what appeared to be a red fright wig, but was actually his own growth; he had enough hair for three or four regular people. His magnum opus was a poem called "The Bricklayer's Dilemma," already thousands of pages long, with no end in sight. From the choice bits I'd heard him read aloud and the things he'd said about it, it was written with one eye on posterity and the other on a potential movie deal. He used archaisms such as "shan't" and "doth"; he invoked the Muse; he had his poor bricklayer look within his humble breast and quail to see the darkness there, but he also embroiled him in car chases, shady schemes and affairs with double-crossing femmes fatales. And still the monster grew. He didn't seem to mind the lack of closure; actual success would have been distasteful to him, because he identified piously with all underdogs, with the suffering downtrodden masses. He cried at news stories about Rwandan orphans. He told homeless men, "I have nothing to give you, my brother, we're in the same boat," with a world-weary, owl-like sadness that was for the most part genuine, but was also interlarded with a certain amount of secret pleasure.

I reached up and removed his hand, stifling the urge to remind him that we had had some fairly entertaining sex, it was true, but there were several very good reasons why we had stopped. First, he was married, and second, although reasonably good-natured, he was no prince, and a prince was what I still, even after all these years, longed for.

"Well, if it isn't Miss Frieda," Gus was saying. "Don't you look adorable. Little Miss Muffet meets Maria von Trapp." He pinched the fabric of her smock.

Frieda cringed and leaned against the wall, glaring at the band. Gus sidled off to the bar without a glance in my direction just as the band launched into an up-tempo circusy number. It felt wild and festive in here suddenly, like a gypsy camp.

When the song ended, Frieda turned to me with a rapturous smile. "I love the oboe," she said. Her glass was almost empty. For her, this was guzzling. "He's so good! What's he doing in this stupid band?"

"His name is Cecil Sperduley," said John.

"You know him?"

"We were bike messengers together. We used to drink beer in the stairwell. I bet he'd love to meet you."

"I'm going up there where I can hear better." She disappeared toward the stage, leaving John and me alone.

"That girl is one olive short of a martini," he said. "Gorgeous, but—" He waggled his hand. His whole body felt as if it were pressed against mine, although it was just his shoulder.

"But nothing," I said. I relaxed, which involved inadvertently returning the pressure of his shoulder. "What are you doing here?"

"I ran into Gus on the street a couple days ago," he said. "He said he needed a site for his play, I mentioned Cecil's mother's building, one thing led to another, and here I am at the fucking Blue Bar. At least you're here."

The Blue Bar was designed to attract people who had money, namely European tourists and Wall Streeters who wanted to hang out in the East Village without actually having to slum it, and keep away those who didn't, namely me. The bar was a long glowing blue tube with mushroomy stools whose glowing blue seats rose from black opaque stalks. Set into the cobalt depths beneath the surface of the bar was a long aquarium, paved with phosphorescent greenish-blue gravel, filled with tropical fish who slid their fan-shaped or ribbon-bedecked or polka-dotted bodies through neon-bright coral. The jukebox was stocked with rare vintage 45s by long-dead Delta musicians, "Little" Willie this and "Blind" Jimmy that. Neon tubes ran around the periphery of the little dance floor and stage, and along the backs of the booths. The walls held various framed movie posters (*The Blue Angel, Betty Blue, Blue Velvet*). This might have been someone's idea of a hip and happening place, but it gave me a deep, unscratchable itch just under the surface of my skin. I finished my vodka and plunked my glass down hard on a nearby tabletop. Several goateed, ponytailed men sitting at the table looked up, then realized that no one had fired a gun and went back to their conversation. One of them was actually wearing dark glasses. Germans.

I handed John a five. "Vodka on the rocks, please, if you're going that way. The good stuff." The good vodka cost six dollars; this was my way of teasing him, because John lived on a narrow but largely self-imposed tightrope. He scrounged up freelance copyediting jobs for a living, which were few and far between, and given mostly to post-collegiate go-getters on their way up. Like me, he was forced to supplement his earnings with the occasional handout from his mother, which caused him to loathe himself but which enabled him to scrape by without going into debt. I suspected that she bailed him out much more often than he let on, but he also came from that New England tradition which values the well-researched investment over the happy impulse buy. His spending habits were eccentric and fanatically rigid, but they enabled him to live on the edge without actually going over it. He bought three button-down shirts and two pairs of trousers a year. When he ate in restaurants, he ordered a bowl of soup and ate the whole basket of bread or crackers, or showed up at BBQ in time for the $6.95 Early Bird Special and took his leftovers home. He'd finagled a deal with his landlord that involved minor custodial duties in exchange for a very small rent, which had turned out to be almost more trouble than it was worth, and he and his wife Rima split all their shared expenses down the middle like college roommates. His friends teased him for his skinflint behavior, but he took it with a sheepish acquiescence that caused my opinion of him to swing from scorn to comprehension to amused sympathy, because I saw finally that he did this not wholly because he was a Yankee cheapskate, but also because he had carved tight parameters in the world for himself and was bound to stay within them.

As he elbowed his way in and spoke to the bartender, I stood my ground uneasily, in the grip of that same fatalistic languor that had come over me last night at George's. So what if I slept with John Threadgill one more time? I was essentially just the tenant of a bag of chemicals and minerals animated by electricity; my body was going to dry up and blow away sooner or later. What did it matter what another person did to it, as long as it didn't hurt, as long as it gave me a kind of pleasure? Who besides me would know or care?

Anyway, I knew John, knew the limits of what could happen between us. Our affair had followed the same trajectory as most of my relationships: bantering dive-bar pickup, drunken sex, a rushed exchange of phone numbers afterwards on a subway platform, then other nights with more dive-bar bantering and drunken sex. Until John, these affairs had generally continued until the guy went back to his old girlfriend or stopped cheating on his current one. These endings caused me no undue distress; downtown bars were stocked with such men, and when one went down, another popped up in his place. But John was married, and this imbued our encounters with poignancy and depth. He told me that he'd never leave Rima, and because I had no reason to doubt this, the anticipation of heartache lent an air of melancholy self-abnegation to our couplings in stairwells and elevators.

One fine spring morning I awoke in my own bed alone, with an ache in every orifice and a memory of bending over on the Christopher Street Pier at four in the morning with my drawers around my ankles while John stood behind me, holding my hips. As I gripped a piling to keep from tumbling into the Hudson, I gazed down into the filthy water and thought gaily to myself, Well, here I am, and this is me. An open, half-drunk quart of cheap beer sat by my foot, our ubiquitous shared bottle, the cost of which was always without discussion split to the nearest penny. When John banged into me with extra vigor and the bottle flew into the river, I told it silently, Better you than me, and watched it sink.

The next morning I decided, lying there awash in every

detail, that this thing between us had gone about as far as it was likely to go. I called John to tell him so, and Rima answered.

John always talked about Rima with a romantic schoolboy wistfulness I found incongruous but touching, because their marriage was at heart a business deal gone terribly awry. She'd married him with the understanding that she would live with him, sleep with him and support him for the three years of marriage required to establish her American citizenship, at the end of which he would give her a divorce. They each had a different reason for this deal: she made three or four hundred dollars a night as a stripper at Goldfingers and didn't want to go back to Rumania; he was in love with her and too young to know any better. Ten years ago, when they'd married, she had been as hauntingly beautiful as Dietrich or Garbo, at least according to John, whose poetic license was understandable, given the fact that by the time I met her, genetics, gravity and a chain-smoking, hard-drinking youth had put an end to that haunting beauty, and with it the lucrative part of her stripping career. She had been reduced to picking up shifts in sleazy strip joints in the Navy Yard or the nether regions of Queens, places where men catcalled and shoved folded dollar bills in her ass cheeks. After work she cast her sorrows and money into the winds of after-hours clubs, then staggered home at dawn to collapse until it was time to get up and do the whole thing over again.

I had run into her a few times before, at parties. I was a little afraid of her. Her drunken rages were legendary and left their mark; during one late-night attack on John, she caught him just above his eye with the edge of her ring and gashed his eyebrow open; in another, she knocked him down, gave him a good hard kick or two and broke three ribs. John told me that calls came for her at odd hours, raspy, stoned voices asking for

Della or Vera; for a while she'd taken up with one rapper/deejay crackhead after another, then switched to middle-aged junkie jazz musicians, and all of them borrowed money she couldn't afford to lend them, then disappeared. She and John still shared a bed, but they hadn't had sex of any kind in several years and weren't likely to again, John told me, and I had no real reason to doubt him. But there was no longer any question of a divorce. She was his broken muse, his shattered Grecian urn. Unlike everyone else, she needed him. For her part, she couldn't afford a place of her own and no one in his or her right mind would have taken her in except maybe her family, but they were all in Bucharest, and she would rather shoot herself than live there again.

"Is John there?" I asked.

"Who is calling?" she asked in her high, slurred, bizarrely accented voice.

"It's Claudia. I'm a friend of his."

"Listen to me, Clow-dya," she said. "I don't want him to see you any more."

"Okay," I said. "That's fine with me."

"Good-bye," she said, and hung up.

This had been last May. I'd only seen John once or twice since then, and each time I'd run into him, he'd begged me to reconsider; we had such good times together and we both knew exactly where we stood, so what harm was there in continuing? These pleas sometimes ended in tears—John's, that is; he could weep with as much compassion for his own plight as anyone else's. But I stood firm. The end of my affair with John had marked the beginning of my yearning for William, which was of a completely different nature, although equally hopeless. I was through with married men, at least for now. Not only that, I seemed to be through for now with any kind of one-night arrangement, any romance spawned after midnight in a bar.

However, a filament of that old era came sliding back now to snake itself around my ankle.

When John handed me my glass, he said nothing about the fact that I'd stiffed him a dollar or two, not even a dry little wisecrack, which I took to mean that he would do anything to get me into bed, or wherever. As if to prove this, he breathed right in my ear so his breath steamed up all the little hairs in my ear canal and my knees threatened to buckle with involuntary mating-instinct acquiescence, "Where have you been?"

"Around," I said. "We've been through this, John. I'm not hiding from you."

He gazed at me with soft admiration, put his hand on my face, turned my head and, without my permission, kissed me. I pulled back to look him in the eye. He had a lovely mouth, wide and full, the upper lip dented in the middle, a deep dimple in his cheek.

"How's the wife?" I asked.

"At least come for a walk," he said. "I've missed your mind. You always inspire me so much, you spark my ideas. And I like to think I do the same for you. I would love so much just to talk to you again."

Probably because you can't understand a single word your wife says, I thought, but I was feeling down and lonely and I'd had a terrible day, so I said aloud, "It would seem churlish not to, when you put it like that."

Frieda was sitting at a back table with Cecil, who had come offstage for a couple of songs. When they were sitting down it was harder to tell how much difference there was in their sizes, but they still made quite a pair. Gus hovered obsequiously over them, his hands pressed together as if he were praying, waiting for an in. He leaned over and offered his hand to Cecil, who dragged his eyes reluctantly away from Frieda and shook it.

I tapped Frieda on the shoulder and said in her ear, "Will you be all right if I leave now?"

She looked up at me. "Do not go home with him," she said. She looked drunk and radiant.

"Frieda. We're just going for a walk."

"Walk fast," she said, and gave me a light slap on the cheek.

John and I fought our way out of the bar. He squired me along the pavement. A deli lay just ahead at the next corner, its brightly lit tiers of fruits and flowers bristling against the muted wash of buildings and parked cars. "I need a beer," I said. "And one of those little Table Talk pies."

He came back with two bagged, opened bottles and two small square boxes. I checked to see what flavor he'd chosen for me and saw with joy that it was apple. I ripped the box open and sank my teeth into the flaky, gummy thing. He watched me eat it. I felt short of breath all of a sudden.

"I'm starving," he said, and took a bite out of my pie, steadying my hand with his. I watched him chew and swallow. A crumb sat on his upper lip. I wanted to lick it off, even though I wasn't hungry any more.

"Eat your own damn pie," I said. We exchanged a hot, half-lidded stare until I looked away with a huge grin.

He ran a thumb over my eyelids, then put his palm flat against my face and pressed it gently against my nose. "You're so tense," he said. "You should relax your face."

"I should relax a lot of things."

"I forgot to tell you," he said into my hair, "Rima's visiting her family in Bucharest until tomorrow night." An involuntary little grunt came from deep in my throat. He hailed a passing cab and gave the driver his address. We sat side by side on the wide cracked seat, not talking or touching. My head buzzed with internal static. John paid the driver and we got out.

John and Rima shared a cramped two-room attic apartment at the top of a former blacksmith's shop on Pitt Street. We passed through a gate and a courtyard, then climbed a narrow dim wooden staircase to the top floor. The bathtub sat by the door, covered with a wooden hinged lid that served as a sideboard until someone needed to take a bath. There were books piled on every surface, bookshelves crammed full and spilling over. Under the eaves of the pitched roof was John's worktable, haphazardly cluttered with a box of plain white paper, stacks of half-typewritten, half-handwritten pages, a jar of ballpoint pens, a dictionary and a manual typewriter. On a hook by the door was a frilly pink piece of lingerie, the only sign I could see of the missus.

The moment John ushered me in and locked the door behind us, I turned into a rubber doll that could be bent and contorted into any position. I found myself face down on the bathtub lid, my cheek against a box of cornflakes, my thighs spread in his hands, his chin between my shoulder blades, his breath in my ear. Then I was facing the sink, palms pressed flat against the cabinets overhead, one knee up on the edge of the sink. I slipped into a dazed, muted euphoria, squeezed myself into a hard compact ball so tiny it was almost gone, a black hole of antimatter located in my navel. A while later I resurfaced to discover that I had become some sort of ottoman: I was down on the rug, supporting his heavy weight on my back, bracing myself on hands and knees against the rhythmic onslaught while the hairs on his chest and stomach rasped against my skin. He picked me up and I wrapped my arms and legs around him and rode him like a merry-go-round horse while he steadied himself against the windowsill. Anyone looking up from below would have seen his bare butt squashed against the glass, my face rising and falling above the back of his head, and several moments later would have heard him give a yell that rattled the windowpanes.

We lay on the threadbare brown rug, naked, drinking whiskey; we never went near the big rumpled trampoline of a bed he shared with Rima. Why it was less adulterous to slide all over the fixtures and furniture I didn't know, but it was. I wasn't at all sleepy; I almost forgot that I had to be at work in a few hours. John's big stomach sat comfortably in front of his torso and his big soft limbs took up space without apology for their lack of muscle tone. He looked like a member of a cerebral, ineffectual alien species in a science-fiction movie, with hairy sloping shoulders, hands as formless and soft as mittens, eyes far apart in his top-heavy, domelike head. He wrapped his body around me, tugged at my hair as if it were a bolt of cloth he was buying, buried his face between my breasts. My entire body always felt tender and slightly raw after a bout with him, as if I'd been pummeled softly all over with rubber mallets.

"What are you working on these days?" he asked earnestly as he pinned me against the rug. It was time for our little talk about my writing.

I intoned in a quavering falsetto, "That dark-skinned foreign man had a gun, and he was pointing it at me! My heart beat like a timpani!"

He rubbed his cheek against my stomach, laid his ear flat so he could hear all the gurgling noises in there, which he had once told me made him feel as if he were back in the womb. "You were always going to start your own novel. What happened to that?"

"I'll do it when I do it, and if I don't, it's no one's loss." I felt an ache behind my eyeballs and in my leg joints, a prickle along my skin that meant it was almost dawn. "How's the bricklayer?"

"Ah," he said, propping his chin on my breastbone so he could look directly up at me. "Poor man. Poor mule. Every brick has to be perfectly aligned with every other brick or the whole wall will go off-kilter. One fraction of an inch off and the wall gets more crooked with every succeeding course. How does he keep at it, brick after brick, day after day, without going out of his mind?"

"Why doesn't he just get a better job?"

"Because bricklaying is his trade," said John significantly. "It's hard, and it's tedious, and backbreaking and lonely, but he's chosen it."

I had nothing to say to this. I reached for the whiskey bottle.

"Claudia," he said after a while. "I can't leave Rima, you know that, right?"

"I know." I poured a little whiskey into my mouth. "I would never ask you to, don't worry."

"But it's so hard for me," he said. "I miss you all the time."

"Oh, come on, John, no one misses anyone all the time."

"I mean it," he said vehemently, then he burst into tears. He sobbed through his nose into his clenched fists, his stomach heaving. "I'm all she has. I can't take it any more."

I got up on my haunches and cradled his head. His hair was as densely matted and dusty as the fur of an indoor pet. The shed condom, weighted with its tiny cargo, lay curled on the edge of the rug.

At around six, just before the sun rose, we went to an all-night Ukrainian diner and ate plates of potato pancakes with sour cream and applesauce. John paid the bill and left me at the entrance to the subway. "It was sublime in the best sense, seeing you again, Claudia," he said, holding both my hands in his.

I smiled at him, took my hands back, and went down the stairs to the platform. It was almost seven; I had just enough time to get home, shower and change, and walk to work.

In the shower I had to brace myself with a hand against the tiles; as I walked out of the park onto Fifth Avenue, fatigue hit me like a hard wind and I was momentarily so dizzy I had to sit down on a bench. I almost fell asleep, but caught myself just in time and made myself get up and keep walking. My brain felt as if it were wrapped in cotton batting. My eyes wouldn't focus properly and my thoughts bumped around my skull haphazardly. I couldn't imagine how I was going to get through the day in any coherent, orderly manner, but I reminded myself that I'd done it before, which was just reassurance enough to propel me toward Jackie's building.

chapter six

When I walked through the door he held open, Ralph gave me an uncharacteristically restrained "Good morning."

"Hi, Ralph," I said. "What's wrong?"

He looked at me as if he weren't really seeing me and said in a bewildered, lost voice I'd never heard him use before, "The old lady's gone."

At first I thought she had left on a trip I had forgotten she was taking, which could easily have happened, and I stared at him in a panic. "Gone?" I said. "Gone where?"

"Gone gone," he said dazedly. "I can't believe it."

"What do you mean, gone gone?"

"She passed away."

I stared at him. "You mean she's dead?"

"Just like that," he said with a weak smile. "I always thought she would live forever."

"My God," I whispered. "So did I." All at once I remembered the radio, my jubilant and insouciant departure yesterday evening. I stared wide-eyed at him, amazed beyond comprehension. No. Could it be? Impossible. But he'd said—a prairie opened in my head, grass blowing to the horizon, fresh wind, blue sky. "How did it happen?" I asked. "Who told you?"

"Ralph dear," called Mrs. Florscheim, who lived on the sixth floor and was emerging from the elevator, "could you get me a taxicab?"

Ralph gave me a wordless look, then went out to the sidewalk, fumbling in his shirt for his whistle.

I looked through the French doors to the courtyard. I could go out there now if I wanted to and sit on a bench by the fountain. The mirrors lining the lobby were neutral now; I didn't need them any more to warn me of my sagging hemlines and windblown hair. My whole body shifted slightly in the suddenly weaker gravitational pull exerted by the building. I bounded to the elevator and rose just ahead of it to her apartment.

I unlocked her door and stood in the foyer for a moment, stunned by a wild, remorseless joy. An understanding of what I had done tried to force itself into my mind like an ocean liner at the mouth of a smallish river. I oscillated between the two realities, Jackie alive yesterday, Jackie dead today, a keen buzz of adrenaline fizzing through my veins. I whispered the word "murderer" to myself; it had a plummy, luscious sound, completely unrelated to the gavel's whipcrack or the crackle of the electric chair. There on the back of the chair was one red-gold hair, there a lipsticked Kleenex she'd dropped in the wastebasket. The residue of her perfume rode the currents of air eddying in the doorways.

"Juanita," I called, suddenly hearing for the first time the vacuum cleaner roaring somewhere, but she couldn't hear me over the noise, and didn't answer.

Through the arched doorway, the living room was a baroque cavern awash in glimmers and shadows. The two dozen roses Jimmy Blevins had sent yesterday were in a brass jar on the low mahogany table; dark crimson petals already spattered the rug. I plunged in among gold-plated paperweights and bronze horsemen on marble stands. The shining surfaces bent and wavered as if in the play of light from sunlit waves high above. I rubbed a gold dagger-shaped letter opener and left an oily smudge, then leaned toward the roses to inhale their rich perfume. They looked like soft rock-clinging undersea animals, all mouth.

I went down the hall, through her bedroom to the bathroom. The blank tiles gleamed dully. The tub was empty. The air felt hollow, as if a cold dense fog had been and gone.

The shower shelf was in the wastebasket under the sink, and the handle had broken off.

The radio was on the side of the bathtub, no longer plugged in.

I ran my fingers around the inside of the tub. No cleanser grit or hardened minerals came away on my fingers. The porcelain sides were as glossily nacreous as the inside of an oyster shell, and completely dry.

I saw, as if on a movie screen, Jackie reaching up to adjust the volume, her impatient hand tugging at the knob, the radio in mid-air, Jackie frantically trying to catch it. The water twitching with power like a live thing, roiling over her heaving body—her eyes staring emptily at the ceiling. A heightened touch (imagined for my own purposes): bubbling up from the radio under the water, Frank Sinatra's voice, "I've got you under my skin; I've got you deep in the heart of me . . ."

I went out and sat in one of the leopard-print chairs in the boudoir and picked up the phone. I dialed the number for downstairs. Louie answered. "Louie, it's Claudia," I said. "Is Ralph around?"

"He's on break. Can I help you with something?"

"Did you hear about Jackie?"

He laughed. "No, what did she do now?"

"No, Louie, it's not that. Jackie's dead."

"What do you mean, she's dead?"

"You haven't heard? Ralph told me this morning when I got here."

"No, I had no idea," he said.

"Could you ask Ralph to call me right away?"

"I'm on my way up to fix a leak on three," he said, "but you could try him in a few minutes, he's due back soon. So how did she, uh—what happened to her?"

"I don't know," I said, "that's what I'm calling to find out."

"I'll leave him a note to call up there," said Louie.

I hung up. This was serious; I had to think, and I was unable to think. My muscles seized up and my face went rigid. A teak chest crouched next to me. On a stand just above my head lurked a silk spider plant, ready to spring. The daylight was blocked by red velvet curtains and inadequately replenished by standing lamps with heavy fringed silk shades. Acorn-sized bulbs burned dimly in sconces along the wall opposite the mirror. The walls were papered with a hand-painted fantasia of enormous genitalesque crimson flowers on leafy stalks; a fecund array of fake ferns and bamboo trees was doubled by its reflection in the mirror-covered wall behind it. Everything seemed cartoonish and unreal in the theatrical pomp of this room. "She made me look through the trash," I could hear myself whining in court, "and all along the picture was upstairs in an envelope where she herself had put it."

"It's called a job," I could hear the judge saying dispassionately, "and you could have spoken up if you thought you were being treated unfairly, or you could have quit. I'm sentencing you to life without parole, and I hope that your incarceration will be a lesson for you."

When I crossed the room and opened the curtains, razor-sharp sunlight slashed through the air and flattened all the rich winy colors to washed-out shadows, obliterating the lamplight, glinting in the mirrors. My reflection was the only vivid thing in the room. Who needed Jackie? She had been a liability, really. Now all that ladylike white-gloved crap could be thrown right out the window. The book could be witty and straightforward and maybe even have a cohesive plot. Eventually, once I'd convinced Gil that I could write a real book, I would start publishing under my own name. I could take William to dinner at Nobu, I could pay off my debts and move downtown, I could travel and sleep late and throw parties and do whatever else I wanted.

My spirits, so long compressed into a tight coil, burst forth like a released spring. I got up and prowled through her closet, rifled through her dressers and nightstand, went into the dining room and opened her liquor cabinet, ran my hands over the objects on the big desk in the living room. As I did so, I found myself accumulating a number of her things, all of which seemed to come into my possession of their own volition. They leapt into my hands like abandoned pets looking for a new owner: bottle-green suede pumps, gray cashmere sweater, gold watch, tortoiseshell fountain pen, gold-plated cigarette case inlaid with semiprecious gems, and an unopened bottle of rare and expensive Scotch. From my hands, they found their way into my canvas shoulder bag by the same force, guided by some mysterious magnetic pull.

As I stashed the bag of loot in the pantry, I heard Jackie's voice somewhere in the apartment. I froze in my tracks, wide-eyed and terrified. She wasn't dead after all. Ralph had made a mistake—I cocked my head to hear what she was saying and realized that it was her answering machine, picking up a call. I hadn't heard the phone ring. I stood over the phone, poised to pick it up if it was Ralph, but after the beep came Mr. Blevins's voice: "Well, hello there, my dearest. I've been thinking about you all morning. How are you today? I'm at the office if you need anything."

I leaned against the counter and closed my eyes, holding on to the countertop, wishing I'd had some sleep last night and hadn't drunk so much. A thick, slow haze of unreality was coloring all my perceptions. I felt like a rudderless boat.

I shook myself awake and set up my office in the dining room, then sat down at my desk. My head was beginning to ache in earnest. The whiskey I'd drunk in the early morning hours had metabolized enough so that my body was suspended in the precarious gully between intoxication and hangover. Given a choice, I preferred to go back over to the drunk side, especially for the task ahead, so I got up and went to the liquor cabinet, found an opened bottle of Scotch and a tumbler, and sat down again with them on the table in front of me. I called Ralph's number again. He answered. "Ralph, it's Claudia," I said.

"Oh, right, Louie left me this note to call you," said Ralph. He sounded out of breath. "I'll call you right back, okay? I have to deal with something right away."

"Call me as soon as you can," I said urgently.

After I'd downed half the good-sized slug in my glass, I braced myself and called Jimmy Blevins. Poor old man, now his life would be so sad and gray. "Oh, Mr. Blevins," I said when he answered. "It's Claudia."

He wept when he heard the news, and to my astonishment I found myself weeping with him. He reminisced eloquently about her beauty, grace and charm, her inspiring rise from her husband's ashes on the wings of her literary career, her endearing vanities and foibles. In a way, it was true; there was no one else like Jackie, she had been one of a kind.

"What happened?" he asked.

"I think she died in the bathtub," I said, my voice dripping with a thick purple emotion I tried to modulate into condolence. "She was there when I left at five. She'd had such a hard day, and she was exhausted."

"I always told her she had to be careful, not to work so hard, not to worry so much. But she wouldn't listen to me."

One afternoon not too long before, I'd said good night to Jackie and Mr. Blevins, who were fiddling with her CD player in the dining room, trying to get it to work. Halfway down the block, I remembered that I'd left the outgoing mail on the dining room table. I went back up to Jackie's and let myself in; I heard swishy, romantic music. I barged into the dining room saying, "I'm back, I just forgot—" and saw them dancing, Mr. Blevins and Jackie. I stopped in the doorway, as embarrassed as if I'd caught them in bed together. He held her in his arms and swirled her around, dipping her, holding her close, then turning deftly and bending his knee to turn again. She cleaved to him like silk. Her eyes were closed. Two flutes of champagne bubbled on the windowsill. She opened her eyes and said, laughing a little, "Come on in, Claudia, we're just practicing for Cafe Society tonight!" I retrieved the mail and went back out, and on the way down in the elevator I thought about the way Mr. Blevins hadn't missed a step when I'd come in or even seemed to see me.

I said, "Oh, Mr. Blevins, I'm not sure she ever told you this, but your friendship meant so much to her."

"She was so fragile underneath it all," he said. "I knew how hard it was for her. I tried to protect her as much as I could."

"She appreciated that more than she could ever tell you."

"She's really gone?" he said wonderingly.

"I know, I know, it's hard to believe."

"Oh, Jackie."

"Mr. Blevins, please let me know if there's anything I can do for you."

"If only you could bring her back," he said.

Juanita wheeled the vacuum cleaner into the living room and whisked it over the rug, sucking up the rose petals, knocking its hard rubber nose against chair legs and coffee tables. I watched her solid figure move energetically, encased in pink uniform and thick panty hose and white sneakers. I wondered what she would do now, how she would survive. How was I going to explain to her? And everyone else?

I dialed another number. No matter what had happened recently, no matter what he currently thought of me, he was still my friend. "William," I said when he answered.

"Claudia!" he said; my heart leapt at the frank gladness in his voice. "I meant to call you yesterday. Did you make it home all right the other night?"

"Yes," I stammered. "William, I have some very strange news. I might be in a lot of trouble, actually."

"Why? Tell me."

"She's dead."

"Who's dead?"

"Yesterday she made me dig through bags of garbage because she lost a photograph. And then she was just—struck down, after I went home. It's like the gods were punishing her. Or someone."

"Jackie's dead?"

"I got here this morning and Ralph told me, and now—"

"What happened?"

"I don't know yet for sure," I said, "but—"

"Oh wait, shit, sorry, Claudia, I have to take this other call. Don't go away."

"I'll hold," I said. I pressed the receiver into my ear as tightly as I could. It was the only thing that tied me to the world of normal life.

"I'm back," said William. "I have a call in three minutes with a big fat cheese, but I can keep him waiting for a couple of minutes. Claudia: she's really dead?"

"You have to swear not to tell anyone," I said. "Attorney-client confidentiality or whatever it's called."

"What did you do?"

As briefly as I could, I told him. There wasn't much to tell; I'd left the radio dangling from a broken shower shelf over her bathtub, and now she was dead.

When I finished he was quiet for a moment, then he cleared his throat. I had a sudden horrible feeling that he was laughing at me. "But," he said then, "do you know for sure that's what actually happened?"

"William, the shower shelf broke; it's in the wastebasket."

"But who told you she was electrocuted?"

"When I got here, Ralph, the doorman, told me she was dead, then I came upstairs and looked at the bathtub and the shower shelf was broken and someone, maybe the paramedics, had unplugged the radio."

"Find out for sure before you go confessing to anyone else," he said, and I was sure I heard a smile in his voice. "I think the fuse would probably short out before enough juice went into the water to kill her. Oh, here's my call. Don't forget to come to my party. I'll tell Ian to call you for an interview, just say the word."

I sat motionless then for a long time in my straight-backed

chair, staring inwardly without blinking at a harsh and unambiguous desert. Finally the phone rang, the two short rings that meant someone downstairs was calling. "Ralph," I said. "Finally."

"Sorry, Claudia. What a day, boy. On top of everything. It just keeps hitting me, you know. I'm thinking of going home early."

But he had called her a loon, a bat, a daffy duck; he had commiserated with me so many times and with such sincerity. I noticed that my glass was empty; I poured another good-sized shot and drank it straight off. Then I said, "I didn't know the two of you were so close."

He sighed. "We weren't *close* close, but you never know how it's going to hit you when someone dies. I should have listened to her more, helped her out more. I hope she knew how much I cared about her. I never told her. I complained about her all the time. Now it's too late."

"What happened, exactly?"

"Hit by a car," he said. "Hit-and-run."

My heart flew from its black cage back out into the broad skies of ordinary human emotion. "When? Last night?"

"Yesterday afternoon around three o'clock," he said, "but I didn't hear until I got home from work. Her neighbor was waiting for me on my front—"

"Whose neighbor?"

"Her friend, Mrs. Marengo. She was crying, 'Oh, poor Ralph,' on and on and I didn't know what had happened, then I go inside and my phone is ringing and it's my brother, telling me—"

"Wait a minute. Who are we talking about?"

"My grandmother, Claudia," he said reproachfully.

I paused while my entire sense of reality rearranged itself, then stammered before the implications could hit me, "Your grandmother died. Oh, my God. Oh, my *God*. That's just terrible. Oh, my God, how absolutely awful. I can't believe this."

"It's nice of you to feel so bad, Claudia. She was a great lady, believe me."

Just then I heard Jackie's front door open and shut, and someone's heels tapping through the foyer, along the pantry, and into the kitchen.

"I'd better go," I said in a rush.

"Thanks for calling," he said.

I dialed Mr. Blevins's number as fast as I could. When he answered I said, "Mr. Blevins, I made an awful mistake, I'm so sorry."

"Who is this?"

"It's Claudia, Mr. Blevins, I misunderstood the doorman, Jackie is alive and well and she just walked in. The doorman was telling me his grandmother died and I thought he meant—"

Mr. Blevins said in a thick drowning voice, "She's not really dead?"

"She's alive, Mr. Blevins, it was all a stupid misunderstanding, and if you wouldn't mind, I think it's best if you don't mention—"

"Jackie is alive?" he said again, uncomprehendingly, and then I heard someone pick up another extension and begin punching in numbers. They beeped loudly in my ear.

"That's her now, trying to call out," I said, "so we'd better hang up. I'm so sorry, Mr. Blevins, I don't know what to—"

"Hello," came Jackie's impatient bark. "Is that you on the line, Claudia?"

"I'm just hanging up," I said, "good-bye."

"Jackie," came Mr. Blevins's strangled cry, "Jackie, I can't believe it's really you, I can't believe you're really there, you're back, oh Jackie." Apparently I wasn't the only one who'd been holding a private whiskey wake this morning.

"Where else would I be, Jimmy? Okay, Claudia, you can hang up, I'll talk to Jimmy for a moment although I must get ready for my meeting—"

In the split second between hanging up the phone and leaping into tracks-covering action, I felt three things simultaneously: gnawing hunger, a desire to laugh hysterically, and a strong resolve to behave to myself and everyone else as if nothing out of the ordinary had happened here. I stowed the whiskey and tumbler in the liquor cabinet, then turned on my computer and opened the file that contained the chapter I was currently working on. I scrolled through it, taking a running leap, correcting things here and there, adding and deleting words, moving sentences from one paragraph to another. When I got to the end, my fingers leapt over the keyboard, out of the gate like racehorses. Ten minutes later, when Jackie stuck her head into the dining room, I had written a whole page. I stopped and looked up at her. I was pretty gonzo from the whiskey, I realized all of a sudden. Everything had a mellow, fuzzy glow around it except Jackie, who seemed unnaturally in focus.

"I can't find my sweater," she said, "the cashmere cardigan, the gray one. Or my gold watch, the one my brother gave me for my birthday. Have you seen them? They were where I left them, and now they're not, and I wanted to wear them to my meeting today with Gil Reeve." She exhaled sharply. "Sometimes I think that girl steals from me. I've been missing things, little things, and that isn't like me at all, I'm very well-organized. And what was Jimmy going on about? He didn't sound like himself. The poor man was almost crying! I had to tell him to stop making such a scene!"

"I'll look for your watch and sweater," I said.

"What were you saying to Mr. Blevins just now?" She came into the dining room to stand directly over me, her favorite vantage point for inquisitions. She gave a sniff just as I exhaled a blast of whiskey breath; her nostrils were two little fully flared vacuums sucking the fumes from my lungs. "I don't like the way you got him all riled up, he seemed to have got the idea from you that I was *dead,* and then I wasn't, what can you have been thinking?"

I gave a bark meant to sound like a carefree laugh. If I could throw up a smoke screen of meaningless chatter, she might just get bored and let it drop. I often used this technique when she confronted me directly with something I'd done; her short attention span generally did her in before we got to the heart of the matter. I always knew, though, that she had filed this latest transgression away in the vault with all the other ones. "Oh, that," I said airily over the hot coals burning in my stomach. "Ralph was all upset when I came in this morning, something about his grandmother—"

We had a staredown; what else was I supposed to say? I looked away finally, and she said, "See if you can find those things, would you?" She went back to her bedroom to do whatever the hell she did in there.

My whole body had gone into some kind of deep freeze from all the various biochemical substances it had been forced to produce today, each one canceling out the next, shock, euphoria, fright, craftiness, venality, weepiness, shock again. It had run out of juice for the time being and I didn't blame it. I got up, went numbly into the pantry, took from my bag all the things I'd stolen from her, and set about returning them to their rightful places, the fountain pen and cigarette case to the desktop, the whiskey to the cabinet, the suede pumps (damn it, I'd really wanted those) to the shoe closet in the hall. I went into her bedroom and handed her the sweater and the watch. "I found them," I said.

She took them without a word and put them on. "I've been meaning to tell you, Claudia," she said. "My great-niece is coming next week from Italy to learn English and meet some of the young people in New York. She's a famous aristocrat in Italy although you'd never know it; she's absolutely unspoiled."

"What's her name?"

"Gianbattista Santa Maria Lucia di Paolo del Castellano," Jackie rattled off in her hard-edged Italian. She was a different person when she spoke Italian, scarier and more legitimate. "She's called Lucia and she's only twenty years old. I'm afraid she won't have enough to do while she's here. I want to set up a dinner party, we'll talk about the guest list later. I set up an interview for her on Monday at eleven with my friend Frances Gray, she has a modeling agency. Did you get that?"

"Frances Gray," I said. "Monday at eleven."

"Of course she's done a lot of modeling in Italy. She's terribly famous there, everyone always recognizes her on the street. That's one of the reasons she wants to live for a year in New York. 'I have to escape the paparazzi, Aunt Jackie,' she told me; they're very bad in Italy, like mosquitoes. Make sure she brings her portfolio with her." She put her hands on her waist and looked over her shoulder at the mirrored wall, one leg extended behind her in a 1950s cheesecake pose. "I'm putting on weight," she said. "I've got to take it off immediately. No more cream sauces for me. Claudia, what exactly did you tell Mr. Blevins?"

This was one of her interrogatory tactics, to lull me with blather, then blindside me with a direct question. I had been anticipating this; I'd sensed, behind her monologue, the ticking in her brain—one, a weeping Mr. Blevins filled with wonderment that she was really still alive, two, the missing items so quickly restored by the whiskey-reeking secretary—she knew they added up to something and she would ferret it out eventually.

No plausible lie presented itself. "I misunderstood Ralph," I said frankly and apologetically, my heart like a trapped quail against my rib cage. "When I came in he looked really upset, and I asked why, and he said, 'She's dead, she passed away yesterday.' I came upstairs thinking the worst. I called Mr. Blevins to let him know immediately. But then, when I called Ralph to find out how it had happened, he said it was his grandmoth—"

"Who else did you call?"

"No one," I said; William didn't count.

"I can't have it getting out all over town! This is just too preposterous. Jimmy told me that he'd already notified some of my friends! Well, I gave it to him. 'Always verify anything that girl tells you,' I said to him. 'You can't take anything she says at face value, she gets very mixed up sometimes.' I'm just beside myself, Claudia; this makes two days in a row. What on earth is the matter with you?"

"I'm sorry, Jackie," I said.

"This whole thing is absolutely crazy. You sound like a crazy person. It upsets me very much, Claudia, I don't know quite what to—and you smell as if you've been drinking."

"I had a little whiskey, Jackie. I thought you were dead and I was upset, and I needed to steady myself."

The picture clicked into place then, I could see its ugly shape cohere in her head: the person she most depended on could not be trusted for a minute. The illusion of my essential integrity had allowed her not to fire me so many times I'd lost count; my mistakes were just the careless errors of a well-intentioned and devoted if deeply flawed employee. I saw the knowledge come to her that I was no good, and then I saw the shutters close on that knowledge. If she played it out to its inevitable end, who would finish this book and write the next one? She blinked several times, shook her head as if to clear it, looked me right in the eye and said firmly, "This is unacceptable."

"I know," I said.

She nodded as if something had been settled and sat down at her vanity table to inspect the damages our conversation had done to her face. Whatever she saw in the mirror reminded her of something else. "Oh, and one more thing, I almost forgot. You broke my soap holder yesterday, putting that heavy radio on it. It came down right on my head, it's a lucky thing I didn't get a concussion. Please go out now and get me a new one at the drugstore. Get a good one this time, that old one was so shoddy."

"All right," I said, "I'll go right away."

I took a twenty from her change jar in the kitchen and put on my coat. When I came out of the elevator, Ralph was sitting slumped on the bench by the door.

He looked up with a wan smile as I came through the lobby.

"Maybe you should take the rest of the day off," I said to him, glad to have the opportunity to worry about someone else for a little while.

"I wish I could," he said. "She complained a lot about her arthritis, her Social Security didn't come, her lightbulbs burned out, and I tried to listen but sometimes I just—"

"You can't always be a saint," I said.

"Yeah, but sometimes I got on her, 'You shouldn't be so negative, Grandma, visualize your potential!' I got into this thing, Lifespring. She told me to get off my high horse and go to confession. We didn't speak after that for a time. But I stayed close by."

"That's all that matters," I said. "I'd better run along. Her Highness needs a new shower shelf."

"Don't want to keep her waiting," he said, and opened the door for me and gestured me through.

I went immediately to a phone booth and called William's office. "I'll hold," I told his snotty little bitch of a secretary, Elissa, when she informed me that "Mr. Snow" was in a "meeting." She took it upon herself to treat me like William's out-of-control neurotic sister, and I took it upon myself to roll right over her. Forty cents into the call, William came on the line. "Claudia," he said.

"William," I said. "You're going to think I'm a total idiot and I am. Not only did I not kill her, she's not even dead. You didn't tell anyone, did you?"

"She's not dead," he repeated.

"William, I can't explain now, it was a perfectly understandable mix-up. It's not like I do this kind of thing all the time. Did you tell anyone?"

"Um," he said, and paused. "Actually, I mentioned it to Margot a few minutes ago. You might want to call her and set her straight. I invited her to my—"

"Oh shit," I said, "will you call and tell her? I'm at a pay phone."

He laughed. "I can't, I have another meeting in two seconds. Anyway, she's probably going to call you any minute. Don't worry, Claudia, we all make mistakes. See you tomorrow night."

"Wait," I said, but he had already hung up. What was Margot's number? I called Information and was told it was unlisted; no big surprise. I had it in my little red book on my desk upstairs—Margot was probably calling me there right now.

Things couldn't get much worse with Jackie than they already were. I went to the drugstore on Lexington, bought a sturdy metal shower shelf and headed back to Jackie's. My conversation with William had sent me into a prickly heat of self-loathing. I wished suddenly, not for the first time, that I didn't have any friends. Friendship was so risky, so painful and tentative. How could you ever trust anyone? Conversations were a series of leaky, fragile paper boats launched with foolish optimism toward a distant shore, too heavily freighted to do anything but sink or flounder or go blundering into other hemispheres. It had been a mistake to call William just now; it had been a mistake to tell him every single awful thing about myself for the past five years. The way he had laughed made me see myself the way he must see me, the way everyone must, and I couldn't afford to see myself as a total joke because all I had was the frail hope that I wasn't. How could I have actually thought Ralph had meant that Jackie was dead? It seemed impossible that I could have made such a mistake. Maybe I was really crazy. Maybe my perceptions, all of them, were the semi-hallucinations of a permanently addled brain.

I crossed Park Avenue and headed toward the familiar facade of Jackie's building. There it sat like a big protective dog, surrounding her with its burly and respectable flanks. She was still alive, I still had a job, nothing had changed.

I took the new shower shelf into her bathroom and hung it carefully on the shower rod, then arranged on it her bottles of shampoo, her fancy lavender soaps, her back brush. I put the receipt in the household receipt folder in the files, put every penny of the change in the change jar in the kitchen, made myself a cup of tea, and sat down at my desk.

117

I had written a paragraph when Jackie came in.

"Claudia," she said, "it's all just too much. Who do you think called while you were out?"

"Margot?" I said.

"At first she thought I was you. 'No,' I said, 'it's Jackie.' She said, 'Jackie! You wouldn't believe what I just heard about you!' Of course I knew very well already. She said she had heard that I was dead! Which someone, she couldn't say who, had told her just a few minutes before. Claudia, there is a rumor circulating now about this, and I want it stopped immediately before anyone else hears. This is truly the most unsettling thing that has ever happened to me. So unsettling I'm not quite sure what to do. Margot, telling me she thought I was dead!" She fluttered around me, pacing over the old rug, smoothing her hair nervously.

"I'll call her right away."

"She's a good girl, that Margot. I could count on her every minute; I trusted her with my life. No matter what happened I knew she was honest and loyal." She sighed, eyeing me unhappily. "I just can't fathom how this happened."

"I know."

"Really, Claudia, this time it's not something I can just overlook. This puts everything in a different light. It makes me feel as if I can't leave you alone in my house, and that makes me so uncomfortable, I can't tell you."

"I understand."

"Do you? Well, maybe you do." She took a deep breath and said without looking at me, "I'm thinking of hiring a full-time secretary and having you work only on the book, maybe at your own house. Mr. Blevins suggested it, actually, and I think he's right. What do you think?"

"It's a great idea," I said. I considered this a promotion, in a way.

She looked at me then, obviously relieved. "Do you think so? I'll have to see if I can afford to pay two salaries, of course. I think it might be the ideal solution to all the troubles we've been having together. I like you very much, please don't misunderstand me, you're a very sweet dear girl, but you must see that I can't have these rumors that I'm dead and so forth."

"Oh yes," I said. "I do see that, absolutely."

"Good," she said, "oh, good, I'm glad we agree about this." She gave a nod in my direction and went off to meet with Gil Reeve.

I called Margot and got her answering machine. "You've reached the home of Margot Spencer," came Margot's fluted tones; of course her junior four on West End Avenue was a "home," unlike my rathole on an airshaft, and of course her tones were fluted on her outgoing message when everyone else's, mine for example, sounded as if the speaker were trapped at the bottom of a well, "and I'm either out or unable to take your call at the moment. Please leave a very brief message and I'll get back to you as soon as possible."

"Hello, Margot," I said in a singsong like a playground taunt, then hastily lowered my pitch and tried to sound a little more adult, "it's Claudia, calling to apologize for the false news; I didn't know William was going to tell you. As you discovered yourself a few minutes ago, Jackie's alive and well and in quite a state about this whole misunderstanding, which I caused single-handedly and which I've now been instructed to undo. So if you told anyone else, I'd appreciate it if you'd let them know it was a mistake. Thanks. I guess I'll see you tomorrow night; William mentioned that he'd invited you to his—" Her machine cut me off with a scolding little beep.

One more call. "Hello," said Mr. Blevins.

"Mr. Blevins, it's Claudia."

"I have nothing at all to say to you and I don't know why

you're calling me again. That was a mean trick you played on me this morning, you know that? You've got a strange sense of humor if you thought that was funny."

"No, you don't understand. I misunderstood the doorman, and it was all a big mistake, and I got myself in a lot of trouble."

"I understand that you ought to have your head examined. I don't take kindly to being made a fool of and God knows I'm a fool about Jackie, but this was different."

"I'm calling first to say how sorry I am and second to ask if you told anyone else. She's worried the whole town's going to think she's dead."

"Well, I did tell some people, and I've already called them back, and they said they'd call whoever they called to tell them, but it seems to me you've already upset the apple cart, no sense in trying to chase after all the apples. The damage has been done and it'll just have to mend itself. I'm glad you don't work for me, and that's the truth. Good-bye now."

I wrote like a fiend all afternoon, feeling as I wrote that this was some of the best work I'd ever done. I finished with a scene in which Genevieve was asked by Tony Roper to interrogate a handsome Brazilian masseur under the pretext of getting a massage at a spa near Monaco. It opened with Genevieve on her stomach on the massage table, naked except for the towel draped modestly around her buttocks. While Raoul vigorously pummeled and kneaded and karate-chopped, Genevieve asked the questions she'd been sent to ask, and elicited a few intriguingly inconclusive answers. But at some point, toward the end of the section, she began to flirt with Raoul, telling him that his hands were the strongest she'd ever felt, that his beautiful, rumbling voice was a perfect accompaniment to a massage because it sent shivers along her spine. Their conversation wrote itself:

"I am flattered," Raoul said smoothly.

"I've never had a massage like this before in my life."

"Your husband does not rub your back like this?"

"Sometimes he rubs my neck, but never like this."

"Every man should massage his wife," said Raoul firmly.

"I'd rather have you do it."

The hussy! Didn't she know any better, after all those years away from New Jersey? How could she make me look through the garbage? How *dare* she be alive after I'd already told Mr. Blevins and wept with him and said all the right things?

Before I could stop her, she added in a low, barely audible murmur: "I sometimes wonder what goes on during all those business trips he takes to New York. He always stays with my sister, even though a hotel is so much more practical."

Raoul was silent a moment, then said delicately, "Madame fears that—"

"Oh, I'm not afraid of anything," Genevieve said stoutly, and leapt up from the table.

Ralph had already gone off duty at five o'clock; the doorman who ushered me out was Grover, the one I didn't like because I always got the feeling that he was spying on me, looking for something he could use against me to get in good with Jackie. I didn't answer him when he told me to have a good weekend; I'd have any damn kind of weekend I wanted. Jackie didn't like him, anyway; she thought he was ugly, which was the worst sin you could commit with her, and no amount of fawning on his part could ever compensate for that.

chapter seven

The air outside was shot through with greenish light and a fine drizzling rain that adhered to my skin like spider webs as I moved through it. I hadn't eaten anything since those potato pancakes with John early this morning. I was so hungry now I felt as if I would float away on the next strong breeze, so I got a hot dog with mustard at the first stand I came to and wolfed it down in four bites, then bought another one and washed it down with an Orangina, which made me feel bloated, and definitely not strong enough to walk all the way home. I climbed onto a crosstown bus belching its way toward Central Park.

I found a seat by a window and rested my hot temple against the cool glass. As the park went by in a brown blur, exhaustion overcame me all at once, and I fell asleep. I jerked awake with a panicky start I didn't know how long afterwards and pulled the cord. I tumbled off the bus, sure I'd gone too far, then saw that I hadn't gone far enough. The neighborhood looked small and brown in the setting sun; the rain had stopped and the sky was clearing. I walked blinking and yawning through a sudden thicket of people with outstretched arms, shaking coffee cups and asking for change in a hostile drone. When I came to my street, it looked barely familiar, like an amalgam of four different streets in a dream. The traffic light behind me changed and a rattling fleet gunned past. Automatically I gave a quarter to the man in the doorway with a sign propped in front of him, and just as automatically he nodded his thanks.

In my mailbox I found a disconnect notice from the phone company and a threat from a collection agency concerning the most delinquent of my Visas. I shoved them into my coat pocket and climbed the stairs, let myself in without turning on the light, shed my coat and shoes, closed the blind that was open, fell onto my bed, and sank into a coma.

I emerged from it the next morning thirsty and groggy, but still alive. It was Saturday, I thought immediately; oh joy, two days off, I could go to the Skouros for breakfast. Then I remembered what had happened in the past couple of days and groaned out loud and put the pillow over my head and went back to sleep. When I next awoke, it felt like late afternoon, but according to my clock it was only eleven in the morning. I had slept for seventeen hours straight. I would have liked to sleep some more, but I was hungry, and so thirsty my eyes had dried in their sockets and my mouth contained beef jerky instead of a tongue. I got up and immediately had to sit down again while the blood rushed to wherever it needed to go to enable me to stand, and then like an old man I gimped into the bathroom and put my face near the sink faucet, turned on the cold water, and drank until my stomach could hold no more, until it bulged at the seams. Then I groped through the shower curtain, turned on the hot water, stood like a zombie with my hand under the stream until it reached the proper temperature. Standing in the shower I thought, Here I am, another day, oh Lord. There was a scratch mark on my left breast. John Threadgill; I had slept with him again. My arms were covered in downy blond hair that sworled like tiny river grasses as the water coursed over it. Were my arms thickening a little? Was that the beginning of cellulite there, on the back of my thigh? My body couldn't withstand this kind of treatment much longer. I needed to get my shit together. What was I waiting for? At this rate I was going to become a crazy old bag lady sleeping on subway-station benches, reeking of piss and howling to myself. My life was a farce, my body accrued debt and trouble and scratch marks, my psyche was a runaway train. Yee-haw.

I got out of the shower and dried off, put on some jeans and a sweatshirt and a sweater, opened the blind and peered out at the airshaft and determined that it was raining again. I put on my raincoat and locked the door behind me and headed up Broadway to the Skouros Coffee Shop.

I should have gone somewhere else, I decided fifteen minutes later. First of all, I spent three of my remaining dollars on a Danish and it arrived leathery and incompletely heated. The guy behind the counter had poured me the sludge from a near-empty pot on the top burner; now he was ignoring me, watching a burger patty on the grill metamorphose from raw meat into melted fat. An oversized mustache rode his upper lip like Don Quixote on his spavined nag, gallantly, its purpose obscure. Its presence on his otherwise unremarkable face tipped me off to the possibility that he had ideas about the rest of his life grander in scope than serving the likes of me. This made me want to sympathize with him, but I couldn't. There was a cruel arrogance to the way he slashed at the grill with his spatula that suggested he would have tilted at windmills and chopped them to smithereens.

The old man two stools away was leaning toward me, staring openmouthed at my calves. His gaze didn't strike me as intentional enough to be lascivious: he had apparently fallen into a trance, in whose blind path my legs just happened to be. We were the only customers. Just outside the plate-glass window, people and traffic went to and fro in the rain like fish in an aquarium. The door had blown slightly ajar; wet bus exhaust mingled with the fried steam rising from the grill.

The *Times* lay beside me on the counter, folded open to the help-wanted ads. It had seemed like a good idea to start getting a sense of what was out there, jobwise, but one quick glance at the ads told me what I already knew—without Jackie, I was lost. Potential jobs for me fell into the following housewifely categories: child care, which didn't pay enough, and anyway, children were serious business and I couldn't hack it, cleaning houses, serving food, typing letters and selling sex in one form or another. A number of temp agencies had put in requests for fresh blood, but I knew all too well what awaited me there: when I sat at those dinosaur typewriters they all had, hearing the clock ticking away, staring at the nonsense they expected me to flawlessly reproduce on demand, my fingers turned into thick stubs that stumbled crazily over the keys. And my devil-may-care sense of appropriate corporate attire made the nice girls who staffed these agencies understandably nervous about sending me out on jobs under their aegis. "Desperately seeking Gal Friday for midtown architectural firm," said another: what was a Gal Friday? Wasn't that someone who could do anything anyone needed at a moment's notice with a cheerful smile? I chewed a hangnail.

I no longer even read the "adult entertainment" ads: years

ago, I'd gone one fine spring day to an "agency" in the Flatiron Building, where I'd stripped obediently to my underwear and gyrated to a cheap disco number on a boom-box at the behest of a chain-smoking woman in her mid-forties. She turned off the music after several bars, leaving me wriggling in silence for a beat or two, and said, "Get yourself a G-string, shave your pubes, and be at this address at eight Saturday night. And be nice to the customers when you're not onstage, that's how you make your money." She handed me the address of a place called Mama's in a part of Queens I'd never heard of; Rima probably worked there. My next stop was Adele's Intimates on Delancey, where I threw away twenty dollars on a tiny spandex contraption I left on the subway "accidentally" half an hour later, to my great relief. Saturday night found me nowhere near anyone I had to be nice to for any amount of money.

A few months later I'd answered an ad that read: "Female Voiceovers Needed—No Experience Necessary," which turned out to be the phone sex industry drumming for rain; this I could do, because it didn't involve contact with any "customers." All I had to do was sit twice a week on a Vaseline-stained couch in the Channel J studio in midtown, reading my hastily written two-minute scripts into a microphone for ten bucks a pop, simulating a histrionic orgasm at the end while Guillermo the sound guy counted down the seconds, three, two, one, blastoff. I hyperventilated every time. After each session I went out and spent my whole check right away, on anything at all.

So far, I had circled one ad: "Make hundreds of $$$ per week stuffing envelopes at home," which I already knew was a scam because I had once sent twenty dollars for further information, and received back a pamphlet that instructed me to run a classified ad like the one I'd answered, wait for the checks to pour in, then stuff the return envelopes with a photocopy of the pamphlet I'd been sent. I had circled it just for show, trying to make as much commotion about it as possible to dislodge the unbroken stare of the old man to my left.

I put the newspaper down and worked on a cottony wad of Danish for a while, then washed it down with the rest of my coffee. There was a full, fresh pot on the bottom burner of the coffeemaker. I looked longingly at it. But when I gestured to my cup for a refill, the counter guy picked up that same old pot, swirled the inch or two of coffee it contained to reassure himself that it hadn't solidified, then splashed a vile dollop into my cup.

"Could you reheat my Danish when you get a chance?" I asked as inoffensively as I could, which wasn't very.

He gave me a limpid glance and returned to the grill to pulverize the home fries banked along its edge.

"Excuse me," I said.

Chop chop, replied the spatula.

"Okay," I said. "I think I know how to use a microwave."

I got up and carried my plate around the counter and put it into the microwave. I was punching buttons and minding my own business when he pretended to notice me for the first time. "What do you think you're doing?" he asked indignantly. "You're not allowed back there."

"So bring it to me when the little bell goes off," I said. I returned to my stool to the roar of the studio audience: Customer, one, Counter guy, zero.

He deposited the plate in front of me two minutes later with a clatter and an averted glare. I dug my fork through the Danish and tried a bite. It was now soft and perfectly hot. The sweet chemical stuff on top had melted into a delicious creamy goop. I leaned over the counter, emptied my cup into the sink, and, curling three fingers around the handle of the fresh new pot of coffee, poured myself a cupful.

"Okay, but I'm gonna have to charge you for a new cup," said my enemy, not looking at me.

"The hell you will," I said back. I took a sip. The slender margin of its superiority to the other stuff was enough to make it all worthwhile.

Out of the corner of my eye I espied the old man. He was laboring now over a word search puzzle book he'd dug up from somewhere. Breathing hard, he dragged the pencil in a narrow oval that no doubt left grooves in the next five pages, a dead-on imitation of my futile perusal of the help-wanteds. I stole a sidelong peek, playing a little game with myself: if his tongue protruded from between his teeth as I suspected it did, I would score another point. Before I could look away, he caught me on the sharp hook of his vehement old stare. The skin on his face drooped as if it had melted. Under caterpillar eyebrows, his eyes were big as hard-boiled eggs in their hoary sockets. He leaned in toward me, his head wagging dangerously, until he came to a trembling halt at the last point of his resistance to gravity. He lifted a forefinger. He seemed to be about to speak.

I lifted my newspaper so I couldn't see any part of him but his two bony knees in their shiny green pants, which he kept turned toward me, not quite supplicating, but conveying a distinct air of offended propriety. He couldn't have known it, but he represented the losing end of an internal battle I was waging. A few minutes later I escaped from the Skouros without paying a cent to anyone, under cover of a sudden influx of hungry customers. A cold gust spattered against me, belly-full of raindrops. I'd left my umbrella under the counter, but I'd just burned the bridge back to the Skouros.

Buses and cabs rolled north and south. On a bench in the island in the center of Broadway sat a figure of indeterminate sex and age wearing a blanket and a pair of sneakers without shoelaces, his or her face hooded by the blanket. That person was shouting at me, gesturing with the ends of the blanket. What did this person have to say to me? What made him or her think I'd want to hear it? Why did they always pick me? I set off fast down Broadway, as if I had somewhere urgent to go like everyone else.

The rain eased a little, then stopped. A wind blew off the Hudson, fresh and cold. I stopped into a deli, bought an orange and put it in my pocket, then walked over to Riverside Park. On West End Avenue I passed Margot's prewar wedding cake of a building, which was only eight blocks from my own but might as well have been in a different city. I looked up at her fifth-floor windows; they winked back at me. She's not here, they said pityingly. She's busy.

In the park, I sat on a wet bench. The river lay flat and sullen, a drenched, dark mineral gray-green. The banks of New Jersey hulked, beaten-down; the sky was several shades lighter than the water, but just as dense. The mastodonic roar of trucks along the West Side Highway was pierced by a bicycle bell on the path behind me, and the voices of children playing nearby on the paved walkway. I felt a fuzzy early-afternoon languor creep into my limbs; a sleep hangover thrummed through my skull.

I took the orange from my raincoat pocket and peeled it, pulled off a section and broke it in half and examined the long, striated sacs of fluid packed like tendons into the tough clear outer skin. What had I eaten this past week? Hot dogs, chow mein, a Danish, a bag of Chee-Tos. I spent my life inside under artificial lights, or out in the streets breathing carbon monoxide fumes, or in bars breathing smoke and drinking alcohol, which was technically a poison even though it felt like just the opposite. Except for my walks to and from Jackie's, I never exercised; I didn't sleep nearly enough and drank water only in the form of the melted ice in my drinks. I was like a tiny version of the city itself: all my systems were a welter of corruption and neglect.

A mouse had been scratching all day under the floor of my more immediate worries, and suddenly it came to me with an intense shock of horror: the scene I'd written yesterday in that Scotch-hazed fury of relief and hysteria. She might be reading it right now. Oh, shit. Oh, *shit*. I writhed on the bench for a moment, unable to believe that I had actually allowed myself to leave such a potentially dangerous scene on her kitchen table in all its naked, subversive glory.

Once, and only once, very early on in my tenure, Margot had told me after swearing me to absolute and solemn secrecy that Jackie's marriage had ended when she'd inadvertently caught her beloved husband of well over forty years in bed with her younger sister Isabelle. Margot didn't say which bed Jackie had caught them in, but for some reason I imagined it was her own; to make matters far worse, Giancarlo and Isabelle had, they confessed to Jackie, been having an affair for nearly twenty years. Jackie had apparently demanded a divorce on the spot and disowned her sister forever. I didn't ask Margot how she knew this. Margot had been much closer to Jackie than I was, so of course Jackie told her things she would never dream of telling me. And since no one else had ever referred even obliquely to Isabelle, I gathered that either everyone knew about the affair and was protecting Jackie by pretending along with her that her sister had never existed, or no one knew about any of it, and it was her darkest, most closely held secret. Either way, nothing good would happen to me if she read that passage.

Even before her divorce from Giancarlo had become final, Jackie had returned to the States to live in their pied-à-terre on Park Avenue, part of her generous settlement. Although

Jackie to ask an acquaintance some leading questions at a dinner party, eavesdrop on various conversations at a charity ball and the like, all fairly tame stuff. But these anecdotes became the cornerstone on which Jackie and Margot had together, over the next two years, constructed *The Sophisticated Sleuth.*

Unlike most detective novels, this one wasn't plotted so much as artificially generated, carrying the reader along with the pointless energy of an amusement-park water ride. Nothing was seriously at stake; actions had no real consequences. A clue dropped on page twenty-seven was sure to have become irrelevant by page ninety-eight. Despite the narrator's frequent panics concerning the great danger she was in, the crime Genevieve was supposed to be solving had no real urgency; it was subsumed by the dreamlike, impervious world of extreme wealth. At the end of the first book, after three hundred-plus pages of high-society gossip and implausible adventures, Genevieve, on her way to powder her nose at a party, happened upon Johnny Abbott, the odious socialist son of her dear friend Bitsy Abbott, in the hallway outside their hostess's bedroom with a stolen ruby necklace in his hands. The case was solved, establishing Genevieve's niche in the pantheon of whodunit heroines: the socialite private eye who attended balls and parties, jetted off to Cairo and Monaco and the Philippines, went skiing with countesses and yachting with senators (frequently pausing to muse at length on her devotion to Giancarlo and her spoiled, darling sons, Gianni and Federico), and happened to stumble on the criminal just in time for the end of the book.

Jackie's agent placed *The Sophisticated Sleuth* at Wilder and Sons with Gil Reeve. Jackie deeply relished the attention and respect she received as one of the most valuable cash cows in Wilder's barn. Gil took her to lunch every so often for no reason except to keep her happy; their discussions about the progress of her books left her glowing with authorly legitimacy.

His assistant Janine fawned over her and fetched her coffee from the good place downstairs because the company swill wasn't good enough for her; I think she may even have called her "Signora."

When Jackie hired me, her second book, *The High-Heeled Gumshoe*, had consisted of little more than an outline of the first half devised by Jackie, Margot and Gil Reeve in the month or so before Margot quit. During the first three months I worked for her, Jackie had made a great show of sitting at her own computer in her study for part of each morning, tapping away. I was afraid that Margot had been wrong, that Jackie was planning to write her new book herself and there would be no alleviation of my tedious secretarial chores after all. But one day she drifted into the dining room when I was working on her accounts and said, all dimples and charm, "I know that's important, Claudia dear, but do you think you could take a minute and see what you can do with this? I just need a fresh point of view. Sometimes it helps so much to see it in someone else's words."

I abandoned with relief the unsavory business of overstating her deductible expenditures and listened while Jackie narrated the synopsis of the first part of the book. She did so with such conviction that I was nonplused when she finished and looked at me expectantly.

"Well," I ventured, perceiving that the autobiographer was open to suggestion, "maybe a creepy guy with a scar could follow you home from the Museum Ball and get killed in front of your house by someone who runs off into the night."

"That's good, that's very scary, Margot!"

"It's Claudia, actually."

"Well, I know that, Claudia, that's what I said."

"Who is the murderer, anyway?"

She clapped her hands together. "We must decide that

very soon. It was never really solved, Martha Von Jetze's murder, but we must change that for the book. Readers like to know who did it at the end, always remember that."

"I will," I promised with a poker face.

She nodded. "You'll find you'll learn quite a few invaluable lessons about best-seller writing, working for me. It's a wonderful opportunity for a young writer just starting out. I wish someone had taught me these things, but I had to learn them all on my own. That's why I don't know all those fancy writing techniques, those complicated words and similes you girls all learn in college."

"I'll throw some in if you want," I said, trying not to sound patronizing.

I shouldn't have worried; my strengths were her strengths. "Wonderful," she said eagerly. "We might as well get started right away."

Half an hour later, having given me as much detail as she could remember about the actual Museum Ball while I took notes, she said, "Let your imagination run wild! You've read the first book, you know how I tell a story. Put something suspenseful on every page, create suspicion about all the characters. And always, lots of glamour. Describe the gowns, the jewels they wear, mention famous people I know, you can look in my little telephone book for names. For the descriptions of clothes and so forth, you can ask me if you get stuck." She buttoned her jacket and swept out the door to buy a heap of things I'd have to return the following day.

I inserted the computer disk she'd given me and opened the file. Margot had written a few pages of Chapter One before she'd quit; she'd thoughtfully left Genevieve dancing with the half-wit son of one of Zurich's oldest families. There were several subsequent pages, a jumble of notes about potential characters, reprises of the plot, unintelligible dialogue and hy-

two, you couldn't have known, but they wouldn't have served that sort of thing, I'll give you a sample menu tomorrow. And I think instead of Gregory Peck we'd better have Cary Grant, because he's dead, and he can say whatever we want him to. Maybe he could drop a clue about that man in the—" Her voice trailed off for a moment as something distracted her, a thread hanging from her blouse, a random itch, "—well, I'm sure you'll figure it out. See you tomorrow morning!"

Jackie's accolades for her ghostwriter were equal in magnitude and frequency to her attacks on her secretary. She greeted each new chapter with cries of excitement, and often read parts aloud to me with as much pink-cheeked gusto as if she'd written them herself. Once the book was under way, her involvement consisted almost entirely of correcting my "mistaken" representation of her life, about which she was the unchallenged expert: "You don't know this world, we never shout at our maids like that"; or "I can't be saying things like that to strange men I don't know, you have me sounding like a fishwife!" Without protest, I deleted the offending passage and rewrote it to suit her. I was careful always to bear in mind that she was the author even though I was the writer, and that her alter ego Genevieve was a model of refinement and elegance even though she herself was not. I was prepared to relinquish every word I wrote as soon as it came into being. Margot had warned me that once the book was finished, Jackie would "forget" that I had so much as a passing familiarity with the general story outline. "It's sort of like brainwashing," Margot had told me. "She'll wear you down until you believe it too."

Naturally, this created an interesting situation for me with Gil and Janine. As the manuscript of *The High-Heeled Gumshoe* progressed, one or the other of them called every so often. Since I fielded Jackie's phone calls, I was usually the one who spoke to them. I had to bite the inside of my cheek to prevent myself from saying, "But the duke *has* to drink too much at that party, because later on he doesn't remember that Genevieve swore him to secrecy, so he lets the cat out of the bag on Klaus von Hasselhoff's yacht, and that's how Felicia knows Genevieve knows about her husband!" Instead, I said politely that I'd check with Jackie, then hung up, waited twenty minutes, and called back. I couldn't tell whether or not Gil had the least idea what Jackie and I were up to; his tone was always vaguely sly and amused, but this could very well have been his manner with everyone. And I was sure he wouldn't have cared at all who wrote the books; why should he, as long as they made money? But for the sake of Jackie's pride, I dutifully kept up the pretense with everyone, including Jackie herself.

When I'd started work on the book, Jackie had induced me to sign an agreement, which Margot had drawn up for herself and also signed, that prevented me from enacting any future legal efforts to gain recognition, more money, or any rights over my work. William was already familiar with this arrangement because Margot had told him all about it; he told me in no uncertain terms that I was prostituting myself. "You're not going to get anything out of this except resentment," he said earnestly. "It's not worth it. I told Margot the same thing." I had laughed at him. Prostituting myself? He'd never cleaned houses for a living; he'd never waited tables. He had no idea. Eighteen dollars an hour had seemed like a lot of money when we'd agreed to the terms of my employment, back when I was grateful to have this job at all.

But he was right. About a month into writing the book, it struck me that I earned the same hourly wage whether I was writing or playing Miss Lonelyhearts on the phone with Mr. Blevins when Jackie wasn't in the mood to talk to him. Jackie had been given a six-hundred-thousand-dollar advance for three books, of which she would pay me about one-thirtieth to write the second one. She didn't need the money; Giancarlo had bought her off with a bundle so big it couldn't really be called a bundle, it was more like a freight. So, with this firmly in mind, I got up my nerve one day and asked for a raise. "I think I deserve it," I said brazenly, "now that I have the book to write in addition to my secretarial work."

She looked at me for a moment, numbers whirling in her eyes. They came up two zeroes. Like many absurdly wealthy people, Jackie lived in utter terror of spending any more than she absolutely had to because then her money would all be gone. And you couldn't pay people too much or they'd get ideas, and keeping people from getting ideas was what made the whole thing work.

"Well," she sputtered, "my advance isn't really so much money, when you think about how much it costs to live in New York. In Paris, I never had to think about money, Giancarlo handled everything. Now I'm worried all the time about whether or not I'll have enough. You can't imagine, Claudia, I used to be able to buy whatever I wanted!" She shook her head.

And that was that. Clearly a ghostwriter was no more than a glorified secretary, who was only slightly more than a maid. Jackie didn't have to mop her own floors or type her own letters, so why should she be expected to write her own books? And why should she have to pay more than secretary's wages to have someone do it for her? Her readers bought her books not because they were well-written, which for the most part they weren't, but because they believed they were true. Jackie's name was the valuable commodity, and the books themselves were merely gross vessels for that breath of immortal ether.

Anyway, she did her part. As Genevieve, she went on talk shows, gave interviews, did book tours, was taken out to lunch. She charmed her audiences and interviewers with her gallant

trashy writers, don't they have anything better to do than inventing these lies and rumors about innocent people?"

Then she deflated like a wineskin. She mooched around in her bathrobe, devouring a bag of jelly beans in the mistaken perception that her despondency was caused by low blood sugar. "I'm usually so energetic," she called to me from the foyer, where she stood looking into the mirror to reassure herself that physically, at least, she still existed. "I accomplish more than any other woman I know." I had to rest my hands on the computer keyboard and tilt my head to hear her, my facial muscles frozen in a bright, fascinated mask in case she stuck her head in to check my reaction. "I'm not like that Dorcas Robles, or that Lucille Patterson, spending all my waking hours at the hairdresser's or having lunch. That's why men like me, because I've got spice, I talk about things that interest them. Dorcas won't even travel without that little dog of hers. *He's* her boyfriend, if you ask me." Dorcas Robles was a pouty and diminutive Spaniard who spent half her time whispering in hoarse distress into the telephone and the other half hand-feeding her lapdog Pepe, a yappy scrap of fur she'd had dyed to match her platinum pageboy. I had no idea why Jackie considered her any kind of rival, but right now everyone seemed to be her rival, except maybe for me. When I heard the click of jelly beans hitting her teeth in the doorway behind me, I twisted around, smiling encouragingly at her. My neck immediately began to ache. "I've had such a fascinating life! Not many people have lived the way I have. I've traveled everywhere, I knew everyone, all the most famous stars, the top politicians. That's why all those people buy my books, because they're dying to know what it's like to live the way I do."

She trailed off to her bedroom to admire certain photographs of herself posing with her titled and famous friends; her voice faded away. I sat motionless, worried, feeling as if this were all somehow my fault. When the phone rang a few minutes later, she whipped to the doorway of the dining room and fastened her desperate, yearning gaze on my face. "It's Lisa Morris from *People* magazine," I said, almost babbling with relief.

Her hand shot out as if for a syringe of heroin. She scratched the back of my hand as she grabbed the receiver. "This is Genevieve del Castellano," she said grandly. As Lisa Morris's voice poured into her ear, she swelled and straightened, a drooping plant sucking up water. "Yes," she said, self-assured again, "I would be quite interested. Let me check with my secretary." She covered the receiver and hissed, "March seventh at four?" I looked at her calendar and nodded. "I think that'll be just fine, dear," she said into the phone. "Now, will you be coming with a photographer, or will that be scheduled for another day?" By the time she hung up, she was flushed and rosy from her nourishing suck at the nipple of public attention.

Her fan mail trickled in at the rate of one or two letters a week. I would have supposed these fans to consist primarily of Republican housewives in Virginia and Southern California, but letters came from foreign dignitaries, retired engineers, college women seeking advice about their own dreams of being female private eyes, gay men who adored her and called her the bravest, most fabulous woman in the world. They took her books seriously, and believed every word; I established affectionate epistolary friendships with some of them. Those who said they were looking forward to seeing Jackie on her book tour made me nervous: I hoped they wouldn't be too disappointed when they realized that Jackie in the flesh knew and cared considerably less about them than did the Genevieve of all those effusive, encouraging letters. I assuaged my fears with the fact that I wouldn't be there to see it happen. I would be where I always was, in Jackie's dining room.

And for the first couple of years, that was just fine with me. I felt safely and vicariously connected to the world without having to confront it myself. It wasn't until *The High-Heeled Gumshoe* was reviewed with arch, coy, not-quite-uncomplimentary condescension by the Sunday *Times Book Review* (appropriately enough, by a debutante-turned-*Glamour* staff writer, the daughter of an old friend of Jackie's) that I began to chafe at my invisibility. A passage from the book, reproduced in a sidebar accompanying the review, looked surprisingly literary out of context, and I was hit between the eyes by the realization that people were really going to think Jackie had written it. As long as this had been an abstract eventuality, it hadn't mattered. Now I felt intimations of a hunger to be recognized for myself.

One day not long after "my" book came out, I looked down at the book on the lap of the woman next to me on the subway and beheld with a small shock of pleasure my own words, in print. I read along with her. The two of us were so engrossed that we almost didn't notice when we reached our common destination. In the final instant before the doors slid closed, we came to our senses, hastily rose as one and collided in the doorway of the train. "Oops," she murmured distractedly. "Sorry," I said, peering closely at her: this, then, was The Reader. She wore large purple-tinted glasses and a burnt-orange wool suit, and her hair had been fashionably frizzed. She looked respectable and not unintelligent.

As we exited side by side through the turnstiles, I couldn't resist. "Excuse me," I said.

She glanced at me, just a dart, to make sure I wasn't asking for money.

I smiled to show that I was harmless. "I noticed the book you were reading."

"What, this?" She showed me the cover. "It's trash, but it's great for the train."

"I'm glad you like it," I said eagerly. "I wrote it."

She stopped walking and looked at me, then turned the book over to show me the photograph of the superbly coifed Jackie, who looked exactly the way the author of such a book should look. "That's you?"

She had me there. I shook my head.

"I didn't think so," she said, perplexed, and started up the stairs to the street.

I climbed the stairs behind her, chuckling grimly to myself. I knew who I was, even if no one else did.

Those books were mine: the one I'd written and the one I was almost finished writing. They were mine, more than anything else had ever been, those preposterous books, riddled with clichés and inconsistencies. I had written them and they belonged to me, and they were all I had.

I fled out of the park, toward home. On the island in the middle of Broadway was the person who had shouted and gestured at me earlier. He had taken off his blanket, revealing himself to be a black man with a grizzled white head and a broad, wrinkled, plum-colored face. He was doing a sort of dance, flapping his arms and rushing at the pigeons who fluttered around him; they lifted off and alit nervously a few feet away every time he charged at them, but they stayed near him, waiting for his next move as if the whole thing had been choreographed. Then I realized that his hands were full of crumbs, and that they were enduring his fearsome dance because he was feeding them.

chapter eight

I came in to find my answering machine telegraphing a line of red glowing dots. While the tape rewound, I lifted the blankets from the bed into the air as if I were making smoke signals and let them settle.

The first message was from John, asking if I wanted to go to Gus's play with him on Friday. "He got Cecil's mother's building. I think your girl Frieda might have had something to do with that. See you tonight at William's, I hope."

"Well, Claudia," Jackie said after the second beep; my heart exploded. "I've found a girl who's going to come on Monday morning, so that's taken care of. Her name is Goldie and I'm not quite sure I like her name, it sounds like a race horse or showgirl, but the agency said she's very reliable. Thank you for those pages you left." I fell bonelessly into my armchair, but then she went on, "I haven't read them yet, I'll do it first thing tomorrow. We must discuss the ending. If you could come on Monday morning to help this girl get settled, it would be a great help, and then maybe you and I would have a chance to figure out how we're going to work together on this next book. That would be just great."

I held the phone, poised to dial Jackie's number as soon as the messages finished playing.

"Claudia," said Frieda in a rush. "Where are you? Call me the minute you get home. I'm in a major panic."

Next came a studiedly neutral female voice as familiar to me in its way as all the others: "We have an important message for Miss Claudia Steiner. Please call the following number at your earliest convenience. It is very urgent that you return our call immediately."

Then came my landlord's voice, asking with thuglike politeness when he could expect this month's rent, as well as the rent for last month and the month before. His name was Miller; he had no first name that I knew of. He had a big solid head and lizardy eyes. He was sinisterly well-groomed. He had feathered hair; he wore a gold chain around his neck; he lived in Saddle River, New Jersey. "Hello there, gorgeous. I hate to keep buggin' you about the rent, don't want to let a little thing like that spoil a beautiful friendship, but what can I say? We all gotta eat." Under his unctuous affection, I sensed a capacity for physical violence that was as inappropriate and hot-breathed as his lovey-dovey veneer. "Give me a call, sweetheart, or page me, we'll work something out. Love to hear your voice, any time, day or night."

The sixth and final message was from William, who sounded self-conscious and muffled: "Hi, Claudia, I hope I'm not waking you up. Just kidding. Listen, could you come a little early tonight? Around nine would be great. Give me a call. Thanks."

When Jackie answered, I made the necessary introductory

pleasantries, then asked in a trembling voice whether she'd read those new pages.

"Not yet," she said.

"Jackie, I think maybe it would be a good idea if you didn't look at them. I thought of a few things I want to change, and it would save you time if you read the second draft instead of having to read both."

"Well," she said, "of course I'm always dying to see every word you write. I meant to read it last night but I've been so hectic, finding that Goldie and getting everything ready for Lucia—"

"Jackie," I burst out desperately, "please don't read that scene. It's so rough, I don't want you to waste your time. You're a writer, you know how it is with first drafts, you just want to burn them before anyone sees them."

She made some inconclusive sounds, and I thought it might be wise to get off the topic to avoid making her suspicious, which would induce her to read the whole thing immediately. I told her I'd see her Monday morning and signed off, still a little queasy.

When I called Frieda, I learned that she'd gone out for dinner and a movie with Cecil and they'd ended up at her place and slept together. Frieda was distraught about this, or so she said. "I'm bad girlfriend material. I always freak out. Oh, God, I like him so much, Claudia. He's so nice to me, in a way I really respect." I could see her sitting hunched over her telephone, a paint-spattered old behemoth as black and heavy as an Underwood typewriter with a slow, wheezy rotary dial, her nervous coltish feet splayed in front of her, fending off anything that might come at her unexpectedly. She sounded suspiciously happy, underneath all her anxiety, as if she didn't really want reassurance. I kept trying to comfort her, she kept deflecting me, and then finally I said good-bye and we hung up. She hadn't asked what had happened with John the other night, and I'd wanted to tell her about the latest fiasco with Jackie. She hadn't seemed at all interested in me.

"I can't go to Gus's play with you," I told John angrily when he answered. "I can't believe you had the gall to ask me."

"Why?"

"Listen, John, the other night was a big mistake."

"I thought we both had a good time." He sounded more amused than offended, as if this were all just a little game I was playing and he would humor me until I lost interest in it and got real. "All I did was ask you to see a bad play with me. You don't have to if you don't want to, but seeing a play is not the same as—"

"Yes it is," I said.

There was a silence, during which I fought a strong urge to inform him that I knew he didn't really give a rat's ass about me, no matter what he pretended to feel; he was patronizing and full of it, and nowhere near as good a writer or as good at sex as he fancied he was, but I managed to keep my trap shut by reminding myself that he hadn't done anything to me that I hadn't let him do.

"If that's the way you feel about it, Claudia," he said finally with a dry condescension that sent my features into manic but silent contortions, "I guess there's nothing I can say."

"You're right," I said, and hung up, still fuming.

I didn't call Miller or the credit-card collection lady. Nothing about my current situation allowed for the kind of conversation they hoped to have with me, and I wasn't sure how to break this to them without getting myself snarled in a lot of lies and excuses I had no interest in manufacturing.

William wasn't home. I was relieved to get his machine. "It's me," I said, trying to sound confident and casual. "I'll be there as early as I can, around nine, unless you decide you want me to come even sooner. If you need me to bring anything besides a six-pack, let me know. Bye." Ugh. What a wormy, pathetic message. I'd made it sound as if I would have held up a liquor store for him, or cut off my arm. I waited to hear Ruth Koswicki remind me passionately that letting people know how I felt about them was a good thing, but there was only silence.

I napped shallowly until early evening, then woke up and rubbed my eyes and stood in a fog before my closet door until I found the warm bottle of gin I'd stashed in there. The eyeliner and black minidress I put on gave me the hopeful sluttiness of a housewife playing a truck-stop waitress in a suburban community theater production. I considered changing back into my jeans and staying in for the night, but as I was putting on lipstick, the gin hit my brain, the lights went down and my costume settled onto my frame as if it belonged there. I shot from my apartment, hurtled down the stairs, burst onto the sidewalk, dropped down the subway stairs and onto a waiting train.

At Times Square I changed to the shuttle, took it to Grand Central and got an uptown local. As the train flew into Jackie's stop and slowed, I watched "68th Street" slide by over and over in block letters in tiles along the walls. The station gleamed, as brightly lit as a public bathroom. The thought of those pages on her kitchen table made me close my eyes for a moment and breathe a prayer to anyone who might be listening.

Two stops beyond Jackie's, I came up out of the ground into the familiar expensive hush of the Upper East Side. I stopped at a deli on the corner for a six-pack, then hiked the long blocks to William's building, a vast glass-and-steel affair that looked like an office building but whose neighborhood was so quiet I could hear the scrape of a dry leaf blowing slowly along the pavement behind me. In the gleaming mirrors-and-marble lobby, three doormen loitered officiously behind a vast desk and a bank of video monitors, fuzzy gray and blue squares that showed the curvilinear oblongs of shadowy, empty hallways. One of them spoke soundlessly into a phone, hardly moving his lips, then gestured me to the elevators.

William had left his door unlocked. I stepped into his tiny hallway and bolted it behind me. "Hey, William," I called. There was no answer. I went into the dimly lit living room and was immediately engulfed in the wide, expansive view, skeletal bridges strung with light, the low-slung industrial glow of Queens. The East River below was streaked with shuddering reflections. The room, all shining blond-wood floor, glass-and-metal coffee table, plush black leather couch, elaborately mysterious stereo components stacked in metal shelves, had an edgy, vacant feeling, as if no one really lived here, like a furniture showroom or a movie set. "William," I called again, then heard water running in the bathroom. I rounded the counter between living room and dining alcove and went into his tiny galley kitchen and stowed the beer in his crowded refrigerator.

He came out of the bathroom a few minutes later. "Hi," he said. "Thanks for coming so early."

"God, I'd forgotten how professional your place looks." I opened a beer and offered it to him. He took it, and I opened one for myself.

He had just shaved. His face had a pale, vulnerable look and exuded a spicy, exciting mixture of chemicals and crushed plants. He rubbed one cheek. "Are you hungry? I've got four kinds of cheese and three pounds of sliced ham."

"Do you have any pickles?"

We were manufacturing hearty, bluff versions of our normal selves while the tension simmered between us like an ignored child. William busily got out pickles, sliced ham and cheese, a jar of mustard and a loaf of cocktail rye, plunking everything down on the counter. I pounced on the food and filled a plate, then sat at the gleaming black table in the dining alcove. He slid a coaster under my beer bottle. I ate. I couldn't read anything in his expression. It struck me how deceptive faces were, how little they revealed of all the weather that went on behind them.

"So," I said finally with my mouth full. "Why did you ask me to come early? Do you need me to pass around canapés and take coats?"

"Moral support," he said tersely. "What made me think I wanted to have a party? Why do people have parties?"

"It's just a bunch of your friends getting drunk in your apartment and using your bathroom."

"It'll be fine," he said, waving it all away.

"Of course it will."

"I meant to ask you," he said then, "what happened with Jackie?"

I swallowed. "She wasn't pleased."

"I can't imagine why."

"What happened when you talked to Margot? Did she get my message?"

"She sounded a little put out about it, actually."

"Margot sounded put out? *Margot* was put out?"

By the time the guests started arriving, I felt nicely removed from everything and everyone; I didn't care, particularly, what I said or did. Harmless, invisible jazz drifted from the speakers like fresh air. People milled about, holding plastic cups. A girl with black curly hair laughed up through her lashes at William: the olive-skinned and bewitching Devorah. I watched her through narrowed eyes. Her date was an innocuous brown-haired fellow who looked like a park ranger. She

150

wore a little dress with a plunging neckline; her cleavage was displayed like deli fruit, so I felt free to stare. She was violently edible. I could see why William had no interest in corporate law or anything else when she was nearby, and why her date kept one woodsmanlike hand hovering near her back.

Rima came over to where I was perched on the heater by the living room window. She crossed the room with her lop-sided gait, her head tilted, her eyes fixed on me. She wore black leather pants and an untucked man's button-down Oxford shirt; her body looked bulky and oddly shapeless, not fat, but strong and unwieldy. Her bobbed hair looked different, blonder, not as gray. She had dyed it. She looked good. "Hi, Rima," I said calmly. My conscience was clear, despite what her husband and I had done in her house two nights ago. I had canceled all that out on the phone with him today. "You look good."

"Oh, well." She ran a hand through her bangs to fluff them, looking sideways down at her feet. Smoke crossed her face. She waved it away and took the cigarette from her mouth. "I can't stand that girl over there; who is she?"

I reassembled what she'd said in my mind until the blurry, accented syllables metamorphosed into words that made sense. I looked over at the person she'd jerked her head at. "Jane Herman," I said, speaking unnaturally clearly. "Why don't you like her?"

She exhaled smoke with a twist of her mouth. She was having trouble staying upright; I knew the feeling. "Oh, Jane. I like Jane. I thought it was somebody else." She leaned on the heater next to me. The two of us sat there in silence for a moment, watching everyone. I caught John's eye; he looked away, no doubt unsettled to see his wife and me sitting amicably together.

"Can I have a cigarette?" I asked her. I hadn't smoked in

years, but I wanted one now. Without a word, she shook her pack and offered it to me; I took a cigarette, then let her light it for me. It tasted awful but wonderful, and seared my lungs as if they had needed a little searing to work properly. The lighter flame illuminated Rima's hands, square and strong, her nails clean and blunt-cut.

I saw Frieda and Cecil then, still with their coats on, newly arrived. Frieda looked gawky and shy. Her big head hung forward on her frail, sinewy neck, and her spiky hair looked vulnerable and half-grown, like the down on an adolescent bird. Cecil stood by her side. He came up to her shoulder. His skin was as burnished and dark as hers was pale; he looked like a cocky little grackle who'd alit next to a skittish loon. He took her coat and headed toward the bedroom, down the hall. I waved at her; she made a beeline for me. "What's wrong?" I asked her.

She looked as if she were about to cry, then to my horror she burst into manic laughter and put her head on my shoulder.

"Are you okay?" I asked her.

"I don't know what I am!" she said intensely into my ear. "He came over right after I talked to you and we spent the whole afternoon in bed. Oh my God, Claudia, fuck all that Canadian stoicism! Fuck Canada! I feel like myself for the first time in my whole stupid life."

"Good," I said dubiously.

"My mother called today and you know what? I didn't even pick up the phone. She went on about how my father won't take any interest in her fucking lawn ornaments and all I could do was lie there laughing at her. Isn't that great?" She flung her arms around me and accidentally jostled Rima, who looked sideways at her with a complicated expression and sidled off to the dining room table, where the drinks were.

"Claudia," Frieda breathed warmly into my ear, "I think I'm in love."

"Good for you," I said, hating myself for sounding so dry and pent-up. "That's so exciting. Here he comes."

Frieda looked at Cecil rapturously, without the slightest hint of coyness or subterfuge. I had a small twinge of fear for her when Cecil came into the room with a self-consciously impassive expression; it gave me the feeling that he would be put off by her naked ardor. But when he caught sight of her, his own face turned into a shining beacon that matched hers exactly. As Frieda and Cecil disappeared into each other I felt mean-spirited, toward whom or what I wasn't sure. The party felt like a crowded subway, the way parties get when they haven't quite begun yet but everyone has arrived, a tense waiting for the crowd to become a temporary village with mores and traditions and squabbles. We were in the history-making stage. People were cracking uncomfortable jokes, rubbing their tentacles and antennae against everyone else's.

I went to the drinks table and examined the available bottles. Finding none to my liking, I went to William's freezer and dug out the bottle of extremely expensive yuppie vodka he always had in there and poured myself a good slug.

"What you doing, Clow-dya," came a hiss at my shoulder. "Give me some of that good stuff." She elongated "good" and spat out "stuff," but I heard her just fine. I poured an equally hefty amount into Rima's glass and we clacked them together and drank deeply. A little while later she headed with fluttering eyes and lurching gait toward the bedroom.

Immediately—literally, two seconds—after she had rounded the corner, I heard another voice behind me. This one was stilted and upper-crust and said, "You know how it is in midtown when you're walking around looking for Broadway? Is it west of Seventh Avenue? Is it east of Sixth Avenue?

Where the fuck is Broadway? It screws up the grid. It makes things more complicated, but more interesting by far. Well, I'm the Broadway of this party."

I wanted another cigarette. "Your wife just passed out, in case you're interested."

"Come with me. Who is this, a Marsalis brother? William is such an unbelievable middle-aged square. Was he always like this?"

"No, he wasn't," I said, and allowed John to lead me over to the stereo. A few minutes later, some dirty old funk was on, the woofers boomed and the lights had been lowered, and John and I were engaged in some sort of dance that was half rhumba, half funky chicken. The crowd had made room for us without even seeming to notice, they had just softly shrunk closer together, leaving a space big enough for us to dance in; the party had coalesced in the last few minutes, and now we were like bees in a hive, thinking collectively with our bodies. William was nowhere in sight. The song changed to a slow groove and John shifted gears, his right hand firm on my back, his knees nudging mine so imperceptibly I began to think I was a pretty good dancer myself. He looked down at me; I studied his succulent mouth, his eyes sparkling under lazy eyelids. His stomach was pressed against mine. The hot, springy bass line and the singer's grunts and moans implied that nothing mattered except fucking, so why didn't we just get right down to it?

"Watch it," I said. "I meant what I said on the phone."

"I assumed you did," he said promptly, without missing a beat, and the semi-sleazy amorousness between us fell away and we became two friendly animals on a dance floor.

"Would you do me a favor?"

"Anything."

"I need some more vodka. The stuff in the freezer, not the shit on the table. Sneak it when William's not looking."

He planted his hands on my shoulders and said, "Stay."

"Oh, hello, Margot," said a girl in cat's-eye glasses I knew vaguely from several other parties.

"Oh, hello, Margot," I said with a grin that felt loopy and half-crocked.

There she was. She very pointedly didn't smile back at me. The blunt-cut tips of her dark hair brushed the shoulders of her black velvet jacket. Her blue eyes were like marbles shot through with ribbons of clear glass; her nose was as small and perfect as a child's.

"Did you get my message?" I asked her.

"She was so upset. I couldn't believe you'd done that."

"She fired me," I said. "Basically."

"Did she," Margot said, in a tone that told me she'd already heard all about it from Jackie herself and was completely on Jackie's side. "Excuse me, I'm going to get myself some seltzer."

John bounded up to me and handed me my glass.

I tasted my new drink. "This is the shitty vodka, John."

"You can tell? How can you tell? I could have sworn you'd never know the difference. William's in the kitchen; I couldn't get near the freezer."

Margot was inspecting the bottles on the table with a snooty furrow between her brows; I could see her as a child, fiddling in consternation with her oysters Rockefeller, her hair in a big bow. "John," I said, "my life is over."

"Tell your Uncle Threadgill," he said amiably.

I'd had about enough of him. "Maybe I just need some air," I said.

"Breathe, my child," he said, and let me go.

I went into William's dark little bedroom and began digging around on his bed for my coat, intending to take a long solitary walk down to Times Square to stare at all the neon-lit perverts stumbling out of movie theaters, to feel the thick breath of the city's intestines on my face. Something moved under my hands, something warm and soft that gave a strangled yelp. "Sorry," I said. I gave up looking for my coat, having lost interest in walking all that way. I flopped down next to Rima on the pile of coats and stared up at the ceiling. My head was ringing.

"You're crazy," she muttered through a thick mouth.

"You should talk," I said back. "What are you doing in here?"

"I'm at a party," she said.

We lay there for a while. She lit a cigarette. Every so often the tip would hiss and brighten, then a cloud of smoke burst from her side of the bed, but other than that, we might have been asleep. My eyes were fixed on the ceiling, but my field of vision kept narrowing until it nearly blacked out, then expanded again, as if I were repeatedly zooming through a funnel to find myself on William's bed once again. I had never lain in William's bed before; I had never spent much time in his bedroom. Even through the coats I could feel how comfortable his bed was, how firm. The solidity of the parquet floor and low ceiling gave the room a kind of neutral coziness. Light filtered through the window, the artificial radiance of the city overlain with the dim supernal light of moon and stars. I inhaled deeply through my nose. His smell was everywhere, emanating from his shoes, his sheets and pillows, any laundry hidden in the closet.

A bulky shape, its head backlit with a red halo, appeared in the doorway. "Rima," said John.

"What *you* want."

"Do you want me to take you home?"

"I don't need to go anywhere."

"Come on, let's go home."

She sighed elaborately and fought her way upright in the mass of coats. "Don't always tell me what to do," she said.

He went over to her and helped her stand up, found her coat and his, and tried to help her on with hers. She shook him off roughly and jammed her arms into her coat sleeves. I lay there, invisible, watching.

"Do you have your keys?" John asked. "Don't lose them again."

She fished around in her coat pocket, then swiped him across his face with her key chain. His hand went to his cheek. "Yes, I have my keys, mister. My fucking, fucking keys."

As they left, Rima staggered against him, I thought on purpose.

I got up and went into William's bathroom and splashed my face with cool water.

Someone rattled the door handle, found the door unlocked, and came in.

"Oops," said Jane Herman. "Sorry, Claudia." She waved and began to back out of the room.

"That's okay," I said, glad to see her. "Come on in."

She perched on the counter while I dried my face. "Having fun?"

"Not really."

There was a brief, odd pause. "I've been wanting to ask you this for a while, and now I'm drunk enough. Is there anything going on between you and William?"

"Going on?"

"You know. Are the two of you an item?"

The old two-headed snake of hope and pain turned in its lair. "Me and William?"

"He's always telling me about some bar the two of you went to, something you said. You're together, right?"

We were looking into the mirror together, addressing each other's reflection. Jane was too thin and she had a large beak of a nose and a low brow, but she carried herself with careless, glamorous self-assurance. Tonight she wore a tight red dress, cut low to reveal an elegant breastbone; her caramel-colored hair was piled into a loose knot on top of her head. She stood with one hip thrust slightly out, her hands at the back of her head, adjusting her hair. Next to her I looked pale and insignificant, but I was beyond envy tonight, or at least any awareness of it.

"Don't I wish," I said frankly.

"Yeah, well, don't we all." Her mouth was curved and humorous, her teeth small and charmingly discolored. "Who is he seeing right now, if not you?"

"No one that I know of." I thought a moment. "No one, actually."

She ran a finger over the dark red lipstick on her lower lip. "Well, he's the most attractive man I've ever met and I've gotten nowhere with him, all these years."

"All I can tell you," I said, "is that Margot could do whatever she wants with him but she doesn't appear to give a shit."

"Maybe that's the key," she said. "Oh, well. What can I do? Me hungry, me eat." We smiled at each other. She turned to me and ran her hands up the sides of my head and gripped my hair close to my scalp. "Cut your hair short. That's another thing I've been meaning to say to you. Cut your hair short on the sides and full on top, like a French boy, and get yourself some good clothes, well-cut, to show off your sexy little body and the lovely bones in your face. You look like an overgrown freshman, like you haven't rethought your look since college."

"I didn't know I had a look," I said, pleased. Her hands felt good on my head. And Jane, of all people, had called me sexy.

"Of course you do. You just need to take control of it." She bunched my hair into a ponytail and used her grip on it to usher me out the door. "My bladder's about to blow up," she said. "Scoot." Then I was out in the hallway and the door had been locked behind me. My scalp glowed. I was starstruck. I wanted to loiter in front of the bathroom door until Jane came out, but I wanted another drink even more.

I made my way into the living room and saw William and Margot sitting together at the dining room table, under a pool of light from the recessed bulb right above them, their arms folded on the table in exactly the same way, talking intently, dark heads close together. Margot was tracing a pattern on the table with her finger. William watched her, and from where I stood I could feel how much he wanted her to look back at him. He looked gangly, rawboned, the way he'd looked in high school. As I fixed my gaze on Margot, a ghostly second Margot glided up from the first and hovered there just above her. I squinted, trying to figure it out, until the two Margots resolved themselves back into one, and realized that I had reached the point at which the authentic and the alcohol-induced had become indistinguishable.

I veered into the kitchen, gestured to three people to bend their heads so I could open a cupboard, took out a cut-glass tumbler and poured from the freezer bottle, which was now almost empty. I took a sip. It went down like distilled ether, icy, poisonous, divine. I ambled over to William and Margot and stopped a few feet away from them. Without meaning to, I began to eavesdrop on them; I had intended for them to notice me so I could join their conversation, but neither of them looked up, so there we were. They were talking, I soon gathered, about a magazine article Margot was writing.

"One tree," she was saying. "Apparently that's all it takes for them to be made aware of the sanctity of life. That's why these Fresh Air programs are so essential."

To his credit, William looked skeptical. "You're telling me that a crack baby gets one look at a tree and he's healed?"

"Studies indicate that he's significantly less likely to perpetuate the cycle of violence if he understands that he belongs to a larger world."

"One tree is a larger world?"

"Not to put too fine a point on it, but nature seems to be the source of morality." She looked at him significantly. "If you don't know you're part of a larger order, there's no good reason not to play God and shoot anyone who looks at you funny."

"That strikes me as just a little simplistic," said William.

"Or," I said—they both looked up at me, startled—"if you surround yourself with fake ferns and cut flowers and bathe in distilled water, you might get the idea that the world exists solely to please you."

I could see a slender green vein jump in the milk-white skin of Margot's temple. "I'm talking about twelve-year-olds in the projects with automatic weapons," she said.

"If you handed Jackie an AK-47 and told her you'd sent a letter to the wrong address, tell me she wouldn't take you out."

William laughed. "Is that one of my brand-new crystal tumblers?"

"Crystal?" I flicked the rim of the glass with one fingernail to produce a dead clicking sound. "Well, it sounds more like glass, but what do I know—" Naturally, I dropped it, but it fell on my foot and rolled, and didn't shatter. My shoe got wet, though. I bent down to retrieve the glass, taking care to keep my rather short skirt from riding up too high. "Oh, damn," I said.

In the kitchen, which was empty now for some reason, I leaned against the counter and pressed the glass to my eyes and took a few deep breaths. Jane wandered in, looking dreamy and focused at the same time.

"Jane," I said. "Hi."

"Hello there," she said huskily. She'd taken her hair down and fluffed it into a wild, predatory mane. Her eyes were half-slitted. "You haven't seen William lately, have you?"

I gestured to the dining room. "At the table," I said, "talking to Margot."

"Thanks," she said, brushing a soft hand over my cheek. I stayed close behind her. She sauntered over and held her hand out to him, her gaze confident and direct and just a bit menacing. "William," she said. "Remember dancing to this song at the beach house?" The song was a decadent mid-tempo rock ballad sung by an androgynous Brit with a tuneless, raspy little voice. What beach house? I took a hard disk of salami and a couple of green olives from a plate on the table and chewed them, riveted.

William flapped his hand at her. "Go away, Jane, we're discussing morality."

"Come and dance," she said. "I don't know a thing about morality and neither do you." I could see him wavering: the lady or the tiger? Then he stood up and took Jane's hand and let her slink him a few feet away to an empty patch of floor by the speaker. She slid her arms around his neck and tilted her hips. He put his hands on her waist and they turned in slow circles. She leaned her forehead against his, and smiled at him, close up. I knew what he looked like from that perspective: his eyes turned into one long eye. She said something to him, something quick and sly, and he laughed with his head down on her shoulder and said, "You're so *bad*, Jane." As she talked, she rocked her body back and forth against his and leaned her head back so her hair fell in a shining stream and caught the light like water. The arch of her throat matched the curve of her small hard stomach, pooching sexily out between her hipbones; she looked glossy and lithe, and I wondered how William could resist running his hands all over her.

"Look at that," I said.

Margot looked up at me then, and I was startled by the coldness in her face. I realized then that I was standing right next to her chair. She held our gaze for a beat longer than necessary, then got up. I moved to let her by, then slid into her empty chair, feeling chilled. I looked down at my hands, folded on the tabletop.

A shiny shape to my right lowered itself to the chair next to mine and handed me a postcard, which I took and examined. The picture on the front showed a lantern-jawed transvestite in a jeweled turban and glittery platform shoes, holding what appeared to be a Tarot deck, opened like a fan, offered to the viewer. "Those are pearls that were his eyes . . ." read the caption. I turned it over, and saw a blur of information, time and place and whatnot.

"Speaking of death by water," Gus said, "I heard about Jackie's miraculous resurrection."

"Who told you?"

"Oh, a little bird. A little golden bird."

Something dawned on me: a memory that included the word "schmoozer." "You told Margot what I said about her, didn't you," I said in disbelief.

He looked sly. "What did you say about Margot?"

"I said it in context, Gus," I said with a flash of helpless anger. "You knew I didn't really mean it the way it sounded."

"Then you shouldn't have said it. The context doesn't matter if you mean what you say, and if you mean what you say you shouldn't care if people repeat it. And if you don't mean it, you should be prepared to take the consequences." His eyes were glittery slits; his face was flat as a mask. He looked like a mean, louche, small-time gangster. "That's how I operate," he added.

"Not me," I said, getting up.

Margot was buttoning her coat, peering down at the buttons in the dark, when I came into William's bedroom. She must have known it was me when I came in, because she didn't look up.

"Margot," I said insistently to her bent head.

"What?" she said without inflection.

What was there to say? "Good night."

"Good night," she said back, and walked past me, out of the room. I lay down again on the pile of coats, just for a moment, I thought, but I must have dozed off for a while, because the next thing I knew, a crowd of people, among them Cecil and Frieda, were all rummaging around and laughing, and then I had my own coat on and was being shepherded out the door with them all, waving good-bye to the far end of the living room, where I caught a blurry glance of William, still dancing with Jane, or embracing her, I didn't see.

The elevator was lined with mirrors; it looked like there was a whole crowd in here although there were only five or six of us. Outside, I followed Cecil and Frieda to a big boat of a car parked along the curb and got into the front seat with them. Maybe they had offered me a ride, or maybe I had simply imposed myself on them; in any case, I watched the streets roll by and leaned my head against Frieda's shoulder. I noticed admiringly that Cecil drove with elaborate, almost exaggerated courtesy. Instead of honking madly at people who meandered into the path of his car while he gunned the engine and tried to hit them, he slowed down and waited for them to cross. He calmly let a taxi swerve in front of him at a yellow light, cutting him off and stranding him at the red light. It didn't seem to be out of meekness, it seemed as if he had studied some kind of martial art of driving where you used the other guy's strength against him.

"You're not from New York, are you," I said.

"How can you tell?"

"You don't drive like you're from here."

For some reason he took offense at this. "I'm just a firm believer in staying out of trouble," he said with a slight bristle in his voice. "I wouldn't say one way or the other that that's a function of where I'm from; I like to think I drive the way I drive because of who I am."

"I meant it as a compliment," I said. "I'm sorry. New York drivers are usually so aggressive."

"Not that I don't stick my neck out when called upon," he said. "I simply believe that everyone's got a right to politeness. Do unto others, like the man said."

"Right," I said fatuously. "That's a very gracious attitude."

"Claudia," said Frieda.

"Well, it is," I said.

"Don't listen to her," Frieda said to Cecil.

I tried to think whether I should take offense now, but it was too complicated, so I simply abandoned the whole exercise and fell asleep before we even made it to the park. I awoke at dawn to the wet, raspy sound of Delilah licking herself under the bed. I still had my coat on. In the pocket I found a crystal tumbler and a postcard. I hoped Frieda hadn't had to help me up to bed, but I thought I remembered hearing her say, "I never knew you had such a cute cat," then raising my head from my pillow, where it had fallen automatically the moment

I'd come in the door, to see Delilah purring thunderously, trai-torously, in Frieda's arms. I hoped Cecil hadn't thought it was his duty to help Frieda escort me upstairs, then suffered a corollary memory of a very dark hand against Delilah's fur, stroking Frieda's very white hand, the three of them having a cross-racial, intra-species love-in. "Delilah," I said forlornly; the licking sound immediately ceased.

chapter nine

I read so much poetry that day my thoughts marched in metrical lockstep by nightfall. I didn't touch the remainder of the gin even though a nice cozy nip or two on a bleak, lonesome Sunday evening was just the sort of ritual I most highly prized. I didn't watch any TV, and I tried all day not to think about William. I didn't call him the way I normally would have, to confer about the party; he didn't call me either, and I didn't want to think about what that might mean. No one called me. I spent the day alone with my invisible cat. I should have just drunk myself into another stupor and passed out cold around three in the morning, but instead I went to bed early and slept deeply for an hour or two, then snapped awake and stayed that way for hours, seeing with the pure clarity of the darkest part of the night that everything I'd said and done my entire life had been completely worthless, and everything that had ever happened to me had been part of one big tragic joke on me.

At eight o'clock the next morning, I crept from my bed and drank coffee at my table. It was time to go and face Jackie. That she hadn't called me to convey her shocked incredulity was not necessarily a good sign. Long after I should have left my apartment, I hovered over my table with a butter knife, slashing open all the envelopes heaped there like a haul of slippery fish. As I gutted them, I thought about the money I'd given the cabdriver, a stupid, spiteful, pointless, empty gesture I'd made out of a sense of nettled pride. It was ironic, I thought without any amusement whatsoever, that love brought out my basest qualities, whereas indifference made me noble. Or did it? Was I ever noble? Well, I'd ended my affair with John, for example, which I couldn't have done if I weren't indifferent to him. But I obviously wasn't the least bit indifferent to him, and ending an adulterous affair couldn't really be considered noble because it only righted an imbalance. God, I made myself weary with endless quibbles and justifications and regrets. My moral terrain was an unnavigable swamp.

All right, I thought, let's get it over with. I marched grimly across the park with my eyes on my shoes, oblivious of the birdsong, the sweet, sun-filled air. I didn't get to her building until nearly a quarter to ten.

"Claudia!" she said when I came in and found her in the foyer, as if she had been lying in wait for me. "Am I glad to see you! I was afraid you'd misunderstood me and you weren't coming."

"I'm sorry I didn't come right at nine, but I thought you might want to—"

"Come and meet Goldie," she said, taking my arm and leading me into the dining room as if I'd never been in there before. "Goldie, this is Claudia. She'll help with anything you need to know. She knows everything and she's invaluable, this girl."

She hadn't read a word, I thought with a profound relief as heady as a swallow of cognac.

"Hello, Claudia," said Goldie, striding over the carpet toward me, giving me a robust handshake. She looked like an apple. She was just over five feet tall and wore a bright red suit with matching pumps. Her torso in its neat blouse and jacket was a solid squat cylinder, her chest and stomach clocking in at about the same circumference; her calf muscles, encased in beige panty hose, were wide and round. Her hair was cut in a saucy, hennaed shag. She had set up the desk in a different spot from the one where I always put it. I could smell her perfume.

"Hi, Goldie," I said with a brilliant smile. "How's it going?"

"Yes, you two figure everything out," said Jackie, and backed out of the room as awkwardly as I'd ever seen her do anything. "I'll be in my room if you need me."

Jackie's whole apartment seemed different today, both brighter and shabbier. Goldie generated a mood of hard-nosed reality, a bright, commonsensical cheer that made the hand-painted wallpaper look dreary, the peeling gilt chairs spindly and impractical. The catchpenny effrontery of her perfume made the atmosphere in here seem slumbrous and old-ladyish. "Have you been able to find everything you need?" I asked her.

"This is not exactly rocket science," she answered with a quick sideways flip of her hand. "Jackie told me she wanted some new chair cushions, I called around and ordered her some. She wanted me to straighten up the supplies, I straightened them up. She doesn't like me and I don't like her, don't get me started, but as far as the job goes, it's a breeze."

"Good," I said. "I'm glad you think so."

"She's a fruitcake, isn't she? I know I'm not telling you

anything you don't already know. And I've worked for some real whack jobs, I could tell you stories."

I laughed.

"Let's see. Her accounts, I just glanced at them, they're all falsified, am I right? You make it all up? I need to meet with her accountant. His number's in the little red book here?"

"It's a she," I said. "Her name is Doris Loewenstein."

"Get out! Doris Loewenstein from Canarsie?"

"I think she lives in Westchester."

"I don't care where she lives now, she's from Canarsie if she's the Doris I'm thinking of. About my age, forty-five, with a nose like a vacuum-cleaner attachment?"

"Could be her," I allowed.

"I'm gonna call her right now. Thanks for your help, Claudia, nice to meet you."

What help? She needed no help. In her first forty-five minutes on the job, Goldie had come in, sized Jackie up and taken over. My naive dim-wittedness on my first day struck me now as insufferably anemic.

I headed down the hall to Jackie's bedroom, inhaled deeply, squared my shoulders and sailed in. She was at her vanity table with her hands poised in midair, one holding a small porcelain pot, the other brandishing a tiny brush. Her face was frozen in the careful, alert amusement of a mime.

"Oh, hello, Claudia," she said, meeting my eyes in the mirror. "How is that girl working out?"

"Fine," I said. I sat down on the very chair I'd sat in on Friday to contemplate the potential fallout from murdering her. It was strange to remember that now; I was a whole other person today than the one who'd stolen her watch and sweater and guzzled her whiskey.

Jackie leaned back, examined herself carefully from every angle. She rubbed her lips together, then opened her mouth wide and carefully removed a stray fleck with her pinky nail from the corner of her mouth. "Well, we've certainly had a difficult time of it lately, haven't we?"

"We certainly have," I said, feeling a bone-deep exhaustion at the thought of all that lay ahead in this conversation. I squeezed my eyes shut for a split second and then opened them again, a few times, ticlike. "I'm not sure how that happened on Friday, Jackie."

"Well, it was terribly upsetting."

"I know it was."

"It can't happen again."

"It won't."

"Now," she said briskly, "about that scene we're working on—"

"You read it?"

"You know, I haven't had a spare minute all weekend, with getting ready for that girl and organizing all the—"

"No, that's good, that's great! Where is it? I'll get right to work on it."

Jackie's answer to this was a stream of enthusiastic, gesticulating Italian, to which I nodded and smiled politely until someone directly behind me answered her in a light, girlish voice, and I turned to behold a tiny young woman wearing only a T-shirt and a pair of white boxer shorts; her hair was unbrushed and she wore no more makeup than I did but even so, she was as lovely as a princess in a Renaissance painting. Her hair, skin and eyes were the same warm shade of pale brown, her forehead was round and high, her hair rippled in gold-shot waves to her waist. She was perfectly proportioned, but in miniature: she couldn't have been much over five feet tall. Her shins and forearms were small and delicate as a child's.

"Oh, Claudia, this is Lucia, my great-niece," said Jackie in her flat American tones, then, without missing a beat, introduced me to Lucia in Italian.

Lucia smiled politely back at me. "Hi, Claudia," she said thickly, the words sounding uncomfortable in her mouth. "My English is very bad, forgive me, please. Nice to meet you."

"She's going to take an English class," said Jackie. "She wants to go to NYU, but I don't want her going all the way down there, spending all her time with all those interracial students."

I said blithely, "Maybe Goldie could look into it." I was almost giggling. The welter of dread I'd been in all weekend! All that poetry! That dark night of the soul!

"Goldie," said Jackie, going back to her face in the mirror. "I'm not sure she would know. She doesn't have your sophistication, Claudia; she's not educated like you."

Interesting how everything had shifted. "She's smart, though," I said primly, as if Goldie were outside eavesdropping.

"She's impossible," said Jackie, lowering her voice as if she also felt Goldie on the other side of the door. "Just impossible. She doesn't understand at all what it means to be a woman in my position, with my responsibilities, not the way you do, Claudia." She was romanticizing me already, and I was enjoying it far more than I should have. "That perfume! I told her if she didn't go in and wash it off immediately I'd be sick. It smells like a saloon in here."

Lucia watched Jackie throughout this diatribe with a blank, polite expression, balanced on one leg like a stork, running a hand up and down one arm and then, as soon as Jackie stopped talking, she asked a brief question that had the word "caffe" in it. When Jackie answered her in the affirmative, she was off.

Jackie began powdering her face with slow, precise little pats. "What am I going to do with her? Her father will never forgive me if anything happens to her. He was Giancarlo's favorite nephew."

"You said something about a dinner party," I said.

"Yes, but who would I invite? I don't know anyone her age. Well, Bitsy has a granddaughter a little older than Lucia; maybe she could bring some of her friends. Could you call her and ask her if she—"

"Maybe Goldie will," I said. Amazing how easy it was to be bossy once you got into the swing of it. "Gil Reeve is expecting the final chapters next month. I was thinking: what about the unknown woman in the limousine? We haven't seen her in about eighty pages, since Ali was shot, remember?"

"Ali," said Jackie.

"The Moroccan guy, Fatima's husband. He was shot in the back and fell off the roof of the castle."

"Oh, Ali! But who was the woman in the limousine? I don't—"

"She could be an Argentinean, the daughter of a Nazi." Nazis were Jackie's favorite villains, along with Communists, Arabs and dope smugglers. "Her father escaped to Buenos Aires in 1945 and renamed himself Martinez, but privately he raised his daughter on Nazi ideology, which he never gave up."

"That's good," said Jackie.

Of course it was good. "And Ali's wife Fatima was their housemaid in Buenos Aires. She found some secret documents revealing his Nazi identity and linking him with war crimes."

"Oh yes," she said, "and Ali and Fatima are blackmailing her, and so she has to kill Ali, and maybe we should have her kill Fatima too. Write all of this down immediately so we don't forget."

I fetched a pad and pen, and soon we had hammered out both the next chapter and an understanding that I would stay at home and write and that she would pay me by the chapter rather than by the hour. As we were wrapping up our negotiations, her phone rang; it was Mr. Blevins, checking in for their daily chat. Jackie gave a guttural laugh at something he said; I gathered I hadn't caused him any permanent damage. I glanced at her, struck by certain smutty undertones in that laugh, wondering for the first time whether she'd ever slept with him. She was so discreet with me about how far she actually went with these men she dated, and of course she had always scornfully deemed Mr. Blevins too far beneath her for serious consideration. But for the first time it struck me that they might, for all I knew, be lovers; I remembered that day when they were doing the fox-trot and drinking champagne at five in the afternoon, the masterful way he'd held her body against his, how she'd told me gaily and innocently that they were only practicing. It occurred to me now that I had almost certainly underestimated her. And him.

She hung up and gave the phone a satisfied little pat. "Well," she said. "Mr. Blevins wants me to spend a week in Southampton with him! Imagine! At my age."

She had once dated a famous financier, some hoary old Wall Street lion I'd never heard of, a white-maned oily-voiced wheeler-dealer with big fake gleaming choppers; she'd told me with girlish prurience that he couldn't "become erect" any more, so he had to use a pump. I had simply assumed that she knew this through hearsay; I now saw that I had been naive, as usual. She'd slept with him! She'd slept with all of them! And she was over seventy! Well, why shouldn't she?

"It sounds like fun," I said, grinning.

She laughed. "Oh, it wouldn't be. It would be so boring to be stuck in that big house in the middle of nowhere with Mr. Blevins. I don't know why the Americans think so highly of Long Island; it's nothing compared to Marbella or the Riviera. And why does he have to moon around me like that? I wish he'd discuss interesting topics. All he ever says is that I'm *beautiful* and he *adores* me, as if that were interesting in any way. Well, it isn't! Now," she said sternly. "I hope you haven't forgotten Lucia's appointment at Frances Gray's modeling agency at eleven o'clock today. Frances values punctuality above everything else, she's very English."

"We'll be on time," I said as I gave a swift but penetrating glance around the room. Those pages weren't in here, at least not where I could see them. I gave a cursory but thorough search through the rest of her apartment: she must have squirreled them away, because I didn't see them lying about. Oh, well, no use getting into a lather at this point in the game—if they weren't in sight, she wouldn't remember them, at least not if I knew her. She had an aerobics class at eleven, and at one she was meeting Lucia and some of her cronies at Mortimer's for lunch. Once she and Lucia were out of the way, I could find and destroy them and make a clean getaway with her laptop. It all seemed safe enough for now. As I passed the dining room doorway, I heard Goldie laughing, saying something about Susie Lefkowitz and prom night.

I went down the hall to collect Lucia, and found her in the guest room brushing her hair. She had decked herself out in a spanking-clean pair of jeans with a crease ironed into the front of each leg and a white T-shirt several sizes smaller than the one she'd slept in. She still wore no makeup. She looked like a very clean, very pretty ten-year-old. "One minute, Claudia," she said. She made a face as the brush snagged on a tangle.

Her equanimity nonplused me. If I had been fresh off the boat, about to have an interview at a modeling agency, I would have been in a vastly different mood and outfit. I might have even thought to put on a little lipstick. Of course, it helped to be the daughter of an Italian marquis or whatever he was, but I'd never seen anyone so purely and unquestioningly sure of herself. Her attitude toward me, polite and even casual, was without the slightest hint of real equality, which put me strangely at ease; she obviously carried in her bones the knowledge of the precise gradations of behavior toward the just-replaced American secretary of an American-born relative. Although she was nine years younger than I was and had just arrived for the first time in the city I'd lived in for years, Lucia was in charge and I was given the command, wordlessly, through a slight rearrangement of the molecules of the air, to be deferential only when necessary, and otherwise to treat her with a detached but casual courtesy, laughing at her jokes if she cared to make any, helping her in any way she required. I found this incredibly refreshing after three years under the irrational dictatorship of her great-aunt. I breathed easily as I waited for her to finish her minimal preparations. She didn't seem to mind being watched; she seemed to inhabit a rarefied state far beyond self-consciousness.

She zipped up her red silk bomber jacket, ready for her interviews; I seemed to recall that these were called something like "go-sees," but couldn't bring myself to refer to them as such even privately because it smacked too much of something, I wasn't sure what. We went down to the street, where Ralph hailed us a cab. I gave the address of Frances's agency, which was less than fifteen blocks away; it would have been faster to walk, I realized, but oh well. We still arrived with three minutes to spare. When the driver hit the meter, I wondered whether I should pay, as her great-aunt's servant or whatever I was, but Lucia solved it for me by taking out her wallet. "I have," she said.

We rode the elevator up to the twentieth floor, where we found ourselves in a bright little waiting room littered with fashion magazines. We sat silently in two small red armchairs until a chesty brunette came through a door with her hand outstretched. A cuticle-shaped curl was pasted to her forehead over her left eyebrow, and she wore a mustard-colored suit whose jacket had a plunging neckline that showed plenty of cleavage and no blouse. "I'm Andrea," she said.

"I'm Claudia," I said, "and this is Lucia."

"I figured," she said with a quirk of a smile. I snuck a glance at myself in the mirror and experienced that ancient feeling I always got during work hours: I belonged to Jackie, even here, and it showed, even now that my days of drudgery were essentially over. I wore a black skirt and a white blouse, black hose and a pair of cheap, badly made loafers I'd found in a bargain shoe store off Canal Street. I looked like an usherette at a small-town movie theater; my posture was all pulled into itself and my face was frozen in an expression of bland diffidence, as if I were acting on behalf of someone else, which I was.

Andrea sat down next to Lucia, who handed over her portfolio without a word, as if she had done this many times before. The two of them murmured, knee-to-knee, in Italian, as Andrea turned pages. I looked at some of the pictures: an ad for perfume, showing Lucia standing in the doorway of a barn, streaming sunlight catching dust motes and illuminating her hair. Why was she wearing that black evening gown in that barn? It suggested an illicit rendezvous with a farmhand or a large handsome bull. Next came another perfume ad, this time with Lucia in a white dress on a swing, her knees fetchingly exposed, her skirt tossed up just so to show a swatch of white panties. What could that perfume possibly smell like? In the next one, Lucia was in a skimpy bikini on a beach somewhere, sticking her little rump out in a totally unnatural posture. She looked indescribably silly. Who stood like that? There was a red sports car in the background, parked on the sand with the driver's door flung open, as if Lucia had driven herself right onto the beach, leapt from the car, walked ten yards, then exhilarated by the thrill of it all, stopped to thrust her hip sideways and smile provocatively at the ocean. The picture made no sense unless you took into account the presence of the photographer, which completely destroyed the illusion.

Andrea lingered over this one, stroking Lucia's glossy image with a manicured pointer finger. Her blood-red fingernail was as long as a small dagger; she wielded it deftly and ostentatiously. I could tell that she loved her fingernails and admired them, posed them against certain backgrounds when no one was looking, and tended to them in her leisure hours. They were her pets. Maybe even her lovers, for all I knew. I caught another chastening glimpse of myself in the mirror, and immediately wiped the supercilious look off my face. It was useless to pretend I was above all this; on the contrary, Lucia and Andrea were speaking a language I didn't understand, besides Italian, some essential, universal code that had nothing to do with actual words.

After a while, an older woman with silvery hair tied with a Chanel scarf materialized from an inner sanctum and perched on the edge of the chair next to Andrea; Frances Gray was obviously much too busy to sit all the way back. The whole process repeated itself in English, the low murmurs over the photographs, Lucia's graceful, blasé presentation of herself. Frances put out a hand (her nails were blunt and colorless: she was powerful enough to forsake polish) and lifted Lucia's T-shirt to peer at her torso through stylish tortoiseshell bifo-

pointed at the lower half of Manhattan. "You know good places?"

"Clubs?"

"Yes, clubs, and—places to go, at night."

All of a sudden New York seemed like one big urinal. I tried to imagine where someone like Lucia would want to spend an evening. I pointed to the map. "This part of town is called the East Village. That's where people go."

Lucia smiled and handed me a pad and pen, and obediently but not without misgivings I scribbled the names and approximate addresses of a few bars and clubs, including the Blue Bar, since all the Europeans instinctively honed in on that place; if she didn't like it, she could leave.

I checked my watch: almost twelve-thirty, perfect timing. Lucia would be back in time to change for lunch; Jackie wanted to show her off to Bitsy Abbott and the Countess Robles, otherwise known as Dorcas, who would surely have her little dog Pepe stuffed into her Chanel pocketbook like a furry hankie. I didn't envy Lucia this outing. While she sat imprisoned at Mortimer's between the emaciated and alligator-skinned Dorcas and the quivering wattles and quavering voice of the frightening Bitsy, I'd be free and clear and on my way home, whistling through the park, concocting the next installment of the adventures of Genevieve.

When the cab pulled up in front of Jackie's building, Lucia looked into her wallet, then said, "Oh! I have no more American money. You can borrow me some?"

Of course, I was low on cash myself, but I paid the man as if it were no big deal. As we walked through the lobby, Ralph gave us the formal smile he gave all the ladies in the building, and sent us up in the elevator without a word. I felt a disturbance in the air between us, a breach in our usual easy rapport, which I attributed to Louie's having told him that I'd said he'd told me Jackie was dead. Ralph had probably thought I was joking, which he would have seen as disrespectful to his grand-mother. On my way out tonight I would explain everything to him and apologize. Not in front of Lucia, though.

Jackie was hovering in the foyer when we came in, waiting for us, but this time she didn't look even slightly relieved to see me, she looked—distraught.

"Oh, hello, Claudia," she said, stammering slightly. She had the wild-eyed look of a spooked racehorse, as if she might start to foam at the mouth any minute. "Lucia, dear, I can't wait to hear all about your interviews, but first I've got to—"

She caught herself and switched to Italian. "Okay, Jackie," called Lucia over her shoulder as she dashed off to the guest room.

I could feel the exact instant that Jackie's attention re-turned to whatever terrible thing I had done; the air drew up around us, sealing us off from the world, from everything but the business at hand. Maybe Goldie had found a mistake in last year's taxes, maybe I'd forgotten to follow up on a refund from a store—I felt the way a sky diver must feel in the door of the plane, staring down at the earth.

"What's wrong, Jackie?" I asked.

She took a shaky breath. She looked haggard and tragic. "Well," she said in a hoarse, hollow voice, "Claudia. You'd better come in here." She turned with her usual brusqueness and led me down the hall toward the room she called her office but used primarily as an adjunct dressing room. As we passed the closed door of the guest room I heard a hip-hop beat from Lucia's radio, faint but steady as a cricket in the underbrush. I stepped into Jackie's "office" and she shut the door.

"While you were at those agencies, I read the new pages,"

she said, grazing both palms over the shellacked cuirass of her hairdo, not quite looking at me, or rather, looking at the general area of my collarbone and avoiding my eyes, which were trained on her face in hot little pinpoints of stunned but newly comprehending panic.

The day went dark. My heart began to thud slowly and a cold, glue-thick clamminess welled from all my pores and encased me in a bind of sweat. "You didn't go to your aerobics class?"

"My aerobics class? What on earth does that have to do with any of this?" I hated that stare of hers, hated it so much I wanted to put my hands around her goosey neck and wring the life out of her, then throw her like a rag doll to the ground and leave her to be discovered by Juanita. "Claudia, I don't understand at all what led you to write those things about—I find it completely incomprehensible that you would—how could you think—I'm not sure what you did think, frankly, and I don't like what it implies about your loyalty, your character—what if I hadn't read it, what if it had gone to Gil Reeve and been published? Can you imagine? It horrifies me, Claudia. It makes my blood run cold."

She stopped. It was my turn. What was I supposed to say? What could I say? I'd written the accursed scene, I'd already admitted it, and I'd already acknowledged that I knew it would upset her, so I couldn't pretend I'd done it by accident.

"Friday just wasn't my day, I guess." My attempt at a laugh sounded like no human sound ever made before.

"Well, we all have our bad days. We do." I could see the flicker of neurons firing, like the lights in a pachinko game. When she was thinking, I knew that she was particularly vulnerable to suggestion.

"I can delete the whole thing," I said with sham decisiveness. "We have a lot of good ideas for that chapter. The strange woman in the limousine, the Argentinean Nazi's daughter—"

"Mr. Blevins has convinced me that it might be the best thing for everyone if we stopped working together on this book." She looked me right in the eye then. "And I agree with him, Claudia, I really do. It isn't so much those pages, although they did tip the scales. I've been feeling for quite a while that I'd like to do all the work myself from now on. I've been very uneasy about having you write so much of my books. It's kept me awake at night, honestly. My readers believe that I wrote them, and it isn't right to give them less than they expect."

Never mind the insult to my writing skills, such as they were. And never mind that she had every right to write her own books, every reason to boot me out. Where would I go now? What would I do? "Well, I could still help you with editing and revising," I said hopefully. "You'd do the actual writing. That way it'll be all your own words."

She sighed and shook her head. "That's what Gil Reeve is for. I wouldn't want to step on his toes. And Jimmy, Mr. Blevins, has offered to look over anything I have doubts about. No, I think it's best if we simply make a clean break. Which isn't to say that I don't deeply appreciate all the work you've done—" I could feel how excited she was to be getting rid of me; she was almost exploding with relief. "I just don't feel any more that I can trust you, and if I can't trust you, there's just no way we can work together. It just isn't possible, I'm afraid, Claudia."

If she said another word to me I would burst into terrible, desperate sobs and cling to her ankles. I put my hand on the doorknob.

"Oh," she said, holding up a hand to forestall me.

"Please write yourself a check for the money I owe you, Claudia dear."

"We're all caught up," I said, "except for today."

I turned the knob and opened the door and was almost out when she called after me, "You know, I could have you come in the mornings, just for this week, to help Goldie with anything—"

"She doesn't need any help," I said. I paused, struck by what I thought was nausea and then identified as words stuck in my craw. "I'm glad it's come to this," I blurted, "because frankly, Jackie, I can't take it any more. Do you have any idea how impossible you are? Any idea? A person would have to be a *saint* to put up with you. Maybe Margot was a saint, but I'm absolutely not. *You* lost that photograph, not me. *You're* the one who pretends to be an author and can barely read the newspaper, not me. You drive me up the wall and I hope I never have to work for someone like you again as long as I live. Good-bye."

I went out without giving her a chance to answer. I closed my eyes and braced a hand against the hallway for a moment. I could feel her in there, mentally brushing me off, reminding herself that she was much better off without me.

All at once I had a plan.

I pulled myself together and went into the dining room. "Hi," I said to Goldie.

"Hey," she said. "You know, it was the same Doris? I couldn't believe it! After so many years!"

"That's amazing," I said with a horrible grimace I hoped resembled a smile. "Listen, I'm on my way home, but I forgot to finish one small thing on the computer. It'll only take a second."

"It's all yours," she said. "I've got to go report on a couple things to the crazy lady, so I'll be out of your way."

I sat down at the computer and in under a minute had deleted all the files containing the new, almost-finished book. Then I got my coat from the closet and put it on. On my way out I pocketed, as if in a trance, one of Jackie's spare checkbooks, the only existing backup disk of the new book, and the agreement I'd signed promising I'd never try to get credit for my work or more money from her, which wasn't even remotely legally binding, according to William.

The next thing I was conscious of was waving with manic, phony cheer to Ralph on my way out. He tipped his cap to me, coolly, I thought, but it wasn't worth defending myself now. I'd probably never see him again.

chapter ten

I spent the next several days dawdling around the city in a fog, spending money I didn't have on various small and cheerful nonessentials—lipsticks named Lust for Life and Siren Song; lavender-scented soap that gave off a sharp chemical reek, but whose wrapper reminded me of an English garden in full bloom and calmed my soul with intimations of Wordsworth; pink platform jelly sandals I might wear in another life but almost certainly never in this one. These purchases momentarily cheered me up, like little bumps of cocaine, but let me down hard right afterwards.

At night I slept solidly for eight, then ten, then twelve or fourteen hours at a time, awakening in a panic, feeling as if I'd been heavily drugged into a near-death coma and had barely managed to drag myself back from the brink of total annihilation. I had to sit up and hold my throbbing head in my hands for several minutes before I was oriented enough to begin my day, then drank cup after cup of strong coffee as the window-shade darkened. I came to know intimately my old armchair, a fusty behemoth I'd rescued from the sidewalk years ago, its nubbly worn rough-weave plaid, its sagging but capacious seat. Constantly at the forefront of my beclouded brain was the plan I'd hatched just before leaving Jackie's, but I couldn't quite bring myself to go through with it. I held the disk in my hands as if it could give me the answer: it was as hard and black as a June bug, with the same sinister sheen. I had never done anything so purely self-interested before, so utterly Machiavellian. This was a corner I hadn't decided whether or not I could turn.

Things had to get worse before I could act, and they did. Toward midnight on Thursday, I found myself at a rathskeller on Avenue A where a very loud, very raucous band was playing. I turned to the man who'd been buying me drinks in exchange for whatever dipsomaniacal maunderings I'd been shouting into his ear, his face a shiny blur in the refracted lights from the stage. I shouted something else into the air between us, he shouted something back, and we laughed. Far away, as far below as the sewers, I heard the slimy wash of everything I didn't want to think about.

I finished my drink and set it on the edge of the bar. He put his hand on the back of my neck and we spun slowly around to the music, our mouths connected by twin warm fumes of breath. What seemed to be a few minutes later I followed him several flights up some stairs somewhere to an apartment, where I must immediately have passed out. I awoke thirsty and confused at daybreak to find myself lying under someone's coat on a couch with all my clothes on and no memory of the previous night. I didn't recognize the skinny guy in white briefs who emerged tentatively from another room and looked at me with equal befuddlement. Politely he sent me on my way, and politely I went.

As I went down the stairs to the subway, I caught the eye of a man coming toward me. He was slightly shorter and probably slightly younger than I was. His dark receding hair was combed back from a broad forehead that rose over concise features, sharp nose, hint of a double chin. His eyes were a faded denim blue; I knew without looking that his body was slope-shouldered and haunchy. "I can't believe it," he said, smiling. "Claudia. Do you remember me? Ned Keller."

Ned Keller? He did look familiar, some night last summer —oh, no, Ned *Keller*—"Hello," I said, my eyes widening. "What are you doing here?"

He quirked his mouth at my obvious discomfort. "I'm on my way to work," he said. "And you?"

One evening last August I'd found myself attending an outdoor performance of *Madama Butterfly* in Central Park. I had gone to the park in search of relief from my furnace-hot apartment, and found it in the form of Ned Keller, opera buff. He'd entertained me during the first act with a running stream of derision: the soprano was shrill and elderly, the violins were out of tune with the woodwinds. He'd had little trouble persuading me to go with him to an air-conditioned bar. One drink had led to another, which in turn led to my bed, where the night had ended rather badly for both of us: I had thrown up on him. He was very gentlemanly about it; he'd extricated himself with a minimum of fuss, showered and dressed and crept away. I hadn't seen him since; I'd hoped never to lay eyes on him again.

"I'm on my way home," I said.

"Late night?"

"Well, sort of—" Oh, fuck it all, why did I have to explain

myself to him? "Anyway," I said with a horribly awkward little wave, "take care, Ned, nice seeing you again."

He gave a nod, then turned and headed up the stairs to the street.

When I stood on the platform and leaned over to see if the train was coming and saw the light plunging toward me, I felt a familiar prickling of the hair on the back of my neck: as I so often did, I sensed a pair of hands just behind me, beady eyes boring into the back of my head. It would be so easy: one slight push at the right instant.

My presence in my own life had become so tenuous, so half-hearted, that I had simply fallen through a tear in the flimsy fabric, slid into an alternate universe where only I existed, or conversely, where everyone existed but me. And it didn't matter. I felt a sucking undertow, pulling me down: I had failed to engage, I had failed to connect; I had failed.

Worse than that, yesterday morning, all at once, I had run out of toilet paper, shampoo, toothpaste and coffee, and had been forced to use instead, respectively, a dirty sock, a gray sliver of Ivory soap, some old baking soda from my refrigerator and a tea bag so old it was practically dust and contained about as much caffeine as a stick of licorice. I found this extremely demoralizing, but the idea of replacing everything depressed me even more. How wearying and pointless it all seemed. All I ever did was produce waste in one form or another, Jackie's books being the most egregious example. I measured out my life in toilet paper rolls.

I leaned a little further over the tracks. Please, I thought, and waited as the train rushed on. I willed it to happen, silently begged whoever it was to deliver me from all this.

Then I realized that I could jump. Such a simple idea, but it hadn't occurred to me until now—I didn't have to depend on those invisible hands at my back: I could do it myself.

A pang of wild longing ripped through me. I closed my eyes and swayed in the thundering wind. As the train plunged through the mouth of the tunnel into the station, I felt myself begin to let go. My mind was ready for it, had accepted the necessary bone-crunching pain before the release. Ahhh, I thought, finally—I looked into the yellow eye and spread my arms to embrace it.

Then some wholly involuntary reflex made me lean back and regain my balance. It felt as if the train itself had pushed me back out of its way. I boarded with everyone else, shaken. I had never before wished for extermination quite that intensely.

On the way home I bought coffee and toilet paper, toothpaste, milk and shampoo; this cheered me up a little. I came into my apartment and turned on the overhead light and allowed the roaches to slide into their cracks, then jumped, truly startled. I'd caught Delilah in her cat box; she was hunched over the gravel, her spine steeply curved, her daily turd halfway out. She looked up at me, I looked down at her. There was in her gaze something of Jackie's imperiousness when I'd walked in to find her naked on the toilet. I looked away apologetically, as if I were the one caught in an awkward position, while she finished her business and stalked under the bed. Only then did I dare cross the room to the phone.

"I need to talk to Gil in person, as soon as possible," was all I would, or could, tell Janine. At first she didn't want to even bother Gil with such a vague request, but I wore her down on the strength of our three-year association. She had a Southern accent; I'd always pictured her with a sulky Cupid's-bow mouth and a fetching cascade of golden curls, although I'd never met her. She put me on hold for a few minutes, then returned to say, politely enough but with her usual miffed undertone, that "he" had an opening on Monday at five o'clock, actually, and he could give me fifteen minutes. I was used to that tone by now and didn't take it personally. I knew how it went; Gil was probably hovering over her with a stack of manuscripts he wanted her to read and a reservation he needed for tomorrow's lunch and folders to file and messages to return for him. She must have heard that I was out of Jackie's life for good, so she no doubt wondered what the hell I could possibly have to talk to Gil about now, but she said only, "All righty then, Claudia, see you then."

I put down the receiver, out of breath for some reason, as winded as if I'd just sprinted away from an attacker on the sidewalk.

I went out and found the nearest beauty shop and plunked myself down and told the woman what to do. Half an hour later, I walked out with a strange light-headed feeling. I'd had the lady cut it exactly to Jane's French-boy specifications. Longish layered bangs fell forward to brush the tips of my lashes; the sides and back lay in pinfeathers to the bare nape of my neck. All the way home I kept peering into plate-glass windows to inspect my unfamiliar reflection; I wasn't sure whether or not I liked it, but it was certainly a change, and at the moment, all change was for the better.

By five-thirty, the windowshade was almost dark and the evening loomed like a mine shaft I would have to descend without a light. I could see a movie or go downtown and drink with whoever happened to be on the next barstool, I could take a walk down Broadway, I could call Frieda and convince her to meet me for a sandwich somewhere, there were always a hundred things to do to fill time, but I was tired of filling time.

As I ruffled through the opened envelopes on my table, I unearthed the *Waste Land* card Gus had given me, cast an idle eye over it, and realized that the first performance started at eight. For the first time in days, I felt something almost akin to anticipation. A disco extravaganza, campy and awful and more ludicrous than anything I'd ever done or thought of doing. I was saved. That was just what I needed. I dialed William's work number and told Elissa in my most officious voice that I was calling from the White House with some vital top-secret classified information for Mr. Snow. She wasn't fooled, I didn't think, but William came on the line right away. "Claudia?" he said. "Where have you been? Why haven't you returned my calls?"

" 'What shall I do now? What shall I do? I shall rush out as I am, and walk the street with my hair down, so.' "

"Are you drunk already? It's not even six o'clock."

"William! Am I really that bad?"

"Worse," he said. "I can't believe you haven't called me back. You're lucky I still take your calls. Are you calling about Gus's play? Where should we meet?"

I decided to dress as if William and I were going on a real date. I put on a dress I'd bought a long time ago on a whim and never worn, an old-fashioned dress in a silky material, gray with a pattern of tiny dark blue flowers and a row of pearl buttons down the front, whose gently pleated skirt came almost to my knees and made me feel like a sexy librarian about to take her bun down and wow the world. I wore some of my new lipstick, the one called Lust for Life, which I found rather apt just now; I managed to apply a little mascara without getting any on my cheeks. After thrusting an arm out the window to gauge temperature and precipitation, I put on a dark gray cardigan sweater. From deep in my sock drawer I dug up a pair of sheer champagne-colored stockings and from the inky hellhole of my closet a not-too-battered pair of high-heeled Mary Janes that made me walk with a cantilevered daintiness. Then I was out the door and on my way to Brooklyn.

I got out at the Bedford stop and met William at the noisy, narrow Thai place across the street from the subway.

"Don't you look swell," he said, smiling, when I came in.

"Don't I just," I said.

"I like your hair," he added earnestly after a moment, sounding surprised and bemused, as if he were taking it personally that I'd cut it.

I smiled enigmatically and let it go at that. I'd never fully understood why men were so funny about women's haircuts.

We sat side by side on stools at the counter, ate a couple of oily, ambrosial curries and drank cold bottles of Thai beer and watched the silent cooks toss handfuls of diabolical red powder into smoking woks. I didn't tell him I'd lost my job; I didn't tell him anything, I just kept up a running patter of nonsense to avoid all the unwholesome, undesirable topics: my rupture with Jackie, his dance with Jane, anything to do with Margot, my recent bout with John Threadgill. William acquiesced to my mood with a parallel and complementary banter of his own.

After dinner we walked west toward the river and then north along Kent Avenue. It was a warm, windy evening, the sky heavy and pink, spitting a tepid little rain, but in a friendly way; we walked past old warehouses and factory buildings whose broken rain-beaded windowpanes were the same color as the sky. I breathed the saturated, enlivening air that came off the river, filling my lungs with it, moving my limbs easily through it. My head felt shorn and downy, like an invalid's. I felt weak but newly alive, as if I had been suffering from a severe and debilitating illness and had just begun the upswing back into normal health. My skirt blew against my legs; William walked calmly by my side, tall and handsome in his suit, close enough to me so that I could have taken his arm if I'd dared. We hardly talked, but our silence was comradely and even affectionate, or so it seemed to me.

The Waste Land Site, as Gus had portentously dubbed it on the card, turned out to be a squat factory building on a littered lot right on the water. The river looked menacing and inimical in the rain, swollen with riptides, glossy with industrial runoff. There was quite a crowd already gathered outside the building. Without looking directly at anyone, I sensed that I knew several of them. We barreled through until we found the ticket seller at a table near the door to the building, who was, I realized, the hatchet-faced, beturbaned Madame Sosostris on the card; tonight he was wearing a low-cut evening gown and false eyelashes, but there was no mistaking that chin, as long and heavy as an andiron.

The tickets were ten dollars each. I paid for both, money that wasn't mine, a credit-card cash advance, because I couldn't stand being William's charity case any more. "Oh—I forgot," said William. "Sorry, I think I'm on the list. Hector," he said to the ticket guy, "I'm on the list." So much for trying to treat him to something. "Here, Claudia, it's on me."

"No, stop," I said. "I wanted to treat you, for once."

"Why don't you just thank me and shut up?"

"Thank you," I said grievously, and shut up.

We were in a long, low-ceilinged room with a concrete oil-stained floor. A curtain hid the back section of the room, a big black cloth with diadems glittering on it; a hundred or so metal folding chairs had been arranged in front. Almost all of the chairs were still empty, since the entire audience seemed to be loitering outside. William and I sat off to the side, in the next-to-last row. Hector had handed William two programs; William gave me one of them now and we read them to ourselves, waiting for the rest of the audience to straggle in. Our shoulders touched. I could feel his warmth through several layers of cloth.

"I can't believe this," I said, pointing at a note at the back of the program. "Listen to this: 'The composer wishes to thank the librettist for his insight and compassion, for being so far ahead of his time, for shaping the pain of a generation and a culture and giving it voice.' Excuse me, William, is he serious? I'm going to gag."

"Well, try to control yourself," said William swiftly. "He's HIV positive."

"Oh," I said, shocked, immediately contrite. "So that's why." I wasn't sure what I meant by that, and William didn't ask. Everyone came crowding in. The lights dimmed. The huge disco ball overhead, with its thousand mirror shards, began to turn, shedding beads of light through the room. A swelling tremolo synthesizer chord resolved into another chord, the drum machine kicked in with the relentless beat of a piston. The audience whooped as a chorus line of men in tight spandex sailor suits came scissor-kicking onstage, singing in reedy unison to a flimsy and fatuous tune: "April is the cruelest month, breeding lilacs out of the dead land, mixing memory and desire . . ." All the scorn that rose in my throat had to be tamped down right away. I wished William hadn't told me. What difference should it make to my experience and opinion of this play that a life-sapping virus had taken up residence in Gus's immune system? He was still a vicious, snide, egocentric prick; it wasn't fair that I was now required to feel sympathetic and open-minded toward this piece of crap. "Stirring dull roots with spring rain," they sang, Adam's apples bobbing, hips twitching, biceps swelling as they raised their arms above their heads and pumped them to the beat.

A lithe bewigged sapling in a red strapless evening dress and long black gloves, carrying a basket of flowers, sashayed in from stage left while the chorus line sank to its knees and hummed. The spotlight picked "her" out and sent the chorus into semi-darkness, where their teeth and white trousers glowed. She struck a pose, hand on jutting hip, and pouted at the audience as the key shifted to a brighter mode, "Winter kept us warm," petulantly, as if she found the whole thing just too annoying for words, "covering Earth in forgetful snow, feeding a little life with dried tubers," toss of the head and roll of the eyes at the audience, who laughed in a self-conscious ripple. The drum machine thudded; the voices of the chorus rose on a glissando to a high wail while the Hyacinth Girl gave a mock swoon and intoned with as much limp suburban jadedness as if she were recounting her latest junket to Miami: "I read, much of the night"—drumroll—"and go south in the winter." She was finished, thank God: applause all around, followed by the quick pattering exit to stage left of her and her sailor-swains.

The stage went dark. The disco ball went dark. The "band" was silent. I whispered to William, "I like this part," and he knocked his head against mine, meaning that he forgave me for being so irreverent, which caused me to swoon a little. My eyes fluttered shut, then opened to see an apparition, naked and blindfolded, walking from the rear of the stage toward us in the frank glare of one spotlight, striding with the remote casualness of a model on a runway on long, knob-kneed, spidery-coltish legs. There was a hush in the audience, silence. The figure walked surefootedly, with a calm, inward expression. A swelling of tears rose in my throat, and my heart beat a little faster: we beheld the perfect body: strong and young, lithe, curvaceous and muscular, with lovely high round breasts and a limp but shapely penis bobbing gently as she walked; she was somehow essentially female, despite her vestigial male baggage. A large, papier-mâché oyster shell opened in the footlights and she walked with grand sureness toward it, stepped into it and struck a pose. She stood for a moment as chords crashed one after another like wavelets, then as the tempo quickened and a darting little melody swam in, she stepped out of the shell and went over to the watchtower that loomed at stage left, a lifeguard's chair draped in black cloth. She climbed the ladder and arranged herself in the seat and turned her blindfolded face down toward the stage as if she could see everything that happened there, and would mete out judgment as she saw fit. Then the lights came up and the show continued with swirls of gold lamé and glittering platform shoes and silly tunes and sillier dance numbers, but I couldn't take my eyes off Tiresias, sitting motionless on her throne. I was stunned by the fact of her. Even the dancing Tarot deck couldn't distract me. What was her life like? What on earth did she do for a living? How did it feel to inhabit such a body?

At intermission, William and I stayed in our seats until most of the audience had wandered out to smoke and kibitz. "Want to go around the back?" I asked him.

"Sure," he said. We snuck out a side door and skirted the outside of the building. The rain had stopped for now; the heavy red fog over the city gave way high overhead to a clear sky and the light of an almost-full moon. Toward the rear of the lot we stumbled on a little garden amid empty crack vials and broken glass. We wiped rainwater off wrought-iron chairs and pulled them over to a low table, sat down and put our feet up. The lights of a rapidly moving boat skimmed upriver, headed for the Bronx. The island of Manhattan lay just across the river.

"That's pretty shocking, about Gus," I said.

"He's taking that multi-pill cocktail, every four hours around the clock. It's like having a newborn infant to feed."

"How long has he known?"

"Eight months."

"Why didn't you tell me before?"

"I wasn't supposed to tell anyone. It just slipped out."

"He does this whole AIDS melodrama and he doesn't want anyone to know he's positive?"

"He thinks it would make people feel sorry for him, and he doesn't want that to color their view of his work."

"Ecchhh," I said, but under my breath so he wouldn't hear.

"I remember when Stella was still Steve," he said. "She's an old friend of Gus's, I think they went to high school together or something. Gus said she was a real jock back then."

"Tiresias is supposed to be old," I said.

"Well, maybe Gus couldn't find an old pre-op transsexual." He leaned back and looked up at the sky. "Remember that time when your mother got into a fistfight with the visiting shrink?"

"Oh, God, what made you think of that?" She'd punched a red-faced, shambling bear one night after too many schnapps or whatever the hell she drank, just because he'd had the temerity to ask her if she'd like to have a drink with him in his motel room. "You think I'm as obnoxious as she is?"

"Obnoxious?" He looked startled, as if he hadn't been thinking along these lines at all.

"She has a bug up her ass about men."

"Well, from what I've heard about your father, she had good reason. Charles Kirby. Isn't a kirby a miniature cucumber?"

"What do you have against my father?"

"Nothing," he said. "I should talk."

"You honestly think I'm like my mother? Please say no."

"Actually, no. In fact—" He cleared his throat, paused a moment while I waited in agony, then said, "She's pretty bitter, isn't she? And you're—"

"Say it."

"I've always thought of you as essentially untouched. Even though you've slutted yourself around the block three or four times—"

"William!"

"—you haven't lost that quality that you've had ever since you were a kid."

"What quality?"

"I can't explain it."

"Try," I said urgently.

"You haven't been scarred yet. You're unmarked in a way. You're still kind of wholesome." He wasn't kidding around, or trying to get a rise out of me. He said it reluctantly but precisely, as if he had reached these conclusions after observation and reflection.

"Wholesome?" I said scathingly, and made a face. "I'm not wholesome. I think it's just that you've known me since I was five and you don't see the ill change that life hast wrought in me, who laugh no more nor lift my throat to sing."

William was the only person I ever quoted poetry around; I suppose I hoped to impress him, but he usually treated me like a zealot championing a pointless cause. "Which second-rate Victorian said that?" he asked.

"Edna Millay was Edwardian," I said, "if Americans can be called Edwardian. Do you mean wholesome as in spinsters and nuns and schoolmarms?"

"How did we get on this subject? All I intended to say was that I've always liked the fact that your mother punched that guy and I thought of it just now for some reason that might have had nothing to do with you at all."

"Whatever," I said, my voice prickly and cool. "I'm sorry about Gus."

"So am I," he said.

We were quiet for a few minutes. I could hear laughter and voices, the smooth near-silent pulsing of the river at our feet. Reflected city lights hung below the island like roots or icicles, glowing squiggles that moved outward toward us with the tide. The reflected city was more alluring than the real one, which looked dim and almost unremarkable in comparison. The moon's reflection lay in the eddies near the bank where we sat, its white light diffuse and messy as an oil slick. I didn't want to bear the rough, unwieldy burden of these hurt feelings. I wanted to scrape them off and throw them away from me like scales from a fish.

"William," I said, "you can't possibly think this show is good. You're just being nice."

He laughed. "If you'd lighten up about it, you might actually let yourself be entertained."

"Let's go in," I said, and sighed.

The second half of the show began with a solo from Tiresias. Her voice was cracked and plain, occasionally off-pitch, but she sang unaffectedly, almost as if she were speaking, so that the words stood out clearly and the melody seemed incidental, which it was: "I Tiresias, though blind, throbbing between two lives, old man with wrinkled female breasts, can see at the violet hour, the evening hour that strives homeward, and brings the sailor home from sea . . ." The lights came up on the lonely typist, awaiting her "young man carbuncular": "I Tiresias, old man with wrinkled dugs perceived the scene, and foretold the rest—I too awaited the expected guest."

I slumped in my chair, bathed in a persistent cold turmoil as I suffered through various would-be showstoppers, the Hanged Man singing his number upside down while dangling by the feet from a scaffolding, the drowned Phoenician Sailor rising white-faced and motionless from a tank of water to intone in a hollow, watery, prerecorded voice, Thunder swooping down at us from the ceiling on wires, throwing lightning bolts, his voice reverberating through special effects.

At the end an old man sat fishing on the banks of a river, wearing a bloody Gandhi-like diaper, singing "London Bridge is falling down" in a plaintive drone. I recognized him from

Wolfram von Eschenbach's *Parzival*, which I'd written a paper on in college—he was the Fisher King, whose crotch had been pierced by a spear for some weird medieval reason. The ignorant bumpkin Parzival finally asked him, "Father, what ails thee?" and won the kingdom, the message being that compassion was important. I'd received an A even though I hadn't fully understood, being only nineteen at the time. And I still didn't, entirely, now that I thought about it.

For the grand finale, the entire cast stood in a semicircle holding their hands together in prayer, chanting "Shantih Shantih Shantih," bathed in the swirling lights of the disco ball. As the music and chanting finally faded away, Tiresias stood up on the seat of the lifeguard chair and took off her blindfold, lifted her arms and stared into the spotlight, and then the lights went out.

"Want to go backstage with me and congratulate Gus?" William asked when the lights came up in the audience.

"See you around," I said. "I have to go."

"You're mad," he said. He sounded surprised. "Because I said you were wholesome?"

"I'll get over it."

"No, let me buy you a drink, I just want to tell Gus—"

"That's okay," I said, "another time."

I ducked out of the crowd the same way I'd ducked in, with my head down, avoiding everyone's eyes. I walked through dark streets toward Bedford Avenue, muttering under my breath as I walked to the trudging rhythm of my footsteps, "Here is no water but only rock, rock and no water and the sa-handy road." I began to look forward to watching people and thinking my solitary thoughts on the train ride home. But on the subway platform, I ran into Jane Herman.

"You took my advice, I see," she said, kissing both my cheeks. "Great haircut! You look incredible."

"Thanks," I said.

The train roared into the station. She leaned against me and said into my ear, "I wanted to tell you about the other night."

I didn't want to hear about the other night, which I assumed meant whatever had transpired between her and William after his party, but I followed her onto the train and leaned against the door next to her.

"Anyway," said Jane, her whole body turned to me, slouching and hunching her shoulders so we were about the same height, "I was sorry you left so early."

"You seemed to be in good hands when I left."

Her mouth had a vulpine quality when she laughed, a calculated, toothy greediness; why hadn't I noticed that before? And there was something pushy and controlling in the way she'd commandeered me and pinned me against the subway-car door, forcing me to listen to this story I didn't in the least want to hear, or rather, wanted to hear only in a masochistic, self-loathing kind of way.

"Where was William tonight?" she asked then. "He said he was going to be there."

"I sat with him. He went backstage afterwards."

"Oh," she said, momentarily at a loss. "Well, anyway. So we ended up on the couch; things heated up, some clothes came off, the question of a condom arose, I just happened to have one, lucky me."

I felt faint. She didn't seem to notice.

"Then in the middle of everything, he got up and started pacing around the room. He went off on a tirade. He said he couldn't do this, it wasn't good for him, and I was like, 'Do what? Have sex?' He said I didn't know anything about him and it was probably better for both of us if we left it that way. So I got dressed and went home."

My knees buckled with joy. He'd extricated himself from her octopus grip and sent her packing. "Weird," I said.

"Claudia," she said, her face very close to mine, "what was he talking about?"

"I have no idea."

"Come on," she urged. "No idea at all?"

"Girl Scouts' honor."

"Maybe he's gay. Maybe he doesn't even like girls."

"He likes girls, Jane. He never shuts up about them." Something of what I felt leaked into my tone. Jane and I exchanged a frankly rivalrous look. The doors slid open; we were at First Avenue. "This is my stop," I said. "Good night, see you around."

Jane took my face in her hands without warning and kissed me on the lips, a real smackeroo. "He's all yours, darling," she said warmly, and smiled at me. "Good luck."

I stared mutely at her, obscurely grateful (he was all mine?), then left the train and watched it trundle off down the tracks until it was nothing but a vanishing point of red light. I sat on a bench in the paper-strewn, pee-smelling station and watched the furry, humped backs of rats scurrying over the tracks, foraging for their supper. I discovered that I was singing under my breath; the song had continued running through my mind, keeping its own time. "Here is no water but oh-honely rock, rock and no water and the sa-handy road."

When the next L train appeared, finally, I watched it come without the slightest urge to throw myself under its wheels. I climbed on and sat down and read the shiny Scotch ads that filled the whole car from one end to the other, pictures of young professionals in their twenties with their first real apartments, their first real girlfriends and boyfriends, wondering which drink went with their new adult lifestyle. Lucky for me, I'd never had any problem with that particular equation, but no matter; I stared in curious fascination at all the post-collegiate up-and-comers with their snappy Scotch-and-sodas. They were hopeful and spruce and brave, as industrious and clear-sighted as little chipmunks. They wore suits all day, sitting at computer terminals in offices as artificially self-contained as space stations, all beige laminated surfaces and subfusc low-pile carpet and fluorescent cubes recessed into miles of fiberglass ceiling tiles. Any potted ficus tree who drooped or shed its leaves would be hustled away in the night and replaced with a better-adjusted one. The dress code was as sexless and absurd and unrelated to natural activity as the uniforms they wore on *Star Trek*. How did William do it? How did anyone? I would never have been able to take any of it seriously, all the conference calls and policy-making and hush-hush deals and promo packages and press releases and company letterhead and global offices and outside counsel and managers' meetings and damage control. It seemed indecorous somehow, profane even, here at the wormy, carious butt-end of the millennium, to evince such naked fervor for progress, to believe so blatantly in further despoliation; didn't we all know better by now?

I got off the train at Sixth Avenue, walked through the long bright tunnel to the IRT at Seventh Avenue and climbed aboard an uptown 9 that had just pulled in. My new car was the old, multi-placarded kind, its overhead ad slots filled with wife-beaters, torn earlobes, unwanted pregnancies, bunions. I looked with impersonal affection at the other passengers. "Lonely I came, and I depart alone," I thought, inadvertently catching the eye of an old woman who smiled at me and didn't look away. She could very well have been a horny old bull dyke looking for some nooky, but I didn't care; I pretended she was my grandma for a couple of seconds, and then we got to my stop and I got off the train and left her to ride on without me.

chapter eleven

I awoke the next morning pondering the possible repercussions and moral implications of what I was about to do, but when my phone rang and my machine clicked on and I received still another message from Miller concerning the rent I owed him, these qualms were squashed out of existence by the ineluctable pressure of necessity. I was doomed anyway. What did one more little thing matter? Look at the way I'd stolen her gold watch and shoes and sweater only moments after I'd found out I'd murdered her. What did that say about my character?

Swiftly and without flinching, I unearthed Jackie's stolen checkbook and wrote myself a check, predated a month or two in hopes that Goldie would think it was an old paycheck I'd just gotten around to depositing, and Jackie would never know. I signed Jackie's loopy scrawl of an autograph, which I was better at than she was, not that this was anything to brag about.

I was out the door and heading for the bank before I could change my mind. As I deposited it at the ATM, I looked over my shoulder to make sure no undercover cops were lurking behind me. The machine spewed a receipt back at me, which indicated that I now had a positive balance of six hundred and thirty dollars in my checking account, one hundred of which were immediately available. Unfortunately, I also had a negative balance of one thousand dollars in my cash reserve account, but the receipt didn't mention that and I didn't ask.

I withdrew an ill-gotten twenty-dollar bill, then crossed Broadway and peered through the window of the Skouros Coffee Shop. I recognized the guy behind the counter, Russell, a harmless pimply boy. There was no sign of my enemy with his great big mustache and cruel spatula and beady eyes, so I went in and inhaled with pleasure the comfortingly familiar smells of bacon grease and bleach. I sat somewhat apprehensively at the counter, hoping the whole staff hadn't been instructed to give the heave-ho to any shifty-eyed blondes who wandered in, but Russell just smiled vaguely and asked what he could get for me. Within minutes I had a steaming plate of scrambled eggs and home fries, a fresh cup of coffee and a glass of orange juice. Things were looking up indeed.

I scarfed every bite, paid my check and left a nice tip, which didn't exactly make up for walking out on my last one but at least prevented another black mark against my name. After I left the Skouros, I found myself strolling down Broadway behind a disembarked busload of tourists I guessed were from either Germany or the Midwest; they walked as slowly as a herd of large ruminants, and all of them had the enormous rumps and mottled, marbled, quivering faces of avid meateaters. I became strangely fascinated by them. I followed them all the way down to Seventy-second Street, and learned the following on the way: they were in fact German; they were paired off two by two in married couples; some of these couples were more civil than others; and they were very hungry but couldn't find a restaurant to their liking, so they were forced to march along, a starving, waddling diaspora.

It dismayed me how much German I was able to understand. I'd avoided learning German all my life, or so I'd always told myself, but every word these people said was as clear to me as if they were speaking English. I watched them peer at the menus plastered all over the windows of a diner, arguing amongst themselves, pointing to various items and weighing the merits of American food versus their good German dishes, for which they were clearly pining. Finally a tall round-faced man with psychotically good posture who appeared to have elected himself their leader gave the place the nod, and they began to stuff themselves through the door. When the whole gaggle of Krauts had disappeared into the steamy depths, there was nothing for it but to go home.

I went home. My apartment smelled stale and unoccupied. I fought with the window until it opened; a greasy little breeze ambled in. The afternoon went by, inexorably, as afternoons will. I sat at my table, looking down at a legal pad opened to a blank page, for much of it. I didn't write "Chapter One" at the top of the page; I couldn't bring myself to be so presumptuous. I was badly constipated today, which in my present state of mind I interpreted as a message from whatever low-rent muse had been assigned to me rather than any result of my diet. I pictured all that dense clayey matter adhering stickily to my tender pink insides, which writhed in futile peristaltic exertion, just as I was doing here at my table, confronted by the blank knowledge of the years I had spent not writing. They mounted before me, covered my lined yellow paper with their lined yellow faces, wasted and decayed, staring up at me like death masks. The ingrained habit of that breathlessly vacuous Gene-vieve-voice clung to me like a cloying smell.

When I was caught cheating on a math test in fifth grade, I'd sat in a silent panic at the dinner table waiting for the phone to ring. My teacher had promised me that she would be calling my mother that night to inform her of my crime and ask that she make sure I didn't repeat it. I dragged my fork through my rice, tried to get my green beans to stand upright on the plate like a row of teeth or fence posts; I couldn't swallow. When the phone finally rang, I looked up, white-faced, and said, "I'll get it, Ma."

But she had already answered. I watched her face as she spoke to Mrs. Cleghorn, sat perfectly still until she replaced the receiver and met my wide-eyed, terrified gaze. "Ach, Claudia."

"I'll never copy again," I said.

She sighed. "It isn't the copying, it's that your superego should be more deweloped by now!" I had occasionally heard her speak nearly unaccented English, usually when she was very tired.

"My what?"

"You copied because your superego is too immature. I don't know why this is so; when I was your age I had a strongly deweloped sense of right and wrong."

"But Ma, I didn't do the homework yesterday. I didn't know how to do the problems."

"So?"

"So maybe I'm just lazy."

"That is because of your superego," she repeated.

"How do you know? Can you see it?"

I had never challenged her before. She drew herself up. "Claudia," she said, "it is inwisible. You cannot see it, but it is there."

"But how do you know?"

"Ach," she said, "enough questions. I have too much to do tonight."

"Just tell me," I wailed.

"I told you, it is inwisible!" she roared.

I went up to my room in a funk, vowing to myself that my own children would be permitted to question the existence of anything, even their mother. I sat in my open bedroom window, telling myself sad little stories about orphans and runaways, sad because I wasn't among them. A creaking rasp of cicadas gusted up from the wash in back of the house. I felt the wind leave a film of grit on my skin, mineral flecks in the hollows of my pores. I could almost smell it, like gunpowder, an acrid tang, and imagined that if I touched my face my fingers would come away sparkling. I listened to my mother crashing around downstairs like a beast whose thankless pup had bitten her milk-swollen teat.

Sitting in this seedy little room twenty years later, staring at the blank yellow page in front of me, I considered the burst of audacity that had caused me to set up that meeting with Gil Reeve on Monday. I had no superego at all; my mother had been wrong. I couldn't believe that I'd taken that disk and erased the whole book from the computer's hard drive. And I couldn't believe that I was actually going to present myself at his office and demand some sort of ransom for the book. Maybe there were several different people inhabiting my body, not entirely unlike multiple-personality disorder; but rather than serving to repress some terrible childhood memory, my own pathology seemed to spring from the efforts of one haplessly ineffectual personality to dig out of some hole another equally hapless personality had landed in.

At five-thirty, it was time to go and wait for my mother on

the front steps of the Piermont House. I found the brochure she'd sent me, which I now recognized as a futile attempt to interest me in her work. She was at this very moment sitting on a "prominent panel of discussants" holding forth on the topic of "Messages from the Id: Preverbal Phenomena in the Analysis." She probably would have been pleased, even delighted, if I'd told her I wanted to show up early to hear her lecture. Why hadn't I thought of that?

The phone gave a precipitous jangle that set my teeth on edge. I snatched up the receiver. "Hello?" I said cautiously. It was probably one of the sneakier collection agencies.

"What's wrong with you?" said William. "Why are you answering your phone?"

My heart did its usual trapeze routine. I forgave him completely for whatever he'd said last night. "It was making the most horrible noise," I said.

"What are you doing right now?"

"I'm on my way to have dinner with my mother. Want to come?"

"No," he said, "I'm too agitated. Will you come over later?"

"Why are you agitated?"

"Bring champagne."

"What kind of champagne?"

"The kind you pop," he said impatiently. "Come the minute you're done with Gerda. Don't dawdle."

"I won't dawdle, William," I said. My voice sounded sparkly and ebullient; I couldn't help it.

What was I wearing? Jeans, suitable for all occasions, my best pair, the ones that cleft where they should cleave and hung where they should hang, at least according to *Cosmopolitan*, which I consulted on all such weighty matters. Unfortunately I was also wearing a flowered shirt made of some slippery man-made material, calculated to please my mother, who had given it to me; I hoped that the sight of it would help her get over whatever deep disappointment I was bound to cause her. William would just have to take me as I was. Not that he'd mind; not that he'd notice.

Clutching the flyer in one hand and a token in the other, I ran down the steps of the subway and almost collided with Margot Spencer, who was climbing them. "Hi," I said, stopping reluctantly.

She stopped even more reluctantly. "Oh, hello, Claudia." She said my name as if it were a venereal disease. She didn't smile at me. She looked uncharacteristically ill-at-ease and her eyes bulged slightly, which meant that she was requiring herself to behave civilly because that was what one did, but she was finding it difficult.

"Well," I said after an interminable silent staredown. "I'd better run. See you, Margot."

Without a word, she turned on her heel and vanished. I went down the stairs and stood on the subway platform in a funk. A headlight plowing along a middle track lit the columns between the tracks, illuminating them and plunging them back into darkness as it passed. Then the express train appeared and streaked by, its windows filled with smug heads. My bowels had loosened in the icy shock of Margot's goggle-eyed stare and were now urgently demanding to be voided, but short of losing a token and going back home, there was nothing to be done but clench my muscles and think about my date with William later. At his house. At his request. With champagne. I boarded the train that came nosing into the station on the heels of its swifter counterpart; a while later I emerged from underground into a golden, windless evening and goose-stepped rapidly to the Piermont House, which turned out to be a stately brownstone on West Fifty-seventh Street.

Although I'd had every intention of waiting on the steps, I had to go inside to use the ladies' room. When I came out, I saw, at the end of the rather dim, coat-filled entryway, the glowing glass panels of old-fashioned French doors. Since I just happened to be passing by, I eased one open a crack and peered in. The room looked as if it had been the parlor back in the days when a family had lived here. Past the backs of the balding and blue-tinged heads of the audience, I saw my mother behind a long table with the other panelists. I'd imagined tiers of alert, professional faces in a big modern auditorium; there couldn't have been more than forty-odd people present, including the panelists and me. I saw a few canes propped against chairs, heard wheezing and the shriek of a hearing aid. In this crowd, my mother looked youthful.

She was speaking. Her voice sounded strong and full-throated. I slid into an empty chair in the last row. She leaned forward, her forefinger in the air, her glasses glinting; her voice rose in pitch and volume the way it always did when she was engrossed in her own ideas. And, as always when she was thus engrossed, I found that my mind automatically became a dark wet-walled cave around which her lecture bounced and echoed and resounded nonsensically.

One day in tenth grade, I'd missed the school bus home. Since the institute was a ten-minute walk from Candlewick High School, I walked there to wait outside on the lawn until early evening, when my mother's classes were over, so I could ride home with her. I sat under a tree with my book bag. The sprinklers were off and the campus was quiet and smelled of cut grass. Beyond the grounds of the institute I could see Candlewick's only traffic light, strung across the highway on a wire at the intersection between here and the high school, the orange peaked roof of the A&W, dust rising behind a pickup truck barreling along a dirt road; here, all was peaceful and civilized. I sat through the afternoon, reading a biography of Edna St. Vincent Millay. As a young poetess, she had lived in Greenwich Village; she was small and lithe with a cap of curls, and she rode the Staten Island ferry with an unidentified "you" I pictured as a man in a beret: "We were very tired, we were very merry—we had gone back and forth all night on the ferry." I could imagine nothing more sheerly romantic than standing at the rail and watching the sun rise over the New York harbor, "dripping, a bucketful of gold." This was the blueprint for the life I planned to have.

Motion flickered across my peripheral vision. I looked up to see my mother, flanked by several students, striding along the walk between the administration building, where her office was, and the large pinkish structure that housed the classrooms. This quick, unexpected transition of my attention between my hoped-for future and the actual fact of my mother afforded me a glimpse of her as others might have seen her. As her students disbanded to the parking lot, my mother marched off alone toward the classrooms, a brave, defiant, mannish person in baggy trousers and an unfashionable polyester print blouse with a floppy bow, her spine ramrod-straight, her gaze fixed on a point on the horizon. Was she really so small? I had always thought of her as enormous. I felt a pang at the set squareness of her shoulders, which looked surprisingly narrow and frail suddenly.

I got up. "Ma," I shouted. "Wait for me!" I ran headlong across the grass.

She turned and saw me and waited while I caught up with her. As I approached her, I saw a stain on her blouse. She'd probably noticed it immediately, the moment she'd spilled the coffee on herself, and said "Ach, poo!" and decided it didn't belong to her. This had enabled her to wear it unselfconsciously, even proudly, for the rest of the day; in her mind, it had become a badge that represented her disavowal of all stains, both external and internal. I felt inadequate and clumsy, another of her stains.

"I missed the bus," I said stiffly.

"I'll be done in an hour. You want to wait in my office?"

Her office was dominated by a framed portrait of Sigmund Freud, whose dark unwinking eyes were unnervingly penetrating, and seemed to ferret out every one of my secret urges. "That's okay, I'll wait outside," I said. I returned to my cool patch of lawn and picked up my book, but the words jarred me now: my future wasn't going to happen soon enough. I put the book down and plucked crabbily at the short blades of grass, scratched a mosquito bite on my bare leg, scowled off into the distance. And there was Ed Snow, trundling along the walkway, sweating in a short-sleeved white shirt, his pants bunching up in the crotch because his thighs were fat. He represented everything I hated about the Ventana Valley: he was wheezing, puffing, walking as quickly as his bulk and the heat would allow. Thinking no one was looking, he plucked the material of his pants from the fold between his buttocks, giving himself a good deep scratch in the process: this was the same man who'd whipped Billy more than once with the white belt he wore to church. "Hi, Ed!" I shouted, and when he turned and saw me watching him I felt maliciously triumphant, as if I'd got him back in some small way on Billy's behalf as well as my own.

My mother's speech wound down to her conclusion. The moderator wrapped things up and stepped down from his podium. There was some applause, which I contributed to, and then my mother was wading through a clutch of antediluvian admirers toward me.

"Well!" she said, beaming, her round face flushed, her eyes

bright. She wore an outfit she must have bought especially for the occasion, a suit in a racy electric blue, with three enormous gold buttons on its short jacket and a mid-calf-length skirt that hung straight down from her boxy hips; under the jacket she wore a floral-print blouse that was nearly the twin of the one I was wearing, same pattern, different but equally lurid colors. "What a wonderful surprise, to see you sitting out there! I bet you didn't expect to be the star of my lecture!"

I was the star? "Hi, Ma," I said with a queasy half-smile.

As we descended the front steps of the building, I let her happiness at seeing me override my own dismay at seeing her, and almost managed to conjure some vicarious anticipation for the meal we were about to share together. She marched to the edge of the curb and her short arm shot skyward; I thought of this gesture of hers as "heiling a cab," but now, as always, I resisted the rather weak temptation to tell her so. She tended to treat my jokes, especially the ones I ventured to make at her expense, as an invitation to discuss Freud's views on humor, which naturally involved an inquiry into my unconscious hostilities.

A cab stopped. My mother propelled herself into the back-seat; I slid in after her and told the driver where we were going. She turned to me, her smile still intact, since I hadn't done anything yet to dispel it. "So," she said. "What did you think of the little story about you?"

"Actually, Ma, I got there too late to hear that part. What was the story?"

"Don't you remember at bedtime when you were a little girl, how you would come in my study when I was working and try to distract me?" She chuckled fondly.

"I remember," I said, and was glad not to have had to hear her chalk all those fruitless nightly bids for affection up to some crackpot theory. She could have simply asked me why I'd done it. A heavy weight lay in my stomach like an indigestible wad of dough. All of my apprehension about the meal to come seemed entirely attributable to the fact that I was going to have to eat Ukrainian food, which struck me now as the most dreary, stodgy, depressing cuisine on earth. "Ma, listen, maybe we should go somewhere else for a change. Maybe a Chinese place?"

"Gott knows from what animal that meat comes," she said obtusely.

I sighed. "Righto," I said with mock good humor.

"What did you say? That expression."

"Righto," I said dutifully, the native-born daughter helping her immigrant mother learn the language. "It means okay, all right—"

"Your father used to say that, how very strange, I don't think it's genetic to use a particular expression. But you just sounded so much like him."

"That is strange," I said blandly. We stopped at the intersection just southwest of Union Square. I rolled down my window and stuck my head out. The sky was shot through with light as effervescent and golden as champagne. I got a lungful of gasoline-laden air just as the light turned green and we shot forward, turned left and lurched into east-west traffic. When a truck swerved into our lane and cut us off, my mother's arm shot out automatically and made an iron bar across my breastbone. Looking down at her arm, startled, I saw that the skin on the back of her hand was frail and papery, mottled with brown spots and webbed with thick blue-green veins. This sent a heavy wave of fear and sadness crashing over me. There she sat next to me, my progenitrix, my own future in human form, and all I wanted to do was get a free dinner out of her and send her off to bed. Ashamed of myself, I turned to her and said with some effort, "It just doesn't sound like he was all that great, frankly."

"I never did tell you very much. Maybe because I wondered why would you care about this stupid fellow?"

"See?" I said with equal parts irritation and defensiveness. "He was stupid. What more could I possibly want to know about him?"

"No, nein, that isn't what I wanted to say, I'm no good at this. Maybe we just forget about it."

The driver had inserted his shabby, shockless taxi into a fire-hydrant space in front of the restaurant; he was idling patiently there without turning around, but something about the stolid set of his head made me realize that he was waiting for us to get out of his car. "Ma," I said, "we're here."

She opened her purse, a large and ancient pleather affair with a big brass clasp and a sinisterly gaping maw that looked as if it would bite the hand off anyone besides its owner who had the temerity to reach inside. She pulled out a pink plastic wallet, from which she extracted a neatly folded ten-dollar bill. The sight of such a bill coming out of such a wallet made me sad and fearful all over again: that was the ten-dollar bill of someone who had no one to distract her from needless, fussy, time-filling tasks like folding her money into neat squares, no one to tell her that this wallet was cheesy and broadcast forlornness. I got out of the cab and waited for her on the sidewalk, unable to watch as she carefully calculated the tip to the nearest nickel and handed it over to the driver coin by coin, picking each one carefully from its pink plastic compartment. I leaned over and offered her an arm, but when she disregarded it entirely and hopped nimbly as a cricket onto the sidewalk, the terrible ache in my throat dissolved.

The taxi slid back into the current and rumbled off down the avenue; we went into the restaurant, which happened to be the same place where I'd recently had breakfast with John. It was a big place, as dingy and impersonal as an old hotel dining room, with dark wainscoting, yellowed photographs of bustling Second Avenue in the 1930s and autographed decades-old head shots of unknown actors. Fans whirred overhead like enormous insects. Egg-colored coffee cups sat upside down in a pyramid on a sideboard next to the coffeemaker; pies turned slowly in a lit case by the cash register like cars in a showroom. The rows of white-shrouded tables were set neatly with silverware and napkins, but we were the only customers. It was still too early for everyone else. Torture-chamber sounds came from the kitchen, howls and banging metal.

I planned to order a glass of wine right away, sip casually and urbanely at it as if I didn't care much about it one way or the other, and then casually and urbanely order another one. However, I remembered, as we were seated by an unsmiling waiter who obviously remembered my mother all too well, that they offered no alcohol here, none at all: I could drink water, or hot tea, or the thin bitter bogwater they called coffee, but I couldn't have even the most innocuous little lite beer. This realization almost undid me. I opened the gigantic menu and set it on the table to shield me from my mother's ever-watchful gaze.

"What are you having?" she asked with enthusiasm. "I'm getting the potato dumplings with sour cream and applesauce and those such delicious fried onions."

"They're called pierogi," I told her tersely. I wanted, with every parched cell of my tongue, a glass of red wine. "I'm going to order a hamburger."

She clucked her tongue against the roof of her mouth, a

sound which made my fingers curl inward like dried leaves. "You could go to McDonald's for that," she said. "Why don't you order that good meat loaf they got? Maybe a potato pancake or so, and a cold beet salad to go with?"

"No, a burger's fine," I said, thinking that just maybe, just this once, if I didn't react and kept nice and calm she would leave me alone.

"But a meat loaf is almost the same thing but it's much more interesting, don't you think so? And those beet salads are done very well, I think. Horseradish, remember?"

"Okay," I said through a sudden case of lockjaw. I tried to throw the menu sharply down, but it sank slowly onto the table like a toppled gravestone. "You're right. Why don't you go ahead and order for me?"

She blanched at my tone. "Oh, Claudia, I was only suggesting. Of course I want you to get what you like."

"I *like* a hamburger," I spat out, gripping the edge of the table with both hands as if it might start to levitate otherwise.

"Good, okay, that's what you have," she said in the clipped voice she used whenever she was out of her depth with me. "And I have the pierogi, there we are." She wrestled her own menu shut and set it on top of mine with a little pat. I saw the whites of her eyes as she cast desperately around for the waiter, who now must have seemed to her the staunchest of allies, but he had vanished into the cabalistic, clanking depths of the kitchen. She looked down at the tablecloth, on which she was carefully arranging her knife and fork.

"I'm almost thirty," I said.

"Yes, I know," she said anxiously. "It's a good age, thirty, a pivotal age, and it's important to—"

"I've been supporting myself, living alone, out in the world, for almost ten years."

"Has it been so long? That's quite a—"

"So maybe I learned, somewhere along the way, how to order a meal in a restaurant."

"Oh, Claudia, all I wanted to do was for you to decide on something good so you wouldn't have to settle!"

"Just because your patients take everything you say as the word of God doesn't mean I think you're God and it doesn't mean you are God."

She stared at me, white-lipped, blank-faced. We were silent until the waiter materialized in the doorway to the dining room. We ordered, gave him our menus, and when he had disappeared again my mother said sorrowfully in a low voice, "You are such an angry young woman, liebchen. I wonder how it was you became so."

"There's a lot to be angry about, I guess."

"You were such a sweet little girl."

"Maybe I was just impersonating a sweet little girl."

She gave me a long gaze that was saturated with some strong, particular feeling I couldn't gauge. If I could have, I would have pulled my head and arms into my shirt like a turtle and hidden in there until she went away. "I don't know how, with my training, my experience, I failed to allow you to flourish."

"Who says you failed? Who says I'm not flourishing?"

We were silent for several minutes, looking around the room as if we'd taken a great interest in the head shots, sipping our ice water, clearing our throats. Finally our plates of food appeared, borne aloft in the arms of the waiter, who deposited them in front of us with a sour, hurried expression as if they were a pair of babies with soiled diapers he couldn't wait to unload on someone else. My mother gave a gasp of pleasure at the sight of her pierogis. She busied herself with dabs of apple-sauce and sour cream, then tucked her napkin into her blouse and dug in. She chewed her first bite with great attention, swallowed, lifted a corner of the napkin to blot her lips, and said, "Well, it's a little doughy, but the applesauce is all right. You're not eating?"

I looked down at my hamburger, a thin gray patty on a splayed-open bun with a soggy lettuce leaf and an anemic tomato slice. "I guess not," I said. "I'm not as hungry as I thought I was."

"No wonder," she said. "I wouldn't eat that if you paid me fifty bucks. Send it back, liebchen, get the meat loaf, please."

"Ma," I said swiftly and menacingly, "remember when I was little and I wanted to know what the superego looked like and you yelled at me?"

She gestured to the waiter, shaking her head at me. "Listen," she said to the man when he arrived within earshot, "my daughter made a mistake, she meant to order the meat loaf. Could we get a plate of that, with beet salad and a potato pancake, instead of this hamburger?"

Without a word, he lifted my plate and stalked into the kitchen. I watched my food go back whence it came. "You sent me to my room," I said.

She chewed in silence for a moment.

I said impatiently, "I can't believe you don't remember. It was the time I cheated on a test. My teacher called you that night."

She leaned back with a decisive nod. "Oh, yes, I remember now. I told you the superego was inwisible but the mind can see inwisible things, but you wouldn't listen, you wanted to see it."

"You were furious at me. Your face turned red and you were shaking."

"I would never get mad over such a thing."

"Well, you did."

"But I wouldn't."

We looked at each other. I tried to reconstruct the incident

220

exactly as it had happened so I could accuse her point by point and force her to admit that she'd been a cruel and terrible mother, but I found that her denial had clouded the entire thing.

"Well, I thought you seemed pretty mad," I said after a moment.

"That reminds me, there's a matter I must discuss with you," she said. "About the figurines. Do you think you might have a place for them sometime soon? All those old family figurines from Germany?"

"No," I said, "I absolutely do not want those figurines. You can donate them to the Salvation Army."

"They're your heirlooms. Your inheritance. They were your great-grandmother's, and they're supposed to go to your daughter when you have one. You are sure you can't find room for them?"

I was visited then by the darkest and direst of fears. All my anger evaporated, or rather, it alchemized into the opposite of anger. "What is it, Ma?"

"What is what?"

"Why are you giving them to me now?"

"I thought you wanted them; I thought maybe you would think it was an honor, a privilege, but if you don't like them—"

"Are you sick?" Cancer, I thought. Breast cancer. Or ovarian, one of those mother-killers. She was sixty-six. What would I do without her?

"Sick?" she said.

"How's your health?"

"My health," she said, puzzled. "I got a bit of arthritis, but—"

"But you're all right?"

"Yeah, sure," she said vaguely, thinking about something else. "But, Claudia, if you won't take them, then there's your cousin Charlotte in Freiburg. You don't mind if I send them to her?"

"Not at all," I said, "but why don't you keep them until—I mean, why not keep them?"

"Because," she said, "I'm moving to a tiny little place next month and I won't have room for them, and so I thought, well maybe I pass them along to you. But if you don't like them, there's no reason why you have to take them. I never knew you didn't want them."

"You're moving? Why?"

"I got a little place with a microwave and balcony about as big as a window box, and I sold my house to a big family, three kids."

"You didn't tell me you were selling it."

"I forgot," she said. "We always got so much else to talk about."

"What were you going to tell me about my father before, in the cab?" I asked in a rush of courage.

"Ach, him."

"William said something about him. That he was a jerk, essentially. How does William know that? Is it true?"

"William Snow was a very troubled little boy," she said, shaking her head. "His father was such a big fat nincompoop, did you know he cheated at poker?"

"William is a lawyer now, remember? He's successful and happy and well adjusted and pretty soon he'll be rich. What did he mean, about my father?"

"There was a lot of gossip always in that place," she said. "Small-minded people with nothing better to think about than me, well, I feel sorry for them, they can't find anything else to do. Ja, your father." She chewed and swallowed; I imagined a host of possibilities in the split second before she answered me. He'd left me an inheritance; he'd had other children besides me; he was actually still alive. "What do you want to know about him?"

"Did he have any other kids?"

"Only you."

"What happened between you?"

"Happened? Between us?" She looked apprehensive. "He had to go back to England."

"Would he have married you if he hadn't been killed?"

"I wouldn't have married him for anything," she said, "and anyway, he was already married to someone else."

"I guess that would have been a bit of a problem."

"It was no problem." She put a whole pierogi into her mouth and chewed, her eyelids fluttering with pleasure.

"But there must have been something about him or you wouldn't have—you know, slept with him."

"Sure, he was good-looking. But he was so silly, such a silly man, Claudia. So vain, so selfish and unkind. What was he doing with me? He had a wife. And if he chose me it was only because he wanted a recommendation from me. I didn't understand at first. I was very naive, he must have been laughing at me."

"A recommendation?"

"For a chob."

"Oh, my God," I said, "what an asshole."

She gave a surprisingly genuine laugh. "Yes, what an asshole." I got a glimpse, in the lightening of her face and eyes, of a younger, happier Gerda who probably hadn't existed since before I was born, pecking away at her typewriter in a foreign city, poor and alone but determined to succeed.

"Ma," I said, "Jackie fired me."

She recoiled from this news as if I'd shot a pistol into the air. "Fired you!"

"I deserved it," I said, obscurely gratified by her disbelief.

223

She reached over and patted my arm. "She is a paranoid, neurotic woman. She is reacting to things that are real only in her head."

"No, really, she had good reason. I screwed up all the time; the other day I finally went too far. There was nothing else for her to do."

"Well," she said dubiously.

"Really," I insisted, glad in spite of myself that she was so hard to convince.

"What are you doing now, for work?"

I shrugged, about to trot out a reassuringly bright and hopeful and wholly imaginary future, but I heard myself saying, "I'm not doing anything. I'm still trying to figure it all out." With a pang of hope and self-loathing, I thought of the meeting with Gil on Monday.

"Ach," she said; I thought I could see the words "grad school" and "floundering" and "decide" form on her tongue and dissipate like clouds massing and boiling and blowing away. "You need some money, then."

"I do," I said. "But I can't borrow any more from you, Ma, you're right."

"Not borrow," she said. "I'm giving it to you. I just sold my house. I just didn't know how bad things were for you when you asked me the other day."

"Oh, Ma," I said in a clutch of anxiety. "No, I don't feel right taking your money—" What was I saying? Why couldn't I take my mother's money, offered freely, when I could steal from Jackie with only the slightest twinge? "And some day I'll pay you back what you loaned me."

"Forget it, forget the money, it's not important," she said, and I could tell she was as bewildered as I was; she was also asking herself what on earth she was saying, hearing herself saying it while intending to say something else entirely. "You got more important stuff to figure out."

"I know I do," I said, "but I got myself into this."

"Oh, piffle," said my mother.

Then, as if on cue, my new, improved dinner descended from the waiter's hands to rest on the table before me. I leaned forward and bathed my face in the steam rising from the meat loaf, breathed the savory emanations.

chapter twelve

I rang William's doorbell just before ten o'clock with two bottles of good champagne. I wanted to laugh aloud with nervousness. I'd drunk a couple of beers very fast on the walk over from the subway to gird my loins; this was the night, I had decided, when I would finally say everything I had to say to William as bluntly and directly as I could. What did I have to lose?

But suddenly I wasn't sure any more that he'd really meant for me to come—maybe it had been a momentary whim, maybe he'd called someone else when I said I couldn't come right away and by now she was curled on his couch with her feet tucked under her, laughing with her head thrown back.

When William came to the door I saw that the couch was empty.

"Finally," he said. "What did you girls talk about all

night?" He took the bottles, felt them to see if they were cold, and finding that they were, enveloped me in a one-armed bear hug, pressing me to his chest so that my nose would have nestled in his neck if I'd had the presence of mind to let it, but for some reason I held myself stiffly away from him, perhaps because several beery little burps were working their way out of me right then.

Then just as suddenly I was following him to his kitchenette in a happy daze, listening to him jabber about something while he put one bottle in the fridge, twisted the foil off the other, aimed it at the sink, and eased the cork from the neck of the bottle. He seemed uncommonly animated.

"I had no idea what to expect," he said, and sucked the thick white foam that came boiling up after a wisp of cold smoke. "Never before in four years at Cromwell Wharton Dunne had a partner asked me to lunch. But it turned out to be a sort of picnic in his office, paper plates on either side of his desk, just informal conversation, you know, about this case, that case, when he says, 'So, have you thought at all about your future here?' and I said yes, I'd thought about it and I was looking forward very much to a long and fruitful career, that kind of bullshit—"

"You got made partner?" I said with a pang of envy.

He laughed. "No, unfortunately they don't just tell you casually over calzones, it's a formal process." He handed me a glass. "But I think he's decided to take me under his wing. You don't get mentored by a partner if they don't take you seriously. I feel like I'm in, I could be wrong, but I got a very good feeling, overall."

"Is that why we're celebrating?"

"We'll get to why we're celebrating in a minute. How's your mom?"

"She's moving to a smaller house. She wanted me to have those awful figurines but I told her to send them to my cousin in Germany. She took it surprisingly well."

"Why don't you want them?"

I gave him a look. "Oh, I just remembered, speaking of fussy little breakable items, I still have your crystal tumbler. It insisted on coming home with me after your party."

"Well, bring it back."

"I will, next time I come over."

"If there is a next time," he said. "I'm counting everything after you leave."

I sat at one end of his big leather sofa and tucked my legs up under me with what I intended to be a seductive little slithery motion in imitation of the girl I'd pictured sitting here in my place. William sat at the other end and set his glass on a coaster on the end table.

"Make some chitchat," he said.

"I got fired," I said.

"Did you now."

"It took her long enough. I deserved it."

"You mean because you were the worst secretary in the history of the profession?"

"Something like that."

"Well, good for you, I guess."

"I took the book with me, William. I took it off the hard drive and erased it. I also stole that bogus agreement I signed. I have a meeting with her editor on Monday afternoon."

His eyebrows shot up; he looked amazed. "Really?"

I nodded.

"You're going to ask for money?"

"Is that really as insane as I think it is?"

He shook his head, admiringly, I hoped. "Well," he said, "you're not taking it lying down."

"Well, I may get laughed out of there. Or thrown out."

"There's always Ian," he reminded me. "You would be my private revenge on him for being such a—whatever he is."

"I have a better idea," I said. "Why don't you give him Elissa? Kill two birds with one stone."

"What do you have against Elissa?"

"It's the way she treats me. Like I'm a crazy person, like I'm bothering you."

"You're so paranoid."

"I'd pay you to fire her. I meant it when I said I'd do your laundry for a year. It would be worth it to bring her down."

"I usually drop it off at the corner place," he said, and smiled. "It comes back all nice and folded. But I'll think about it."

I smiled back at him. This is just William, I told myself; I'd known him all my life. The boy next door, so to speak. "I have another confession to make," I said swiftly. There. I couldn't take it back; I had to go forward, it had to come out now or we'd just sit in silence until Old Scratch came in with his pushcart to truck us off to hell.

"Worse than stealing my glass?"

"I think so," I said. I paused, then blurted, "I gave all that money to the cabdriver."

"What money?"

"That hundred dollars."

"What hundred dollars?"

We stared at each other.

"You gave it to me the night I—the night at George's, with Gus."

He sucked on the inside of his cheek for a moment. "Huh," he said finally, "maybe you dreamed it."

"No," I said, "I didn't dream anything that happened that night. I wish I had."

"What do you mean?"

"You don't remember? I hit on you, and you sent me home in a cab."

He leaned his head back against the wall and smiled sideways at me; I basked in the steadfast warmth of his gaze. It was hard to breathe. I felt pleasure and pain and a druglike urge to melt. I closed my eyes, unable to bear it.

"William," I burst out, "how could you call me wholesome?"

He laughed. "Why are you so upset? What's so bad about being wholesome?"

"I'm not *wholesome*. Let me explain something, William. I don't want you of all people to think of me as some kind of sister. I'm no sister."

"I never said you were."

"Well, good," I said. I was really doing this; I was saying these things to him. I felt a little loopy with relief. I also felt as if I were only about halfway there. "Also, while I'm at it, I might as well tell you that I slept with John Threadgill again the other night, which was a complete mistake, but it just confirmed something I've known for over a year."

"That he's still married?"

I ignored this. "I can't have that kind of casual thing any more. I want something real or nothing at all."

"Me too," he said, "that's exactly what I've been—"

"No, it isn't the same thing. Because I—"

"That's what I wanted to—"

"Shut up." I set my glass down on a coaster on the coffee table and slid over to put my hands on his elbows. The room went completely silent. His eyes didn't waver from mine; he had no expression on his face.

"I'm just sitting here waiting for you to get it," I said finally.

"Get what?"

"You know what, William. It's totally obvious and you're not stupid, at least not usually."

"I am right now," he said. "I don't know, Claudia, you're going to have to tell me."

"I love you," I said, just like that; my tone was conversational, almost bemused, but every cell in my body was alight, as if I were in some warm, thrilling dream, the kind I awoke from and tried to reenter with all my might but never could.

"You love me," he repeated, in what appeared to be bafflement. "You mean love, love?"

"Yes."

"Do you really?"

"Yes," I groaned, half with relief, half with dread of what he'd say now.

"No," he said then; my heart almost failed me. "You don't."

"I swear, I do."

"Trust me, you don't."

He sounded so cool and unmoved that I started to cry.

"Stop," he said.

"I can't stop," I sobbed. "I feel so stupid."

He put his arm around me and pressed his lips to the crown of my head. As he spoke his breath warmed my skull, and the warmth spread downward into my entire body. "No, no, no," he said. "It's me."

"Don't humor me," I said fiercely.

"I'm not humoring you. Ask me why we're celebrating."

"Why are we celebrating?"

"I got my results today. I got tested."

My veins flash-froze. I pushed him away and faced him. "And?" I said.

"And I'm negative. I'm okay."

I went to throw my arms around him, but he staved me off with both hands raised. "Wait, I'm not finished. I had every reason to think it would be positive. I'd accepted it, but for years I was too scared to find out for sure. Then recently Gus convinced me to go in. And I'm okay. I don't really believe it."

Gus. Of course. I'd known it all along, somehow. "Pour me another glass," I said.

We tossed off another glass each, then refilled our glasses and downed most of those, too. I was fully crocked already after just two beers and three little flutes of champagne.

"All right, William." We were sitting upright again, facing each other at either end of the couch, the bottle between us on the coffee table. I was interested to note that he'd neglected to place a coaster under a wet vessel. He was agitated indeed. "I'm ready to hear about Gus."

"Oh, that," he said distractedly. "Well, I slept with him years ago, once or twice right after college, but that's not what I have to tell you."

"Oh, William," I said. "How could you? He's so disgusting."

William cleared his throat and started to say something, licked his lips and tried again, ran his hand over his mouth. "Shit," he said, "I can't." He leapt up and walked with jerky steps into the kitchen. I heard him opening and closing the refrigerator a few times.

"What are you doing in there?" I called to him after a minute or so.

"Stalling," he said, and came back in with a bottle of mineral water. "Are you thirsty?"

"I don't drink water," I said. "Come on, William, look at what I just told you, and if I could survive that, you can say anything. Come on, it's your turn."

He stood in the middle of his living room, holding the bottle straight out from his breastbone and capping the top with his thumb. He stood like that for a minute or two, looking at me, mulling the words over on his tongue, getting them ready to come out. I looked patiently back at him, waiting. He made an impatient wrought-up karate chop in midair.

"What is it?"

He sat down next to me and hid his face in his hands. "I can't look at you while I say this. You have to look out the window until I'm finished."

I tilted my head so all I could see was the pale, skewed reflection of the room in the big window.

"I'm a pervert," he said finally. There was a long silence. I sat up slowly and looked at him, waiting. He placed his palms together, slid them between his knees. "For so many years," he said with a mild discursiveness that made me suspect he was extremely nervous and hiding it well, "I've been sort of like Jekyll and Hyde, clean-cut professional by day, degenerate weirdo by night—except that it's essentially voluntary; I don't go temporarily insane or anything, I'm just twisted."

I laughed; I couldn't help it. "You are not twisted, William, you're—"

"Wait a second," he said, and sighed as if he'd been holding his breath and was finally letting it out. He took a long drink of water. I watched him as he swallowed, wiped his mouth on the back of his hand, and stared at me, his eyes dark and hollow.

"What?" I said, really alarmed now.

"Okay," he said. "I do weird sex things." His voice sounded a little hoarse. "I mean I used to."

"What weird sex things, exactly?"

"Uh—well, with prostitutes," he began, his eyes trained on

my face for the slightest twitch or flinch. Seeing none, because I was exerting every ounce of my willpower to keep from showing my horror, he continued, "And people in S&M clubs, those dungeons. And various people I meet through personal ads, a lot of older women, couples looking for a third—"

"Prostitutes," I said wonderingly. "Dungeons. You mean you—what do you do in there, exactly?"

"I—" He looked at the rug. "Everyone's really polite and soft-spoken, actually—I don't know, Claudia, do I really have to describe it?"

I stared at him. "Tell me," I said.

"Okay, well, when someone asked me to do something, I'd do it. Is that enough detail for you?"

"No," I said. "I want to know what kinds of weird things you do. Did. Specifically."

"I'd let people tie me up—"

"Is this women, people? Or—"

"And men," he blurted.

Suddenly I didn't want to hear any more about that. "And prostitutes?"

"They're strangers. They're professional and impersonal. Like nurses; I've always liked nurses."

"What about personal ads? Who did you meet? What's it like sleeping with a couple? I've never really done that."

"Claudia. Quit interrogating me. It's weird sleeping with a couple, what do you think?"

"Have you ever slept with two men at once?"

"No." He gave me a look. "I feel even worse about all this now than I did before."

"Did you think I wouldn't be curious?"

"Last question," he said. "Let's get this over with."

"Okay. Did you ever fall in love with these people?"

He gave a dry little laugh, which I found oddly touching. "No. That was basically the whole point. Look, Claudia, the last time I did anything like that was more than three months ago. I almost—the other night after we left George's—I started to go down to Mott Street to meet a—"

"That night? The night I hit on you? Who were you meeting?"

"Some Chinese couple. But I changed my mind. The next day I made my appointment to get tested."

I stared into his face. It was the same face it had always been, the same watchful, half-smiling, heartbreakingly direct gaze.

"Oh, God, William, you slept with Gus?"

"Yes."

"And all those strangers? Why?"

"I felt useful," he said. "I felt like I was useful to them."

There was a long silence. I could hear the electricity humming through the walls. A lightbulb gave a small tick, expanding in its own heat.

"And I thought you were so perfect," I said. My mouth was dry.

"Why would you think that?"

I said insistently, as if my words could make William go back to the person I'd thought he was, "Look at this apartment. The way you are. You never even have a button missing. And in high school you were so—I don't know, such an odd bird, so antisocial and—"

"I was pissed off," he said. "All I wanted was for everyone to leave me alone, and they did."

"You were my role model," I said in despair.

"Serves you right for having a role model," he said, but gently.

"Ah," I said despondently, and drained my glass. "I can't believe it. All that agonizing about Devorah and Margot and all those normal nice corporate girls—"

"That was real, Claudia. I mean, I wasn't—"

"And always treating me to things. Buying me off. Appeasing your conscience. Allowing me my little delusions."

"No!" he said. "That's not at all what that was about."

"Leave me alone for a minute. I have to think."

I got up and went into the bathroom and locked the door. I looked into the mirror for a few minutes. My eyes looked as huge and shocked as an owl's. William had a life he'd hidden from me; he had allowed sleazeballs and perverts of every age, sex and persuasion to do whatever they wanted to him, including Gus—okay, I thought, I would pretend this was no big deal, I wasn't shocked or heartbroken, I'd never imagined anything to do with him and me except friendship. I was his friend no matter what and always would be, I'd tell him, and then I'd go home.

I strolled back out to the living room. The potted ficus cast a leafy shadow over the rug. William was on the couch, looking into his champagne glass, his legs crossed so that one foot rested on the other knee. If he knew I was there, he didn't show it. He seemed to be wholly absorbed in his glass. The light on his face was soft enough so I couldn't read his expression, but from the angle of his legs and the looseness of his shoulders as he leaned back against the cushions I got the feeling he was lost in his own thoughts, none of which had much at all to do with me. Realizing this, I was so overwhelmed that for a moment I just stood there in the doorway, staring at him.

"Hey," he said, noticing me for the first time, "you're back. Are you okay?"

"Am I okay?"

He furrowed his brow, lawyer-like, weighing his next words

as if they were coins he was placing one by one on a scale. "I'm sorry I upset you," he said. "That was the last thing I wanted to do; I just wanted to come clean. I couldn't stand lying to you any more."

"Couldn't you?" I was surprised at how calm I sounded. My whole body was shaking.

"Sit," he said, and gave the cushion next to him a comradely thump.

"No thank you," I said politely, "I prefer to stand." I continued to stand there, my hands clenching and unclenching at my sides, my tongue tapping idly and ruminatively against my teeth, looking at him.

"Quit it," he said after a moment, laughing a little. "You're making me nervous."

"Am I? Sorry."

"Sit down. Have some more champagne. It's good, by the way. How much was it?"

"I'm not telling. You asked me to bring it, I brought it."

"Yeah, but you just got—"

"It's my fucking treat," I said. "See, that's what I mean. No matter what you do during your off-hours, you have a secretary, you own this apartment and you're going to be made partner, it's just a matter of time. And meanwhile, I'm some kind of poor relation you help along, try to set up with a menial job at your firm, slip handouts to on the sly—if we wore the same size and we were both men you'd give me your old suits. I can't take it any more. It's unbearable."

I went into the kitchen, found the second bottle of champagne in the fridge and opened it over the sink.

"What are you doing in there?" he called worriedly, as if he feared I might be slitting my wrists with his bread knife.

"Slitting my wrists with your bread knife," I called back. When the foam came up I drank it, wiped my mouth with the back of my hand, took a good swig and then another one, coughing a little at the sharp bubbles in my nose. Then I went back into the living room and stood in the middle of the rug, holding the bottle by its sweaty neck. "No, really, it's no big deal. I'm glad to know the truth. I'm glad your test was negative."

He leaned forward so his elbows were on his knees and both feet were on the ground, looking up at me with his empty glass held loosely between his legs. "Can I say something?"

"It's your house."

"First of all," he said, "I had no idea you felt that way about my treating you to things. Why didn't you tell me? Why did you let me keep doing it if it bothered you? I was just trying to be gentlemanly."

"It's not that I didn't appreciate it," I said, feeling absurdly dramatic all of a sudden. "And second?"

"You're the one who put me on the pedestal. I didn't do that."

I went over and refilled his glass until the foam rose in a column that toppled and slid down the sides of the glass onto his hand. "Sure you did," I said. "You created some perfect-guy character and made me think you were him. If I'd known all along that you were a—"

"Pervert. Sit down, why don't you?"

I sat next to him. "A pervert, then I could have, I don't know, I just could have known."

"What difference would it have made?" he asked with real curiosity.

"I don't know whether or not I would have been so gaga over you if I'd known."

"Well, what about now?"

There was a silence, not uncomfortable, during which we just sat there and looked at each other. We both sighed at the same time, then laughed. Then he reached over and cupped my cheek in his palm and ran his thumb over the bridge of my nose. "You're so beautiful, Claudia," he said. "I'm sure you know."

"Am I?" I leaned my face into his hand and closed my eyes. My head nuzzled its way along his arm to his shoulder, my mouth found his neck and rested there. I could happily have drowned in the smell of his skin.

"I like this shirt you've got on," he murmured into my ear, sliding his hand over my back, my shoulder, my breast. "Very slippery."

Here I was, on William's couch with him, in his arms, on the verge of something. But the whole dynamic between us was wrong, or at least, not as I'd imagined it would be; there was that quality in his body again, the thing I'd sensed that night after George's, a cooperative elasticity which held no answering heat, just a desire to intuit and accommodate whatever I wanted.

I pulled away.

"What is it?"

"This is just—my God, how gullible am I?"

"Come back here," he said with some urgency. He had an erection; I could see it outlined in his jeans. How strange, I thought with a detached sense of wonder: I had given William an erection.

"This is just the same thing again, isn't it?" I said.

"What same thing?"

"Have you ever resisted the temptation to give someone what they want?"

"That's not what this—"

"Have you?"

He watched me, and didn't answer.

"Do you have any idea how it feels to be the beneficiary of

your sexual generosity? I'll tell you: it feels like being sent home in a cab."

"But—listen." He stopped.

"Your father cheated at poker," I said. "My mother just told me."

"Please stop taking this personally," he said swiftly and warmly. "What I told you was painful and difficult. I didn't mean to—to hurt you, Claudia, or whatever I did. I had no idea. What do you want me to say? That I'm sorry I did such an awful thing to you? But I didn't do anything to you. I did it to myself."

As he said all this, I had the awful sensation in the pit of my stomach of being taken to task. He was right. He was right, and yet I still didn't forgive him. "I want you to tell me straight out exactly how you feel about me," I said. "Whatever it is, I can take it."

"I'm not so sure about that."

"Believe me," I said through a rising panic, "after three years with Jackie, I've grown accustomed to criticism."

"I have no criticism of you at all," he said bluntly. "That's what I'm not sure you can take."

"But you think I'm wholesome."

"That's a compliment, you idiot. You're always telling me how screwed up your life is, but have you ever done anything you couldn't get out of, or walk away from, or undo somehow?"

"Yes," I said bitterly. "I fell in love with you."

"Man," he said, shaking his head. "I take it back, you're worse off than I am."

I let this sink in for a beat, then stood up and headed for the door. "Okay," I said, "I'm leaving, good night, thanks for telling me the truth, I'll talk to you soon." I didn't look back. I was out the door and down the hall and almost to the elevator when he caught up to me, grabbed my arm and whirled me around.

We looked at each other in silence; he looked ashen and unhappy, and I imagine I looked about the same.

"Let go of me," I said tersely, stabbing the down button.

"Don't go, Claudia."

"I think I've served my purpose here."

"Your purpose?"

"You think you're all cool and bad and underworld, don't you? Sneaking around, pretending to be one thing and actually being another thing entirely. What exactly did you expect me to say? Do you think I enjoy being your mother confessor? Well, I don't. I feel like I can't trust you any more. You were the one person, the only one, and now—"

"Wait, don't—"

"You needed me to think you were perfect, that's why you didn't tell me before. Well, I hope you're not sorry you blew your cover; I hope it was worth it." The elevator arrived with a little "ding." The doors slid open and I got on. "I'm not mad at you, William, I'm mad at myself."

"Liar," he said, stepping back as the doors slid closed. As I sank to the lobby I felt a heady relief. I was free. I walked out into the evening air and stood for a moment on the sidewalk, looking up at the rows and rows of dark and lighted windows, all the way up to William's floor, where his own particular windows were too high up to see. At least all my own foibles and fuckups had always been right out in the open; William's had been festering, hidden all these years behind this expensive, ugly facade. The thought of him all alone up there with his problems and regrets was a dark bruise on my frontal lobe. God damn him. He'd been so profligate with himself, his body, his affections, and all along I had been right there and he'd never even tried to touch me. Why the hell not? Why them and not me? I found to my surprise and annoyance that I was crying again. I wiped the tears away and struck out for the subway.

Before I reached the corner I was tackled from behind, brought to the sidewalk on my hands and knees and pinned there, firmly, but without menace, so I knew it wasn't a mugger or rapist. I struggled, breathing hard. He had one arm across my chest and another around my waist. "Just tell me one thing before you run away," said William into my ear. "Would you rather I'd taken advantage of you up there without telling you everything?"

It didn't hurt, my palms and knees pressed against the sidewalk, but it wasn't all that comfortable either, and his forearm was crushing one of my breasts.

"Let me the fuck up," I said intently.

Immediately he released me and we both staggered to our feet. I flew at him and shoved him so hard he went back a couple of steps. "Are you going to stop sleeping with weirdos?"

"I already have."

I shoved him again. "How could you sleep with a sleazebag like Gus?"

"He's not a sleazebag," said William. "And that was ten years ago!"

I bent over and crashed my head into his ribs; he held on to me as I pummeled him. Then he took my face in his hands and pressed his face against mine so our noses mashed together. He kissed me for such a long time, and so passionately, that I thought I might faint. I bit his lip until I thought I tasted his blood. No matter, he was disease-free.

He pulled back to look at me. "One of the senior partners at my firm lives a block away. Can you imagine his reaction if he walked by right now?"

I bit him again, then pushed him against the wall of his building, slid my hands along his arms, pulled them out to either side so we were sprawled vertically, snow-angel style, squirming and rolling around, straining to press as much of ourselves against each other as we possibly could.

"Are you trying to get me in trouble?" he asked, chuckling.

"Are you trying to invite me back upstairs?"

"God, yes."

In the elevator we clawed at each other; it was a good thing the elevator went straight to his floor without taking on any other passengers. He stepped off first and headed down the hall to his apartment, and I flew at him, landed on his back, held on and rode him to his door, then was carried down the hall, into his bedroom, and deposited on his bed.

He flung himself onto me, covered my body with his and my mouth with his. Something tickled; I couldn't breathe. I started to laugh and he gave me a light pinch on the earlobe.

"Relax," he said. "Jesus, you're squirrelly."

But I couldn't stop giggling. Everything was funny: his confession, my reaction, our being here like this, the way his mouth felt on mine—warm, intimate, hungry—"Stop just a minute. Please. I just have to catch my breath."

Very slowly and with all of his attention, he freed one of my breasts from that ridiculous shirt, covered it with his mouth and breathed warm air on it. Without undue awkwardness or effort, we helped each other take our clothes off. The grainy light in the room was just enough to see by. I admired William's limbs in silence, raising myself above him to look down through the tunnel our two bodies made. He was sinewy and narrow-hipped. His thighs, from this angle, were rounded mounds. His skin against mine was smooth and cool, except for the extremely hot clublike thing attached to his groin, poking me blindly in the abdomen. I reached down and touched it

243

for the first time; doing this to William was so purely strange that I inhaled sharply as I grasped it.

"This feels so incestuous," I said.

His eyes glinted evilly.

"Pervert," I said, laughing.

He held my hips, positioned me over him, and then he was inside me. We stared at each other, hardly breathing, then eased into each other. I felt like a starving person at a banquet, overwhelmed by sudden plenitude, beset by a greed so vast it made me feel a bit demented. I devoured him, gorged myself, wallowed in gluttony. William gave himself up to my hands and mouth, both of us laughing a little at how good it felt.

After I'd vented as much of the past year of frustration and deprivation as could be expelled at one go, something shifted between us. We gazed at each other, our faces nearly expressionless, while our bodies did whatever they wanted. The half-light made everything feel both slowed down and slightly unreal. There was an immense stillness right at my core that wasn't any particular emotion, it was just myself, wholly present, a more concretely and intensely pleasurable sensation than anything I'd ever experienced before. I burst out laughing again from sheer pleasure. He smiled back at me, cupped my face in his hands, looking as stunned and replete as I felt.

Near dawn, without a word, he turned me over and nestled against my back, curled himself around me, one hand holding a breast as casually as if he owned it. He fell asleep, breathing against the back of my neck. How could he lie there so calmly? How could he sleep? All my muscles were twitching. I cast back over the night, replayed every detail of every moment from my tentative arrival onward. Somehow, magically it seemed to me now, I had managed to end up here in William's bed with him. I had very little experience with fulfillment and joy; I found them, as I found most new things, nerve-wracking and potentially dangerous.

I made myself think in lurid and explicit detail about what William had done with hookers, Gus, middle-aged couples and masked women with whips; the images rolled by, a seedy film in my head. More strongly than my own shock and disappointment I felt his loneliness, how degraded and lost he must have felt, no matter how much pleasure these encounters might have afforded him on another level. What surprised me most, in the end, was how little what he'd told me surprised me, now that it was beginning to sink in. It all jibed in an odd way with what I'd already known about William, which struck me now, lying here, as a lot more than I knew about anyone else. We each knew the worst about the other, I thought, for whatever that was worth.

What was he going to make of this? What did I make of it? What were we to each other now? From here on in, it was going to be painful and awkward between us; it was inevitable, that was the way it always went. I already dreaded tomorrow. Maybe he would regret all this as soon as he woke up; maybe I would. Oh, God, maybe I should just get up and go home now and spare us both.

Slowly and carefully I slid my limbs away from his, got out of bed, dressed in the now-daylit room. He didn't wake up. On the coffee table in the living room were two empty bottles of champagne, the bottle of mineral water and two half-empty flutes with no coasters. I carried them all into the kitchen and left them on the counter by the sink, then wiped the coffee table with a damp sponge. I silently let myself out, closed the door of his apartment behind me. I heard the click of the automatic lock.

In William's elevator I stared at my reflection. I looked as unabashedly gorgeous as a starlet: rumpled, bright-eyed, cheeks glowing, lips rosy and bee-stung. My body had a slightly swollen look about it, a soft, sexy puffiness. I decided to walk home. The sun felt good; it was a relief to be outside on the street, in the quotidian bustle of delivery vans and late-night partygoers getting out of taxis and Korean delis doing a brisk trade in newspapers and coffee. The air was fresh and bright. Leaves on young saplings growing between sidewalk and street had just begun to bud; a few early crocuses were opening. My mood lifted higher the further I got from William's building. I almost ran across the park, so glad I'd left William's it was all I could do not to burst out in wild, triumphant laughter, imagining his relief at finding me gone.

chapter thirteen

The Adult Editorial Department of Wilder and Sons, Publishers, was on the sixteenth floor of a medium-sized skyscraper. I landed in an overstuffed violet chair in the waiting room. The receptionist was so charismatically ugly I stared at her as directly as I could without offending her: her upper lip beaked over her lower, her hooded eyes were set in dark rings, and her head emerged from between her shoulder blades. She whispered into the phone; audible words stood out from the general hiss in twos and threes: "told her yet . . . he's been so . . . just awful . . . screaming like a . . ." I strained to hear the rest.

William hadn't called me and I hadn't called him, and now it was Monday and my whole chest felt aching and bruised, as if it had been pummeled from the inside repeatedly and determinedly.

I shared the plush violet waiting area with three others,

a bald sunburned man with a paprika beard who looked as though he could have captained the *Kon-Tiki*; an intensely thin woman quivering slightly like a greyhound, black fedora artfully crowning a long silver sheet of hair; and a young babyish man with pursed lips. They shared an eerie conformity of self-absorption, like figures in a wax museum or a lunatic asylum. The receptionist's phone bleated twice. "Hold on a second. Yes? Okay, I'll tell her." She looked over at me with eyes like black ancient stones over which the hinged hemispheres of her eyelids slid together and apart. "Claudia Steiner? Janine will be right out."

I gathered my bag and coat and made sure my blouse was buttoned properly. A fat, red-haired young woman appeared in the doorway. "Claudia?" she said doubtfully to the woman with aluminum-foil hair.

"Janine?" I said with equal skepticism.

"Oh!" she said, and laughed. "You're Claudia. Come on in."

The framed book jacket of *The High-Heeled Gumshoe* hung halfway along the hallway she led me through. On the front was an artfully out-of-focus photograph of a model who was supposed to be the young Genevieve. She wore a formfitting sheath that gloved her bony frame; her fashionable slouch made her hipbones jut upward at an angle. An absinthe-colored wash (foggy rain, overhead streetlamp) gave her skin a hepatitic tinge. She appeared to be too weak to stand up straight, burdened by the demands of her genre.

Gil Reeve was exactly as I'd thought he'd be: choleric, well padded, his face mottled like a good rump roast. Small crimson veins spidered along the bulb of his nose and threaded through the whites of his eyes. He offered me a warm, thick hand, which I shook with a nervous expression I did my best to ameliorate into a smile. I felt tongue-tied and woolly-headed.

"So you are an ingenue after all," he said in that mellow, ironic drawl I knew so well. "Come on in."

He closed the door of his office behind us.

"Thanks so much for agreeing to meet with me on such short notice," I said as I sank into a chair that seemed to have no bottom. My knees rose around my ears; I resisted the urge to flail. I pulled myself out and moved over one seat to the right, tugging my skirt down.

He leaned back in his own chair, his neat football of a stomach rolling a little under his shirt. "What can I do for you?"

I wrestled momentarily with the slippery eel that was my reason for being here, then pulled from my bag the computer disk I'd stolen from Jackie. I held it up. He peered at it over his reading glasses. The sudden meaty impassiveness of his face made me feel as if I had to talk very loudly to penetrate it.

"This contains the only copy of Jackie's new book," I said.

"I was hoping she'd deliver it in the usual way."

"She doesn't have it any more," I said. "I took it with me when she fired me. I didn't steal it, because it's mine. I wrote it. Here."

I pulled out the agreement I'd signed three years ago and offered it to him, prepared to explain that it wasn't legally binding, but instead of taking it, he swiveled around in his chair to face the window. I waited. His phone buzzed three times and then stopped. Down in the street, an ambulance wailed against a honking wall of traffic. I thought of the passenger, dying in all that noise. Then I noticed that the top of Gil's head was bouncing gently; I heard a small snort, like the sound of a bathtub plug being pulled. When he turned back around, his eyebrows were still knit with mirth, although the rest of his face was all business.

"I take it," he said dryly, "that you're here to sell me the book."

We looked right at each other for a brief moment of charged silence. "Look," I said. "How would you feel if someone else had been taking credit for your work for three years? I know she paid me, I know it was the deal from the beginning. But—" This wasn't coming out right. I started all over again. "You know I can write," I said earnestly. "Jackie's books are the proof."

He burst out laughing.

I had to laugh a little too. "Okay," I said, "but at least you know I can string words together. Eventually I want to write my own books, but for now I'd settle for some money in exchange for this disk. Nothing major. Just enough to bail me out."

He silenced me with a raised hand. "First of all," he said crisply, "the shocking fact that you wrote this book and the one before it is pretty much common knowledge. Second, if you were anticipating my slavering thirst to get my hands on that manuscript you might be disappointed to learn that the general public is finding accounts of unapologetically lavish lifestyles increasingly distasteful. It's not the eighties any more; the tide has turned. People don't care about the super-rich unless they're incest survivors or alcoholics or lost all their money. We don't forward negative letters to Jackie, but they're becoming fairly regular. In fact, a certain amount of energy has gone into protecting her from several unpleasant truths, among them the fact that this will be her last book, and it won't earn out a tenth of its advance. Also, she's becoming something of a laughingstock among our younger editorial staff. It would be a relief, frankly, if she were unable to meet the terms of her contract. Of course, in that case, she would be required to return her advance. Her agent is aware of this situation; I gather that she herself is not."

I opened and closed my mouth.

"It goes without saying that if she submits an acceptable draft, we will abide by our agreement and publish it."

"I see."

"You may find that she's willing to listen to whatever terms you've come up with. I think you're wasting your time here."

"Poor Jackie," I said in a rush.

He nodded over his bifocals. We looked at each other for a moment. I felt like a wriggling bug at the business end of a microscope.

"Thank you for meeting with me," I said, and stood up. He shook the hand I extended to him, but I wondered whether he wiped his own hand on a napkin as soon as I'd left his office. I wouldn't have blamed him.

The receptionist was talking once again with great intensity into her telephone. The chairs were all empty now. As I went by her desk, I was pierced by the keen ray of her gaze: here she sat, as steady as a turtle in the maelstrom of her life. I went soberly out to the elevator.

I walked over to Fifth Avenue and made my way up to Fifty-ninth Street to sit for a while on a bench at the bottom edge of Central Park. Nearly bare trees struggled out of the mud, their branches fuzzed with the tenderest green. Horses stood in line along the sidewalk, hitched to buggies, minding their own unfathomable business and shitting at will, big soft grassy dumps that billowed against the asphalt. A flock of pigeons lifted off into the trees like one huge bird that shattered to bits against the underside of the branches. A man lay upwind of me on another bench. He smelled like grapefruit or paint thinner, the bitter metallic stench of ketones, unmetabolized alcohol digesting his body from within. Some bio-chemist I'd met in a bar had explained the process to me. I felt a rush of fear, thinking of the chain of events that had brought him to this pass.

After a while, I crossed the street to the small plaza where the garish bright-gold monument to General Sherman stood. I circled it a few times, compelled by its frank gilded vulgarity, and by the giant testicles dangling from the general's stallion. A black pigeon perched like a winged helmet on the top of the general's bright-gold head, unfazed by the evident speed at which his horse galloped behind the swiftly flying angel leading Sherman God knew where. She held an olive branch that looked like a gigantic feather, and she looked sly, as if she knew something Sherman didn't. I thought for a moment about various kinds of victory: pyrrhic, hollow, hard-won, certain, winged, final.

The memory of my meeting with Gil was like a tribe of stinging ants just under my skin. I decided to walk all the way uptown. As I strode through the fresh blue evening, I permitted myself to imagine that I was a nice, well-adjusted, gainfully employed person going home to William, who'd made something homey and nourishing for dinner, roast chicken and steamed broccoli, and had opened a bottle of good red wine. On the whole, as fantasies went, this one was pretty good. It acted like a jet pack on my back; before I knew it I had walked nearly all the way home. But it all crash-landed as I stood in line at the corner Chinese take-out place and read the menu I already knew by heart, having eaten everything on it at least three times.

I trudged up the stairs to my apartment carrying my white paper bag of overcooked vegetables in slimy gray goo. I kicked my door open and strode into my little domain, turned on the light and beheld several fat, calm roaches nosing their unruffled way along the floor, the sink edge, the counter, the wall. I stamped my foot and they vanished reluctantly and desultorily, without fear. I had been deposed, toppled, eliminated from their cosmogony in the course of one day.

Delilah lay right smack dab in the middle of my bed, licking herself. Her mouth on her nether parts made a wet clicking noise that disturbed me intensely.

And there were no blinks on my answering machine. The light held steady, like a watchful eye looking straight into my soul.

I set my bag of food on the table and reached for the phone.

Frieda answered, laughing, on the first ring. Her voice sounded warm and ardent. "Oh good, I'm so glad you called back, I forgot to tell you—"

"Frieda?"

She paused. "Who is this?"

"It's Claudia."

"Claudia, oh my God, hi!"

"Is this a bad time?"

"No, no, how are you?"

"I'm—I'm okay. How are you?"

"Great."

There was a silence. The wires hummed. "How's Cecil?"

"Great. Things are just great. I feel so boring now. I have not that much to report. Isn't happiness dull?"

"I wouldn't know," I said with a wry laugh. It came out wrong.

Her voice changed immediately to a treacly coo. "Oh no, really? Why, what's wrong?"

"Forget it. Tell me what's going on with you. How's your work?"

"Remember all those things I kept picking up off the street?

Well, I've started a whole new series, using them. They're supposed to be funny and beautiful, though, not some heavy moralistic eco-thing. I feel like I'm making finger paintings and mud pies again."

"I sense Cecil's influence," I said, trying to keep my tone light. It was very difficult. I felt sour and jealous and lonely.

"Damn it, everyone keeps saying that. Like I can't change on my own?"

"I feel like we haven't talked in years, Frieda."

"The phone works both ways, you know," she said, but lightly.

"You're right," I said. "I'm sorry I haven't called. Do you want to get together sometime soon?"

"Actually, we're leaving for San Francisco first thing tomorrow morning. Cecil's band has a gig there, and then we're taking a little vacation. Maybe we'll rent a car and drive up the coast and go camping."

I couldn't say anything for a minute. I could see the two of them sitting shoulder-to-shoulder by a campfire on the beach. The cliffs along Highway 1. The fog, the Pacific, the stars, the golden light. "Well, roast a weenie for me. Have a great time, Frieda, I mean it. I'm so happy for you."

"Thanks," she said, her voice softening. "I'm sorey I haven't called you in so long. It's just, I don't know, things have changed."

"You mean you've been taken over by aliens and forced to behave like half a happy couple."

"I'll give you a call when I get back."

When I hung up and turned around to look at the bed, Delilah was still there. She was watching me as steadily as the answering-machine light, but she had two eyes to its one, and hers could really see. I sat down next to her cautiously. She stayed where she was. I touched her spine with my fingertips. I stroked her, once and then again. A few strands of fur rose and hung there, riding the current. She lay back on her haunches and slid her eyes half-shut, licked her chops, and then began to purr. I barely breathed as I nuzzled my hand around her ears, and when she butted her head against my hand I almost burst into tears.

When I awoke, I was curled around an empty space on the bed; the whole place reeked of vegetable chow mein. I stretched, got up and threw the take-out bag into the garbage, found my keys and wallet, put on a jacket and went out. I threw the garbage in the can on the sidewalk and headed toward Broadway.

I took myself out to dinner at a bistro on a corner, where I was shown to a cozy little table with a lit candle in a glass jar and cloth napkins; the waiter whisked away the other place setting and presented me with a menu as thick as a program. I didn't need to look at it; I knew what I wanted. After a salad of baby greens and a glass of the Cabernet the maître d' had recommended, I tucked into a plate of roast chicken with mashed potatoes and broccoli. I finished with a mousse au chocolat and a snifter of an old brandy so potent it almost vaporized on my lips. When I'd eaten and drunk everything, I put down my napkin and signaled for the check. When it came I glanced at it without blanching, paid in cash and tipped generously.

I strolled down to Times Square, looking into the faces of the people I passed as if I were new in town and had never seen anyone like them before. As I made my way back up Broadway, I passed a movie theater showing something I wanted to see; by chance, the last showing started in fifteen minutes. I bought a ticket, went in and found a seat, and sat quietly, thinking my thoughts, until the lights went down and the movie started.

I was sucked into the story within the first five minutes,

and remained wholly engrossed for almost two hours. When the lights came back up, I blinked and yawned and looked around, utterly surprised to find myself here in the theater. It had been so long since I'd seen a movie or read a novel; I'd forgotten the salubrious power of a good story. I walked home, grave but carefree.

The moment I woke up the next morning, I cleared my throat, brushed a kernel of sleep from my eye, sat up straight on the edge of my bed with my feet on the floor, then picked up the phone and called Jackie, my heart fluttering at the base of my throat. Just because I felt sorry for her didn't mean I wasn't still scared of her. But for the first time where Jackie was concerned, my sympathy overrode my terror: she deserved her book back, whatever good it would do her now. It certainly hadn't done me any.

Her telephone rang a second time. I hoped she was awake; I wanted to get this over with. I was going to pretend that I'd forgotten to transfer the backup disk to the hard drive because I'd been so flustered when she fired me, which involved the further pretense that I'd been saving the new book to the disk rather than the hard drive all along, which actually was no more or less ludicrous than any of the fabrications I'd spun for her over the years.

"Claudia," she said then. "My goodness, am I glad to hear your voice!"

I hadn't expected this reaction. "How are you?" I said through a small but solid frog in my throat.

"Well, my dear. I have had just such a time." She laughed. I heard a hollowness in her laughter, a hard bright empty undertone that could have meant anything. "That Goldie has left me in quite a state."

"She left you," I said, confused. "You mean she quit?"

"We decided not to continue," said Jackie firmly. "We didn't work together at all well, it was nothing like with you and Margot; we had no rapport at all."

"She's a tough cookie."

"Well, she really is! Anyway, she's not coming back, and I'm through with that agency that sent her; I spoke to some woman there who told me Goldie was the best they had, so they couldn't send me someone better, and she was pretty rude about it. I was quite upset. I suppose by now you've found a job."

I gaped into the receiver. Impossible. There was no way.

"Actually, not yet," I said.

"Here's the thing. I'm leaving today, I'll be gone a week, that tedious Long Island thing with Mr. Blevins, and I must have someone to bring in my mail and answer anything urgent. You're the only one I can count on to do it properly."

"I am?"

"Well, you know, Claudia," she said. "We've had our difficulties. But—I've been thinking about what you said as you left the other day."

"You have?"

"You know," she blurted, "maybe I have been too hard on you sometimes."

"That's true," I said warmly. "I haven't been the best secretary, though."

"We could both try a little harder to understand each other."

"Yes," I said, absolutely amazed, "maybe we could."

There was a pause, not uncomfortable. "I've been trying to work on the scene we discussed last Monday, do you know the one I mean?"

She had not been trying to work on that scene. Obviously

she hadn't even tried to open the files. She had made no effort to continue the book on her own even though the deadline was coming up in three weeks, and she never missed a deadline, or rather, I didn't. She hadn't even known the book was gone.

I paused. "Look, Jackie," I said, "I know you didn't work on that scene."

"I did, I spent an entire afternoon going over those notes we made," she began, then abruptly cut herself off. I waited, feeling amused and sympathetic; poor Jackie, she hated to be caught in a lie, or rather a half-truth, more than anything. "I have some ideas for the ending," she said defiantly.

"So do I," I said.

"You do?" She sounded pathetically eager. "Oh, Claudia, that's wonderful, I'm so excited to hear them. Could you meet with me this morning? I'm leaving at one o'clock, but I could see you any time before that."

"I'm busy today, actually," I lied, because I didn't feel one bit like seeing her today, "but I'm free tomorrow; I could come in the morning and go through your mail, then take the laptop home and write." I was going back to work for Jackie. Her stupid junk mail; the smell of her vestibule; all those awful, oppressive outfits I'd allowed myself to believe I'd never have to wear again.

She sighed. Instead of the snazzy new secretary she'd dreamed of, she was stuck with the same old unreliable one. "And you'll call me with every single important letter or message I get? Every one; especially interesting invitations to dinner parties, or letters from important people. Don't assume you know what's important, I want to hear every one."

Oh, God, what was I thinking? "Don't worry, Jackie, I know what to do."

"Please fax me anything that looks urgent. And the pages you write; I want those at the end of each day so I can look them over, it's terribly terribly important that we finish this book as soon as possible."

"Okay," I said, twisting the phone cord around my forearm, pressing it savagely into the skin so it made a mark. "Have a good trip, Jackie. See you when you get back."

"Thank you, Claudia dear," she said. "See you next Monday."

When the phone rang again a few minutes later, I let the machine pick up, and was very glad I had when I heard my landlord's voice. "Claudia, it's Miller again. You haven't returned any of the messages I've left you over the past few weeks, so I'm assuming you've decided not to resolve this in an amicable manner. So against my will I find that the time has come to play hardball. I need that rent money by this afternoon or I'll have to initiate eviction proceedings. You leave me no alternative. I'll be stopping by the building in a little while, so maybe we can have a chat then. Otherwise you'll be hearing from my lawyers. All right, honey, sorry it has to be this way, I hate to do this to anyone, especially a sweet young lady like yourself."

"I can't pay the rent!" I cried out to the roaches like the heroine of a melodrama, but not one of them stepped forward heroically. The sound of Delilah's determined crunching behind me was making me hungry enough to join her there at her bowl, but instead I got dressed and went to the deli on Broadway.

The air outside was alive. Above the sun-washed buildings the sky was a dense, plastic blue; directly over New Jersey a few clean white clouds lay in parallel ridges as thin as eels or ribs. The sun seemed to come from every direction at once so that the whole street was drenched with light and there were no shadows anywhere. The wind held only a whisper of coldness, like one stream of basement air leaking into a warm room.

As I stood in line at the deli with my English muffins and orange juice, I saw Margot Spencer outside in old jeans and a baggy sweater, trying to tie a very large black Labrador puppy to a lamppost. She had her hair in a ponytail, and she looked almost plain for once, so plain I didn't recognize her until I'd registered her small, impeccably shaped head. The puppy wasn't cooperating. When he jumped up to lick her face, she dropped the leash to regain her balance and he almost got away and bolted into the traffic. She caught the end of the leash just in time to drag him back. I took my change and bag of groceries and went outside. "Hey, Margot," I said, "can I give you a hand?"

"Please," she called back; she didn't see who I was until it was too late to retract her acceptance of my offer.

I knelt down, held the dog's collar and looked him right in the eye. "Hold still, you big galoot," I said firmly. I didn't have much experience with dogs, but I'd read that they responded well to alpha behavior. The puppy cocked his head as if he were waiting for me to play, but he held still. Margot secured the leash with a good knot, then had to step back and acknowledge me. This she did with her usual grace.

"Well, thanks," she said, wiping her hands on the seat of her jeans as if she'd got them dirty holding the leash. "I appreciate your help, Claudia. He was about to get run over."

"You're very welcome," I said. "It was the least I could do."

We looked at each other a moment. Were we going to acknowledge my recent mistakes and get past them, or were we going to say a curt good-bye and be enemies? I had thought all along that this was up to Margot, but the struggle with her puppy had leveled the playing field.

"I mean," I went on, "after everything that's happened lately."

"What's happened lately?" She brushed a shiny strand of dark hair away from her nose.

Good question. I wasn't sure either. Had Gus told her I'd called her names, or was she still upset about the whole dead-Jackie thing, or both, or was there something else I didn't know about? "I know you're very loyal to Jackie," I said slowly, hazarding a guess, watching her face for clues. "But she just called me and hired me again. I think she's forgiven me."

"Jackie always forgives everyone," Margot said with a hint of a smile. "She can never remember anything long enough to hold a grudge."

"I know," I said. "Lucky for me."

There was a silence. She seemed to be waiting for me to say something.

"What did I do?" I blurted, amazing myself.

"What do you mean?"

"We used to be friends. Well, friendly. Something's changed. I think it's because of something I said or did."

The whites of her eyes were perfectly clear, so purely white they had the bluish undertone of flat white latex paint. Her skin was equally flawless, a uniform cream color with a tinge of rose on her cheeks and lips: she had not one blemish or scar, not even a freckle. I had never realized it before, but she had the same sinless, slightly mocking air as my mother's shepherdess figurine, that purse-lipped maid in dirndl and frock eternally leading her snow-white fluffballs to some Edenic pasture.

"You haven't done anything," she said.

"Really?" I said dubiously. "Then it's just my imagination?"

"Well." She paused, then added with obvious reluctance, "No, actually, not entirely."

"Then what?"

261

She looked out at the traffic, which moved along smoothly, as if the snarling, honking, fist-raising winter had never happened, as if those rock-hard banks of sooty snow, those clouds of reeking steam that came boiling up from underground to envelop windshields, had never caused one suburban mother to shriek bloody murder at a single cabdriver: it was springtime in Manhattan. It was clear that she didn't want to have to accuse me of anything; she didn't want to be having this conversation at all. She wanted to go about her business and never think about me again.

I would have let her, but the sky was as blue and shiny as a tarp, and the air was so surreally bright I got the idea that nothing could hurt me right now. Cheerfully I waited, prepared to stand there all day. She was going to have to tell me, because I wasn't going anywhere until she did.

"To be perfectly honest," she went on after a moment, still avoiding my eye, "it's just that I think you're—I can't believe I'm saying this, you're going to hate me—"

"Say it," I commanded, using the same alpha technique I'd used on her dog.

"It's because you're a drunk," she said apologetically.

"A what?" I gasped. "I'm a *what?*"

"Honestly, Claudia," she said. "It's not personal, it's just that people who drink upset me. I can't be around them. I have to keep my distance, for personal reasons that have nothing to do with you at all. My own stuff." She looked small and contrite, a little frightened, as if I were about to clobber her with a bottle of hooch.

"Well," I stammered, "I drink, sure, I drink, but so does everyone, and anyway, it's recreational drinking, I mean it's not like I'm an—"

"Really, I swear," she said. "I'm not accusing you or judging you. I just have to protect myself."

"Against *me?*"

We looked at each other mutely for a moment. I recalled then that her memoir had contained numerous scenes in which her British expatriate parents and their friends drove off in Jags and Mercedeses after cocktail hour to dine at the club. Gin-and-tonics in the summer, Scotch in the winters—it had all sounded so romantic, all those sexy, glamorous, decadent grownups going off into the night in a cloud of laughter and cigarettes, leaving Margot alone with the nanny. But now it dawned on me for the first time that Margot might not have liked her own upbringing any more than I'd liked mine. And that she had been avoiding me not because of something I had done, which would have given me cause for regret and apology, but because of who I was, which was beyond my control. All right, now I knew. It was time to be on my way.

I made myself smile at her. "That's a great dog, by the way."

"I just got him," she said. "He terrifies me."

"You just have to show him who's boss," I said encouragingly. "He wants you to."

"Maybe," she replied faintly.

I turned and headed for home, my cheeks burning in the brisk wind. A drunk was someone to be reckoned with, someone interesting and far-gone. I should have been alarmed and ashamed, should have considered joining all those chain-smokers in church basements—I knew what I was supposed to feel. But the sunlight covered the street with the clear healthy gold of ale, the brownstone faces were burnished the toast-warm color of bourbon in candlelight, the air was clear and lively as gin, and something leapt in me, a persistent little flame of self. Drunks didn't set themselves apart, didn't look down on anyone—they sat shoulder-to-shoulder with everyone in the bar, awash in fellow-feeling, the roar of the surf in their heads so loud it made time stop, washed away everything except whatever was right here, everyone bobbing together on a sweet, warm flood of oceanic feeling. It could either drown or sustain you, depending. As I burbled along the sidewalk, filled with the liquidity of life, a line or two by a fellow drunk blew in on the breeze like a yellow butterfly, darting into view then out—"O world, I cannot hold thee close enough! Thy winds, thy wide grey skies—" that was enough; the sky was blue, it was spring, so the rest of it didn't fit. But I felt a sudden love for the whole shining fragile globe; I would have hugged it hard enough to deflate it if it had been the size of a beach ball.

chapter fourteen

As I went through the door of my building, someone else came in hard on my heels. I turned blithely to hold the door open for whatever neighbor was behind me and beheld instead the big buffalo head of my landlord. He saw me, too, which was potentially calamitous. "Miller," I said stupidly. "I've been away for months."

"I'm glad to see you're still alive, sweetheart," he said, crowding me into a corner of the entryway. "I was worried. I've been leaving you messages."

"Yes, well, I lost my job and had to go out of town to take care of my—my aunt, who's got a brain tumor, she needed me to—" I tried to avert my nose from the stink of his aftershave. "Anyway, sorry about the rent."

He repositioned himself to circumvent my nostrils' escape ploy; his dewlaps quivered with another silent fart of cologne that went straight to my stomach and roiled around the emptiness with all the enzymes and acids. "No hard feelings. Can you get it to me by this afternoon?"

"I'm not sure," I said. "I'll see what I can do."

"February, March, April. Three months." He held up the appropriate number of fingers. His chest hairs were pushing like insect antennae through his shirt's pores.

"The thing is, I don't have any money, Miller, I lost my job."

"Did you? Aw, I hate to lose a good tenant like you. I was just on my way up to see you, actually, so you saved me a trip all the way upstairs. Listen, get me one month's rent today, and I'll wait a week on the other two. Otherwise—" He spread his hands to show how helpless he would be otherwise.

"Today," I repeated. There was about half a month's rent left in my checking account out of the money I'd stolen from Jackie. William would have lent me the rest in a heartbeat, and my mother would have given it to me outright, but I preferred not to ask either of them for anything right now. I could have "borrowed" from Jackie, I supposed, as an advance on my salary, but the thought of her reaction if she found out—"I'll see what I can do," I said again, as if I were planning a flurry of financial activity upstairs.

"Okay, I got someone else to see in the building," he said. "So I'll come by in ten, fifteen minutes and pick it up."

"Listen, Miller," I began.

"Ten minutes? See you then." His broad backside heaved itself up a flight of stairs. His knock on someone's door echoed through the stairwell. As soon as the door opened to admit him and closed behind him, I raced upstairs, the back of my throat meeting my intestines in a clenched handshake. He wasn't going to evict me physically today, he couldn't; these things took time, there were legal channels to be gone through, possession was nine-tenths of whatever, I'd get the money together eventually. He couldn't throw me out of my own home; I didn't even have to answer the door when he knocked, I could pretend I'd gone back to my aunt's brain tumor.

Jeans, toothbrush, legal pad, pen, cat food, cat litter, what else? A couple of paperback poetry anthologies, three shirts, shampoo, bras and underwear. I shoved everything into my enormous old canvas backpack, not breathing. I didn't have time to think it all out clearly, but I knew with a blinding flash of instinct, as much as I'd ever known anything, that the most important thing in the world right now was to get out and stay out and never have to tell Miller another lie again as long as I lived. It was time to move on. I was finished here for good. I found Delilah's cat carry box, which she hadn't been in since she was a kitten going to the vet for her shots; she'd loathed it then and there was no reason to think her feelings had changed in the meantime, but of course I couldn't leave her here because for some reason, I wasn't ever coming back. To my amazement, she went in without a peep, as if she knew.

I took a last look around at the room, saw it as clearly as if I'd never seen it before. I hadn't really lived here, had I, not the way other people inhabited their homes. No, this room had been more along the lines of a holding cell, a way station. Or a launching pad. That was it, a launching pad, that was a much more comforting way of looking at it, as if I were about to fire up my engines and scorch the earth.

In the last seconds before blastoff I remembered William's crystal tumbler. I found it in the cupboard: even though I was in a hell of a hurry, I stood still for a moment and held it to the weak light, turned it so the facets winked and glinted. It looked like Cinderella's other glass slipper, the one that had come home with her while its mate stayed behind at the ball. I wrapped it in a sock and packed it, then turned my attention to the heap of unpaid bills I'd been toying with for weeks. If I left them here, I could just forget about them, because I wasn't leaving any forwarding address, but the same blind instinct that was commanding me to leave told me sternly and in no uncertain terms that those bills were coming with me. So I packed them into an outside pocket and zipped it shut.

I shouldered my pack, picked up Delilah's box, then abandoned ship without a backward glance, nine years of my life left behind, the rest of it a cipher in front of me. I left my bag of groceries on my armchair; how was I going to toast an English muffin when I was leaving my toaster behind? As I locked the door behind me, the phone rang. On my way down the first flight of stairs I heard my own voice explaining that I was unable to come to the phone right now. I wished this narration would follow me like a film voice-over, but it stayed behind with all my work outfits, the shed skins of whatever former self I was leaving behind.

I heard Miller's amiable mumble behind the door of 2B, getting louder as I passed as if he were just on his way out. His aftershave stood guard on the landing like a pit bull. I made it down the last flight and out the door. I stood on the street while people plowed around me and jostled Delilah's box, unwilling to lose their hard-won momentum by cutting a wider swath around us. Here it was. I had gone over the waterfall without a barrel. The man I always gave quarters to was sitting as usual in his doorway behind his sign, and looked up as I went by. I shook my head and kept going.

Jackie had said she was leaving at one, which was in less than half an hour. Once she was gone, I could go to her house and raid her fridge and figure out what to do next. I carried my cargo to a bench on an island in the center of Broadway, across from the pigeon-feeder, who was hard at it. I grinned at him. He was completely out of his tree and had nothing in the world but his blanket and some bread crumbs, but he was a free man. There were worse lives you could have. He caught me looking, and without acknowledging me began to improvise: a dip, some soft-shoe, a batlike flap of his blanket. The pigeons stayed right with him, pecking at the small handful he let fly every now and then.

Out of nowhere, I was hit by an idea for a novel I might write. I saw the whole story laid out before me like a meal in a restaurant, probably because I was near starving by that point, and my low blood sugar was making me a little daft—there it hung like a mirage, superimposed on the pigeon man, who was now directing traffic, or at least he thought he was.

When I next looked at my watch, it was after one o'clock. I hailed a cab and gave Jackie's address to the driver, whose turban looked suspiciously like Madame Sosostris's; he repeated back a garbled rendition and we were off. He muscled the car's nose into a clot of traffic, honked at a chubby jogger crossing against the light, and said, "God damn it" with an odd cadence. I craned my neck to spot openings in the next lane, blanched as the meter clicked off another quarter so soon after the last one, pounded an imaginary accelerator as we burst forward into a clear stretch of street.

In front of Jackie's I allowed Ralph to help me out of the cab. "Hello, Claudia," he said warily. He looked spiffy today, his uniform buttons shining in the sun, his hair freshly clipped.

"Hello, Ralph," I said. "Did I miss Jackie?"

"She just left," he said.

We looked at each other.

"I wanted to explain about the other day," I said.

"I heard she canned you," he said with a grudging smile.

"Only for a little while," I said, laughing. "Did she mention I was working for her again?"

"She didn't say anything about it." He carried Delilah's box through the door for me. "Actually, she didn't mention you'd be coming by today at all."

"She might have forgotten to tell anyone. You know how she is. Can I run these things up? I've got a key."

He shot a glance at the cat carry box he'd set on the marble floor, obviously full of cat, and the backpack, obviously mine: just the merest flick of his eyeball, since he didn't want to be rude. I carried everything into the open elevator and prayed to a deity newly invented just for this. Delilah scratched the floor of her box; her back humped up against the lid and she let out a small pleading yowl I wanted to echo, a yowl which must have confirmed beyond a doubt Ralph's correct suspicion that all was not kosher here. He stood deliberating by the elevator control panel: he had no idea what I was up to, he didn't trust me anyway, the super would fire him. He owed me nothing. But his fellow-feeling prevailed in the end, which was exactly what I'd banked on. "Up you go, then," he said. The doors slid shut and I rose slowly to the fourth floor. "Good man," I whispered to myself, vowing never to forget him, no matter how far my fortunes might take me.

Jackie's apartment smelled as if the windows had been sealed shut for years. I stepped inside and inhaled a thick stew of perfume and dead flowers and trapped city air. It was dark and chilly in here, and too quiet. I freed Delilah, who bolted stiffly for a corner of the living room, then I opened the dining room curtains. The roses on the table had hardened into little knobs on brittle stalks; the fallen petals were as brown as old banana peels. Juanita must have got the sack right after I did. I carried the whole mess into the kitchen and ran it through the garbage disposal. The grinding din did me good: it reminded me that life's functions continued through fair times and foul.

The refrigerator offered a compost heap of half-rotted iceberg lettuce and green peppers in the vegetable crisper, a bottle of expensive champagne, some flat seltzer, condiments in jars with hardened brown stuff around the rims, and a loaf of extra-thin sliced gourmet white bread. The freezer was much friend-lier: four frozen lasagna dinners, a half-gallon of peach frozen yogurt, a bag of mixed vegetables and a wad of hamburger meat. I unwrapped one of the frozen lasagnas and stuck it into the toaster oven to bake, then popped open the champagne and took a few swigs. This reminded me of William, which gave me an intense pain in my sternum that radiated outward in spokes like a red-hot bicycle wheel.

I wandered into Jackie's bedroom, which seemed to be filled with the wreckage left behind by a teenager going on her first date. Bottles and pots sprawled on her vanity as if she'd swirled a hand through them. Drawers had been left open, stockings hanging out like arms and legs dangling over the side of a boat. Her bed was covered with a tangle of hangers and crumpled dresses. More from an excess of nervous energy than anything else, I began hanging up her dresses, folding the stockings, closing the bureau drawers, righting the bottles on the vanity. The very act of doing this caused a tender shoot of some wholly new feeling to poke a pointy green head up through the loam. I felt protective. Of Jackie, of all people. She would have hated to come home to find all her things where she'd left them; I knew exactly how it would have made her feel: let down, uncared-for, lonely. No matter that it was her own fault for being too cheap to hire a full-time maid—she couldn't help that, it was just the way she was. Poor Jackie, she had such a shallow store of self-possession. The news that her career as an author was over would quite possibly bring her whole world crashing around her ears, that was how shaky her world was. Her illusions were all she had, except for Jimmy Blevins. And, it appeared, me.

271

In the wastebasket, where I just happened to glance on my way out, I spotted a receipt from the neighborhood lingerie shop. Picking it up to get a better idea of the nature of Jackie's purchase, I deduced that this morning she'd gone out and bought herself a silk teddy which cost just over a hundred dollars, the very morning she was about to go to Long Island to stay in a secluded country house with a bachelor friend. This was very interesting, although it was not technically any of my business. I hoped they were having a swell time together, waltzing along the porch at sunset; maybe she even held his hand when they walked along the beach. I bet he was in seventh heaven right this minute.

I sighed, then went into the living room and tried for quite a while to coax Delilah out of her hiding place in the dark region under the couch. Finally I gave up and got two mixing bowls and a big flat baking dish from the kitchen and filled one bowl with water, then set all three by the far end of the couch and filled the other bowl with cat food and the baking dish with cat litter. It would have to do until I could convince her to come out from there and get into her box again before Jackie came back from Southampton. If I couldn't get her out, the worst that could happen was that I'd inform Jackie that my cat was stuck under her couch, and she would have to deal. This didn't scare me as much as it would have a month ago, but it still wasn't something I looked forward to with any enthusiasm.

I sat heavily in a chair, drained of all my excitement, beset by an uneasy, horrible dread. Here I was again at Jackie's. I had nowhere to live. How could I ever face William again? What did I have to offer him, or anyone? Nothing had changed, nothing ever would.

The timer bell on the toaster oven went off, and automatically I went into the kitchen and ate steadily for ten or fifteen minutes. The lasagna gave me an instantaneous resurgence of pure animal energy that translated itself into renewed optimism. I threw away the aluminum container and washed the fork and drank some more champagne, surprised by an unexpected sense of relief, an incongruous hopefulness that swelled until it resembled excitement. Jackie and I were even: sure, she'd forced me to look through all that garbage and treated me like a half-wit and made me write her books for a pittance, but I'd stood up to her and stolen her book and now we could start over with the slate wiped clean. She was going to have a difficult time of it over the next few months, and the least I could do was help her through it. Maybe this time around I'd try to knuckle down and concentrate on getting addresses right and remember to give her all her messages. It seemed worth a try, anyway. Some day I'd get a better job, some day I'd have a better life and be a better person. In the meantime, this was what I had to do.

I went into Jackie's pantry and got out the laptop, plugged it in and turned it on. I rummaged around in the outer pocket of my backpack until I found the disk, put it into the drive, listed its files and copied the entire book back onto the hard drive.

While the machine clicked and whirred, I dialed William's work number. Somebody answered briskly, "Cromwell Wharton Dunne." Whoever it was sounded middle-aged and female and had an old-fashioned Brooklyn accent. For a brief joyful moment I thought it was Goldie.

"I'm trying to reach the office of William Snow," I said.

"You got it, honey, but he's out at the moment."

"Who is this?"

"Oh, I'm just a temp. My name is Rita and I'll be happy to tell him you're on the line. Whom should I say is calling?"

"But where's Elissa?"

"I couldn't really say; all I can tell you is that he hired me indefinitely, until he finds someone permanent."

"Please tell him Claudia called," I said, and hung up, grinning like a jack-o'-lantern.

Then I remembered the phone call my machine had picked up as I fled from my apartment, and dialed my own number to see who it had been. I heard the phone ringing in my empty apartment, heard my own voice inform me that I wasn't there. After the beep a familiar male voice said, "You can't hide from me forever, you know. Listen, I'm taking the rest of the day off. No one's here because it's Easter week and they're all playing golf. It's spring, in case you haven't noticed. Meet me in Central Park at three o'clock on the hill by the zoo, you know the one I mean. If you're not there I'll come and hunt you down, Claudia. If you think I'm kidding you'd better think again. See you there."

I was light-headed. I wanted to race like a maniac around the whole apartment, knocking things off shelves and upending chairs and flinging around all the dresses I'd just hung up. Instead, I corked the remainder of the champagne and stuck it into a side pocket of my backpack, hid the cat box in Jackie's shoe closet, whispered good-bye to Delilah and headed for the door.

Just then, it opened.

I froze, prepared to tell Jackie whatever she wanted to hear. I was here to open her mail. I'd thrown out the dead flowers and hung up her dresses. I'd—

Lucia gave a strangled scream when she saw me, then put a hand on her heart and leaned against the table in the foyer.

"Hi, Lucia," I said effusively; I'd completely forgotten she was staying here. "I'm just on my way out. I'm so sorry I scared you."

"It's okay," she said, recovering a little. I noticed that she had a tiny diamond in her nostril; Jackie must have hit the roof. Other than that, though, she looked exactly the same: clean-scrubbed and lovely and self-assured. "Your hair! I like. Is very good."

I touched the top of my head with my fingertips. "Jackie called me this morning," I told her. "She asked me to come back to work for her, that's why I'm here."

"Yes, I know." She smiled with just enough warmth to acknowledge her happiness at my reinstatement as her aunt's secretary without inviting me to tell her any of the details. "I owe you for the taxi."

"Don't worry about it," I said firmly. "Really."

She opened her wallet and handed me a five. "Thank you for the, those places you tell me to go. I am having a good time. Jackie doesn't know where I go."

"Well, I won't tell her, don't worry. Lucia, there's a cat here. Under the couch. I need to leave her here for a few days. Do you understand?"

"Yes," she said calmly, as if cats came to stay under Jackie's couch all the time. "You want me to do something with her?"

"No, I'm coming in again tomorrow. I just wanted to let you know so you wouldn't be scared if she jumps out at you."

"I'm not scared of a cat."

"You got your nose pierced," I said.

She laughed. "It's not real!" She took the diamond out and showed me. "I could never do that! My father would kill me. It's just for fun."

"Oh," I said. I laughed. "All right, I guess I'll see you to-morrow, then."

I rode down in the elevator with a gaunt silent old woman in a black suit and a bell-brimmed straw hat. She stared straight ahead, swallowing with dry effort. In the small descending box our two lives stood apart, not touching.

Ralph stopped me on my way out. "Louie just sent Miss Lucia up," he said, not meeting my eye, carefully not registering the backpack I was still carrying, the frenzied grin on my face, the faint hint of champagne fumes. There was so much not to notice about me I wondered whether he would be able to manage. "He didn't tell her that you were up there. He didn't know." He looked at me then, to tell me the rest with a glance: he was annoyed at me for putting him in this position, I had crossed the line, but he wasn't going to rat me out to Jackie.

"Everything's okay," I said reassuringly. "I left my cat up there, but I'll take her before Jackie comes back."

Seven veils descended over his eyes: he didn't want to know. He looked around the empty lobby. The mirrors and marble and European oil landscapes stared back at him. A fecund wind slid in from the courtyard and ruffled his ruler-straight bangs. "Okay," he said.

"Thank you," I said fervently. I wanted to hug him, which would have horrified both of us.

I departed down Park Avenue with a spring in my step. Tulips grew cheek by jowl in tight squares along the central island of the avenue, forming carpets of waxy petals a foot or so above the ground. Their mouths strained upward in mute, strangulated unison. I crossed the street and picked one and stuck it into my hair. Then I went along a westbound street to Central Park. I entered through a gap in the wall, followed a path through the trees, emerged into a clearing and collapsed in the sun on the hillock where William had told me to meet him. I took his tumbler from my backpack and filled it with champagne, then closed my eyes. I felt my life in pieces around me like an eggshell I'd pecked my way out of. The sunlight glowed rosily on my eyelids; I floated rootless as a milkweed pod over the roaring grid. The air was alive with chlorophyll and insect wings. Miles away, a pneumatic drill blasted at the foundations of the city. It sounded to my drowsy ears like champagne bubbles against a glass, pop pop pop pop pop, celebrating nothing in particular.

Printed in the United States
by Baker & Taylor Publisher Services